TERI WOODS

DUTCH II
ANGEL'S REVENGE

THE SECOND OF A TRILOGY

For information on how individual consumers can place orders, please write to Teri Woods Publishing, Greeley Square Station, P.O. Box 20069, New York, New York, 10001-0005.

For orders other than individual consumers, Teri Woods Publishing grants a discount on the purchase of 10 or more copies of a single title order for special markets or premium use.

For orders purchased through the World Wide Web and/or P.O. Box, Teri Woods Publishing offers a 25% discount off the sale price for orders being shipped to prisons, including but not limited to federal, state and county.

TERI WOODS

DUTCH II
ANGEL'S REVENGE

THE SECOND OF A TRILOGY

Note:
Sale of this book without a front cover may be unauthorized. If this book was purchased without a cover, it may have been reported to the publisher as "unsold or destroyed." Neither the author nor the publisher may have received payment for the sale of this book.

This novel is a work of fiction. Any resemblances to real people, living or dead, actual events, establishments, organizations and/or locales are intended to give the fiction a sense of reality and authenticity. Other names, characters, places, and incidents are either products of the author's imagination or are used fictitiously, as are those fictionalized events & incidents that involve real person and did not occur or are set in the future.

Published by Teri Woods Publishing
Greeley Square Station
P.O. Box 20069
New York, NY 10001-0005
www.teriwoodspublishing.com

Library of Congress Catalog Card No:
ISBN: 978-0-9672249-6-1
Copyright:

Dutch II: Angel's Revenge Credits:
Written by Teri Woods
Edited by Teri Woods and Barbara Colasuonno
Text formation by Group 33
Cover concept by Barbara Colasuonno and Lucas Riggins
Cover graphics by Group 33
Printed by Malloy Lithographing

This book is dedicated to Kwame Teague and his wife LaShonda Teague. Stay strong for yourselves and your family and never give up your fight for freedom. May God Bless you both.

– Teri

ACKNOWLEDGEMENTS

As always my family, my mother, Phyllis, my father, Corel, my fiancé, Lou, my daughter, Jessica, my son, Lucas, Jr., and my brothers, Dexter and Chucky. I would also like to thank the people who successfully help me in this publishing business and with the Dutch II project: Barbara Colasuonno, Coral Tolisano, LaToya Smith, and Lucas Riggins, Tiffany and Kevin at Don Diva Magazine, King Magazine, XXL Magazine, Murder Dog Magazine, Radio One, Vinnie at Barone Press, Sonni and Kim at Citibank, Marge, Ron, Chris, and Judy at Malloy and my distributors who make sure my books get out there to the bookstores, Larry and Gail, Wendy and Eric, Nahti, Bob, Stacey Sharock and Pam Tucker, Cliff Evans, and Joe, thank you for your business and continued support. To all my authors, Kwame, Nurit, Eric, Curtis, and Melvin, thank you for believing in Teri Woods Publishing and allowing me to bring your stories to life. I want to thank Darryl Miller, Esquire. I thank you so so much, you and your wonderful staff. You do so many things for me and I know you do them because you believe in my visions and dreams. You've always believed in me and I'm so glad our relationship continues. Thank you. Don't worry, I'll turn these dreams into cash flow. To Manny Haley, aren't you something? Mr., I wanna be your manager! Thank you for helping me. Thank you for your professionalism, Brooklyn, and for believing in the things I'm trying to do. Also, thank you for helping me and holding me down when I'm out in LA. To Robi Reed, I'm really excited and so thankful to work with you. To Sandra Derrell, girl it might take you some time, but you do come through. Thank you for helping me and introducing me to your Rolodex. No one does that! Thank you! Thank you! Thank you! And to Lou, thank you, thank you, thank you. You really hold it all down and you really keep me focused. I love you.

But mostly I want to really thank you, whoever is reading this. Your support of me, my company and my authors has been remarkable and overwhelming over the past 5 years. Whoever you are, wherever you are, thank you!

TRULY,

Teri Woods

TERI WOODS

Prologue

Get these people out of here!" Detective Smalls bellowed.

The Essex County Courthouse had become a madhouse. Screams of confusion and cries of pain filled the air and seared the ears of the seasoned detective. In all of his thirteen years on the force, he had never seen anything like this. It was like a terrorist had dropped a bomb on the courthouse and transformed it into a war zone. Paramedics, uniformed police officers and Newark's Special Unit along with the Newark Fire Department all struggled to maintain order in the aftermath of the massacre.

"Move aside, please. Move aside!" Smalls commanded as he directed the curious who had filed into the bullet-ridden courtroom door.

"Officer! Officer! My son was in there, please..."

"Please don't let my wife be dead! Someone help me!"

The faces and voices reminded Smalls of a recurring nightmare, one he could not wake up from. He had been one of the first on the scene and had seen the human carnage strewn like discarded waste. As he entered the smoke-filled courtroom, the smell of death hit him in the face. It now lingered in his nostrils as he looked around in disbelief. The tragedy was an unbelievable sight.

Frank Sorbonno's body lay grotesquely twisted against the rear wall. District Attorney Anthony Jacobs' body had been blown to pieces, his headless remains sprawled on the prosecution's table. The judge was slumped over his gavel, and nine of the twelve jury members leaned every which way on top of each other.

Innocent bystanders and the disguised Charlies lay strewn on the floor. Their blood was splattered all over the courtroom and even on the American flag that hung limp in the corner. That sight in particular caught Smalls' eye and etched itself in his memory.

Smalls sat down in the back row of the courthouse and ran his hand through his salt and pepper hair. *How could this have happened?* he asked himself as he continued to inspect the room. Dutch had single-handedly taken the American justice system and slapped it his bloody hand. If gunshots had been applause, the courtroom would have received a deadly standing ovation with Dutch as orchestrator.

Smalls silently watched as ambulance workers rolled corpse after corpse onto soiled gurneys and out the courtroom doors. All he could think of was Dutch. He prayed he would be found among the dead. He'd give his right arm to have Dutch in front of him, bleeding, dying and begging to atone for the atrocity he had inflicted on the flesh of the American justice system. But Dutch was nowhere to be found. The police had sealed off the building and a ten block radius. The Feds had stopped airline flights and bus and train departures. But all was to no avail. Dutch had managed to slip through the tight noose they had meticulously prepared for him and escaped unscathed. He mocked them all.

But more than how he did it, everyone wanted to know where he went.

The question was very simple.

Where was Dutch?

Chapter One

Fuck y'all!" was Dutch's emphatic verdict on the entire courtroom, and the Charlies stood ready to impose his sentence. Bullets filled the unsuspecting courtroom. Dutch pulled out the twin forty calibers strapped under the defense table and fired into the face of the bailiff to his right as he reached for his service revolver. The second bailiff was spun off his feet by a Charlie in the front row. People leapt and ducked but to no avail because there was nowhere to hide.

Gripping both pistols like death's sickle, ready to claim his next victim, Dutch cut the judge down with a shot to the chest. "Guilty, muthafucka! Guilty!" Dutch laughed, firing a second shot that exploded the judge's head like a melon. "Gavel that, pussy!"

Anthony Jacobs felt the muzzle at the back of his head and before he could even pray, lead filled his thoughts.

The jury was mercilessly sprayed with a barrage of gunfire by four Charlies. All the while, Dutch searched the frenzied rows looking for Frank Sorbonno. He found him crouched under a row at the rear of the courthouse. Dutch smiled down on him.

"Frankie Bonno! It's the black Al Capone, muthafucka!"

Dutch quipped as he aimed the muzzle at his bald dome. "Happy Valentine's Day, sweetheart!"

"Dutch please! I ..."

Bonno's cowardly plea was silenced by six hollow point messengers of death.

Meanwhile, courthouse officers had begun to converge on the room. Shots flew through the door, killing two Charlies, while Dutch and six other Charlies made their way to the exit and out the door.

Three more Charlies, positioned in the rear of the building, were exchanging fire with several officers, clearing the way for Dutch and his team.

"Dutch, this way baby," one of the Charlies beckoned before her lungs filled with blood from a gunshot in the back. She fell, silenced forever, as Dutch and the others made it to the stairs.

Outside, police and ambulances had arrived.

One of the ambulances, however, arrived with two Charlies dressed as EMT workers and was conveniently parked adjacent to the rear of the courthouse.

With eyes alert to the police and all their activity, Craze cautiously emerged from behind a dumpster and opened the back door.

To the average eye, the ambulance didn't appear out of place. The mêleé had panicked the minds of everyone and no one knew what to expect next, certainly not an ambulance escape.

"The basement!" Dutch ordered the remaining three Charlies with him. "Make sure my man is compensated for his assistance," he smirked, then shot out the rear door and popped into the ambulance.

Craze looked at his long-time friend, relieved that he had

made it, then screamed at the Charlie in the driver's seat, "Fuck you waitin' for, tomorrow? Drive!" He flipped on the siren and sped off. As the ambulance turned the corner, Detective Smalls and his partner, Detective Meritti, skidded up and jumped out of their car ready for war.

"Where is Dutch?" Smalls demanded, but he became distracted when Detective Meritti entered the room behind him. Smalls could tell by the look on his partner's face that he was the bearer of bad news. Smalls had been dealing with the press throughout the ordeal, keeping them informed on what was going on. But he had postponed leaking any information concerning Dutch until the chief of police got back to him. And today Meritti was the chief's messenger.

"What's the world coming to, eh?" Meritti asked in his Brooklyn Italian accent. "First 9-11, now this?" He scanned the crime scene in disbelief. "This is the beginning of anarchism."

Smalls agreed. "So?" he inquired, studying Meritti's blue eyes.

Meritti sat down and lit a Winston. "I can see the headlines now. *Gangster kills judge and jury and escapes*," he bitterly remarked with a flourish, tapping the ashes from his cigarette.

"Do you know what kind of message that would send?" Meritti continued his rant. "Every fuckin' nut with a gun and half a heart will think he can do the same thing!"

Smalls nodded. "No courtroom in America will be safe. The next thing you know, people will be shooting DAs and judges in the street!"

"And rioting in county jails to bust out the kingpins," Meritti added in a tone of disgust.

Smalls knew where Meritti was going with the conversation.

"I take it chief feels the same way?" Smalls asked, already knowing he did.

Meritti nodded, watching his partner of six years, knowing what the chief was asking of him, and he knew Smalls didn't like to lie. To Meritti, Smalls had always been an annoyingly honest detective.

"If I go out there and tell those people that James is dead...if we cover up his escape and it gets out..."

"It won't get out," Meritti said cutting him off.

"But if it does?"

"It won't."

Smalls saw the logic in the decision.

Even though Dutch had committed a heinous act, if the world thought he was dead, potential copycats would think twice because Dutch didn't survive. But to Smalls, a lie was still a lie.

However, if the truth was told, Dutch would become a legend — the gangster's hero, the outlaw that blasted his way to freedom. No, Smalls' heart decided the truth couldn't be told — yet. Not until James was firmly in his grasp, and for the sake of justice everywhere, the truth had to be concealed.

Smalls rose slowly, feeling the full weight of his fifty-four years in his arthritic knees.

"Okay, let's go meet the press," he said, smiling at Meritti weakly.

Meritti took one last look at the room and wondered aloud, "But HOW did he do it? There are metal detectors on every floor, even right outside this door, and he smuggled in a fuckin' arsenal? How?"

Smalls looked at Meritti with steel in his eyes. "I don't know. But I promise you, I will find out."

With that, they left the courtroom.

Chapter Two

Delores Murphy clicked the power button to her television and heard the reporter confirm her sons demise.

"Thank you," she whispered, grateful that it was finally over.

Delores had silently witnessed the rise of her only child from a petty car thief to a vicious drug lord. Now, she was too numb to cry. Pain and a sense of relief mingled in her soul, and for the first time, Delores questioned herself.

Where did I go wrong?

She had tried to raise Bernard like any other single black mother in the grip of poverty. She tried to instill in him the basic moral principles of love, honesty, and a belief in God. She had also tried to teach him the value of his freedom, of his black manhood, and of his own self worth in a society that wanted to brainwash the black man into believing that he was worthless.

Materially, Delores never spoiled Dutch but she always tried to give him the best, just like any mother would. But Delores still felt that she had gone wrong somewhere. She felt that the hate and rage she carried against the system in her youth had somehow seeped into her son.

She wondered if hate so deep could be genetically inherited.

She also wondered if every lesson she had taught Dutch had been filtered through her own bitterness and resentment. And maybe her very own breast milk had contaminated his soul.

"Nigga, go on out there and take back what them people took from you!"

Delores remembered preaching those words when he came home from prison. He had gone away a man-child and returned a man. Had her words somehow unlocked the fury trapped inside of him and unleashed her son's demons onto the streets?

As Dutch emptied the book bag on Delores' worn kitchen table, stacks upon stacks of rubber banded rolls of money landed with soft thuds.

"Ma, we movin'," Dutch announced proudly, wearing his father's smile like it was his own.

Delores' eyes widened. She was weary from working two jobs, and her son, not even a year out of prison, had brought home more money than she'd seen in her entire life.

"Bernard, where did you…"

Dutch's soft kiss on her quivering cheek cut her off.

"It's what the world owes us, Ma. And I won't take no for an answer. Not even from you."

Her silence became her approval. She knew all about the Month of Murder. She also knew that her son was called Dutch, the black gangsta the mob feared. But she had never said a word. What would she have said? The truth was that a large part of her was proud of him, and she wasn't mad at all.

Now he was gone. He left a wicked memory on the streets and a tragic memory in her mind that joined the memories of his father to this day. Not a single day went by without her recalling her only love's luscious kisses and calloused caresses, and the feeling of his manhood deep inside her followed by the mellow croon of his baritone in her ears.

I love you, Delores.

I love you, Bernard.

If she ever needed his embrace, it was now. She had had other men in her life after Bernard, other friends, other lovers, but none had managed to touch her heart like Bernard had. She never married, refusing two proposals in her lifetime, because she believed in her heart that he'd come back to her one day. But he never returned. Now, the last thing she possessed of his was also gone. Just as she lost him to the Vietnam war so long ago, she had lost his son to a war that unfortunately raged right outside her front door.

Delores felt all alone. The only thought that consoled her was the one of her imagination — Dutch going out like his father, guns blazing, fighting for freedom.

She didn't know how right she was.

The ringing phone brought her back to reality. Delores slowly stood up and picked up the receiver.

"Hello?" her frail voice answered softly.

"Is this the Murphy residence?" a male voice questioned.

"It is."

"May I speak with Delores Murphy?"

"Who's calling?" she asked, although she already knew who it was. His tone and style were a dead giveaway.

"This is Detective Meritti. I'm sad to inform you that your son, Bernard James, has been killed," Meritti explained softly but matter-of-factly. "We need you to come and identify the body. I know this is difficult, and I'm sorry that I'm not there in person to deliver...."

"No," Delores interrupted. "No, it's quite alright. I'm already aware of Bernard's..." she cleared her throat and added, "I was expecting your call."

"If it's alright with you ma'am, I think it would be best if I sent a car for you."

"No, I don't need a car. I can get there. I'll be there within the hour."

Meritti sighed with relief. He didn't want to appear pushy, but the sooner they completed their official charade, the sooner they could concentrate on finding Dutch.

"That would be great, ma'am. Do you know how to get to the County Coroner's Office?"

"I can find it, Detective Meritti," Delores replied, her tone sending the message that the call was over.

"Very good. We'll be waiting for you."

Delores hung up.

"Who's fooling who in here?" Meritti asked.

"I wonder if she'll buy it?" Smalls wondered aloud.

"Please, God. Don't let it be true! Burned beyond recognition? Charred remains..."

The detectives took Delores to a clean room where a body lay covered by a white sheet on top of a table. Detective Meritti introduced himself and recounted to Delores all that had transpired.

"It looks like his accomplices, these, um, Angel's Charlies, were the actual culprits. It seems they started the fire so that your son could escape. But he didn't make it out. And it looks like the coroner has already identified a set of matching dental records," he added as he flashed them at her before placing them back into the folder next to the body.

Then he lifted the sheet.

Detective Meritti proceeded to tell her that the pink-black distorted lump before her was her son.

This ain't my son, Delores thought as her body began to tremble uncontrollably.

Meritti noticed that she was beginning to lose her equilibrium, and he gently grabbed her to support her in case she fainted.

"Mrs. Murphy? Are you alright? Can I get you anything? Please, sit down."

Delores shook off his offer and brushed his hand off her shoulder. She stood very still, silently staring at the body. The nameless lump of flesh they claimed was her son wasn't even the right height. Close, but a little too tall. His build, or what was left of it, was too bulky.

Anxious eyes looking for closure could be easily fooled.

Detective Smalls watched her intently as if he had the eyes of a hawk. He was fully aware of the masquerade he and Meritti were perpetrating. More importantly, he was looking for a sign that Delores was staging a masquerade of her own. He felt that if she identified the body too quickly, too cleanly, perhaps she was already aware of her son's whereabouts, already knew that he wasn't dead. So Smalls watched her facial expressions from the moment the sheet was lifted and observed her eyes as they flicked over the body. He watched her very carefully to see if she had been prepared or had rehearsed her reaction. Crying too hard, screaming for the Lord or shouting for mercy and faking too much drama would be dead giveaways. But to his surprise, Delores did nothing like that. The pain that glazed her eyes was too deep and too real to be an act. She had passed the test, but not for the reasons Smalls had assumed. Delores looked from face to face, and her motherly instincts kicked in.

She knew they were up to something. But what? *This ain't Bernard, but they must want it to be or they want to know where he is. I'm going to pretend right along with them.* And that's exactly what she did to protect her child.

The police were trying so hard to deceive her but they themselves were being deceived. Delores stood in the middle of the cold sterile room trying to figure out their motives while they were trying to figure out hers. The illusion of truth wore a mask of deception well.

"Mrs. Murphy, I know this is hard for you," Meritti said slowly. "But can you ID this body for us as your son?"

Her weak gaze masked a strong resolve as she looked from Smalls to Meritti. Delores lowered her head and subtly nodded.

Meritti was relieved.

Smalls was perplexed.

And Delores' soul was tormented. The pain in her eyes Smalls detected wasn't her belief that her son was dead. It was because he was still alive. Somehow, somewhere, Bernard James, Jr. was still alive. The nightmare wasn't over, and she was more confused and flooded with emotion now than when they had first lifted the sheet. Once again, she had co-signed to a reign of terror she was sure would follow. The nightmare was nowhere near over. The truth was, it was just about to begin.

"Where do I sign for my son's body?" she asked.

"Right here, Mrs. Murphy," said Detective Meritti.

Delores took the pen and signed for the "pretend" Dutch to be released to the funeral director. *I got to pay to bury this muthafucka that ain't even Bernard. I'm going to kill that boy when I see him,* she thought to herself. But her intentions were to cremate the remains so that the secret of Dutch could be scattered to the winds.

Chapter Three

Whose world is this?"

"Mine!"

"Whose world am I?"

"Mine!"

"Then say my name, ma. Say my name."

"Young World," Lana purred as she posed in the bathroom doorway. She had the curves of two letter S's facing each other. Chocolate from head to toe, she stood bowlegged, wet and naked, tantalizing Young World as he laid back on the spacious bed in their Cancun hotel suite.

"Do my dance, yo," Young World told her.

Lana began to slowly and sensually gyrate her hips to the rhythm of her own lust, palming her full breasts and pulling at her tender brown nipples.

"Like this, World?" she smiled, loving the feeling of her man's eyes all over her.

"No doubt. Slow motion, ma. Move it slow motion for me," he replied with gangsta charisma. He licked his lips and grabbed his crotch.

Lana complied as she crawled on the bed like a black panther in the jungle stalking her prey. Young World parlayed like the young Don Dutch made him, wearing only two things, a pair of burgundy silk boxers and Dutch's dragon chain gleaming off the reddish-brown skin of his bare chest.

He watched Lana take his erect member into her warm mouth and wrap her juicy lips around his shaft, relaxing her throat, and curling his toes. Her head bobbed as if his dick was licorice and she was addicted to sweets.

Young World had definitely come up lovely. It had been nine months since the courthouse massacre and things had gone just as Dutch predicted they would.

The streets is gonna be wide open like pussy after this. Niggas you thought you could count on either gonna flip and try and go for dolo or nut up under pressure.

The streets lit up like the Fourth of July as street niggas and greedy crews scrambled for the crumbs off Dutch's table. Young World had one of the sickest teams in the game, but even he took loses. His right hand man, Jazz, didn't have the killer instincts it took to ball on World's level so seventeen shots later found him on a basketball court in the park. Jazz and Young World had come up together so his death hit Young World hard, but there was no time to mourn because the streets wouldn't let him.

The rest is up to you.

Dutch's final words to him replayed in his head and made Young World put his gangsta down in a way that would make Dutch smile in his grave and make the streets bow down. While he relaxed with the love of his life in Cancun, Mexico, the streets of Newark were on fire.

"Young World, muthafucka!" the masked gunman yelled from the chrome black Ducati. His fully automatic Israeli Uzi spit round after round into both the driver of a drop top Lexus coupe and the girl sitting in the passenger seat. They slumped like Kennedy, and the Ducati gunner sped off, leaving the bodies nodded at the light.

Lana's deep throat game had Young World feeling like he was about to bust all over her tonsils, but he wasn't ready to nut. He wanted to feel that bomb shot of hers that had him so in love. He lifted her chin and pulled her up until she straddled his hips and slid down on him, riding him like the stallion he was.

The young hustler wasn't a stranger to the county jail, but with the paper he was making in the McCarter Highway Projects, bail was like candy money. His momma posted his bail. He knew it would be just a few hours more before his paperwork was processed and he was released. He stretched out on his bunk without a care in the world, knowing his name would soon be called. He didn't know his number would come up before his name did.

Youngen closed his eyes to catch a quick nap. He never saw Duke slip into his cell like the Phantom of the Opera, gripping a homemade shank tight in his palm. Duke quickly snatched the pillow from behind the man's head and put it over his face. The short struggle ended quickly when Duke plunged the shank into his victim's heart, giving the it a deadly twist to seal the deal.

"Tell 'em Young World sent you," Duke whispered menacingly.

"Ooh, World, don't stop, daddy. Ooh, I love you, World, I... " Lana groaned as she rode World like she was raised bucking broncos. Her ass slapped against his thighs.

"Say my name, ma!"

"World, Young World, nigga!"

The black clad Charlie bellowed before she let off a rain of black talons into a crowd of Irvington Bloods on the corner of Groove Street. They never knew what hit them. Their bodies jerked and twisted like a crew of break-dancers before they dropped to the ground, dead and smoking.

Just like that, Jazz's murder was avenged and the Charlie sdisappeared into the shadows.

Lana gripped the dragon chain like the reigns of a horse bridle and rode her stallion wildly. Young World grabbed her ass, spread her swollen lips, and plowed into her, matching her, thrust for forceful thrust. Lana screamed out in a mixture of pleasure and pain while Young World long-dicked her into a sensual explosion that drenched her thighs and the satin sheets beneath them. She collapsed on top of her man, covering his face with gentle kisses.

"I love you, World."

"I love you, too."

Young World lay back and relaxed. While he was getting his dick sucked and fucked on all night, he felt secure knowing that back in Jersey he had a team of hungry wolves working to ensure that he had an empire to go home to.

Their murder game was not to be fucked with, but World made the mistake of thinking murder was enough to hold an empire together.

THREE YEARS LATER

Chapter Four

One-eyed Roc stood in his prison cell at his sink, brushing his full beard in the mirror. It glistened with the muslim hair oil he used on it almost as brightly as his freshly shaven head. Roc stepped back and admired himself. His gentle expression reflected an magnetic edge. They say prison preserves your youth, and at 33, Roc still looked like he was in his mid twenties. The only difference was his slightly protruding belly and the extra bulk prison food had put on him.

He was 6'3" and a solid 235 pounds. His celly nicknamed him Suge Knight because of his resemblance to the music mogul, along with his deep booming voice that commanded attention whenever he spoke. Roc was, however, far from a Suge Knight. Adherence to Islam and his sincerity to its beliefs had mellowed him, perhaps not all the way, but enough to be recognized by the prison administrators and his fellow convicts who were well aware of his past street reputation. In fact, no one called him Roc anymore. They called him by his Islamic name, Rahman, which meant merciful in Arabic.

Rahman felt in his heart that he was no longer the murdering gangsta that he was when he had first arrived to prison. He now possessed a sincere passion for Islam and for the plight of the inner city that he had spent so much of his life terrorizing and dehumanizing.

When Rahman had gone to prison, he had a saved hefty stash, a little over five million dollars. But in the three years he had been locked up, he had given away over a million dollars to needy families, single parent homes, battered women and orphaned children.

His wife, Ayesha, who was faithfully sticking by her husband, managed the money, doling out cash as Rahman instructed. Things had been rough for Rahman and Ayesha with Rahman away and Ayesha raising their three children alone.

Despite the distance and the apparent hopelessness of his life sentence, she would often tell him, "You're with me even when you're away. Allah will bring you home to me."

And it seemed that Allah would do just that.

"As-Salaamu Alaikum, Ock."

Rahman turned around to find Akbar standing in the doorway of his cell.

"Alaikum As-Salaam," Rahman replied, returning the greeting. "I ain't even hear you standing there."

"Then you slippin'," Akbar chuckled. "You hear a ninja walkin'," he joked.

Akbar was Rahman's mentor. They had similar backgrounds. Akbar was older than Rahman and also from Newark. Both had been heavily into the game but now both were dedicated to Islam.

Akbar walked into Rahman's cell and held out a magazine.

"What's that?" Rahman asked, looking at the rolled up magazine.

Akbar showed him the cover. It was a copy of the new Don Diva Magazine with a picture of Dutch, Craze, Angel, Zoom and

Rahman himself on the cover. It was a photograph Rahman recognized, but he turned away from its nostalgia.

"Come on, Ock. You know I don't keep up wit' that anymore," he told his friend and grabbed his prayer rug and kufi.

"Naw, nephew, I think you'll want to see this one," Akbar said as if it was absolutely necessary Rahman read the article.

"Page 56, Rah. I'll get it from you after Jum'ah," Akbar said as he walked out the cell.

Rahman sat down on his bunk and flipped to page 56. The article was entitled 'Angel Alvarez'. And read:

What's really good, yo? You know Don Diva always comes with the exclusive exclusive! You heard it here and nowhere else type shit, ya heard? Our topic today? That mysterious street legend, Dutch. It's been three years since his alleged (and we do mean alleged) death. Now we have a one-on-one interview with Angel Alverez, the only female to run with the notorious Dutch. The following came from a taped phone convo from West Virginia where Angel is currently housed.

DD: What's up, mami? What's your life like?

Angel: You know how it goes wit' a bid. You put it on your back and troop it like a boss bitch. Ju don't know?

DD: Aiight, if only these snitch muthafuckas understood the principles of this shit. But yo, I hear congratulations are in order! You won your appeal.

Angel (laughs): I can't believe that shit either. Fuck man, my lawyer ain't even expect it! You know how the Feds get down, they some dirty muthafuckers. No matter how fucked up the case is, they make that shit stick. Even if you innocent, you goin' to jail fo' fuckin' with them, man.

DD: Well, I guess its true. You can't hold a good bitch down!

Anger: What, ju don't know?

DD: So, how does this effect Rahman's case, or should we not discuss that? (Rahman Muhammad was Angel's co-defendant, now also serving multiple life sentences.)

Angel: Naw, yo. Me and my nigga ain't got nothin' to hide. We held it down like family supposed to and now just like cream we 'bout to rise to the top. Me and you, Roc. We all we got!

Rahman lowered the magazine and couldn't help but smile. Angel was still Angel. They wrote each other from time to time, which is why Rahman already knew about her case. After finding out about her appeal, he jumped on his. He was just waiting on a decision. He turned his attention back to the article.

DD: So when do you touch down officially?

Angel: You know the courts. It's a whole bunch of legal bullshit, but it's comin'. And like Dutch used to tell me, they can't stop what they can't see, so it's best nobody know, feel me?

DD: Felt. But speakin' of Dutch, what was son really like?

Angel (pauses then laughs quietly): How many real gangstas you know?

DD: Including myself? One.

Angel (laughed at my quip): Well, dig yo, gangsta ain't enough to make you Dutch 'cause papi is so much more. He had strings attached to the game like a puppet, and he controlled every move. Even now, three years later, niggas still makin' records about this nigga, namin' clothes after him...

DD: Not to mention books.

Angel: Oh yeah, that Teri Woods chick? I respect her pen game. She's real gangsta for puttin' my man's story out there. I read it. It was official.

DD: But yo, one last question. If anybody knows, it's you. We asked Rahman two years ago (see Don Diva July 2003 edition) but he evaded us. Do you think...?

Angel (shouting): Fuck that bullshit! Fuck what you heard! My man ain't dead! Them fake-ass, wanna-be gangstas might want him to be, but he AIN'T! And until he come through, just know Angel gonna hold it down and rep my man and the streets!

DD: You keep saying your man. Thought you were...you know?

Angel: What? I eat fish? (she chuckled) I've had my share of snapper, but let's just say Dutch is my sweetest taboo.

DD: Juicy, Juicy tell me...

(The one-minute warning cut me off just when we were getting to the good shit).

DD: Well, one minute left, any last words?

Angel: No doubt, to Roc. Hold your head 'cause it's me and you. To Goldilocks and Angela Hearn, one love. And to the streets, pick a side and ride or die cause the ride is 'bout to get rough. And let all them bitch ass niggas know whose runnin' them streets for real. Angel's baaaack muthafuckas! Siempre.

Rahman laid the magazine aside and rubbed his face. Angel definitely hadn't changed and apparently thought he hadn't either. But he had, and it made him wonder where that left the two of them. He knew what she was going to do if released from prison. Take back what they had lost. But he had a different mission — to clean up the streets.

What happens when an irresistible force meets an immovable object? Well, the streets would soon find out.

Rahman walked into FCI-Lewisburg's chapel just as the Islamic call to prayer was being chanted.

Hayya alas-Salah. Hayya-alal-Falah. Come to prayer, come to success. In Arabic, heard throughout speakers in the chapel, it represented the Masjid for the Muslim inmates.

Rahman was the prayer leader better known as Imam in Arabic. He led all the Muslim inmates in prayer and advised them on their personal issues from time to time. He prayed his two ra'kahs and then made his way to the podium.

"As-Salaamu Alaikum," he said in greeting to the forty-something Muslims sitting on the floor in lines of straight rows behind one another.

"Alaikum As-Salaam," the brothers replied in unison.

Rahman surveyed the gathering of the men before him. He knew many of the brothers had been stone-cold murderers, kingpins, pimps and boss players. Now they all bowed to one God in perfect unity and harmony. Allah was truly the greatest.

"All praises are due to Allah. We praise him, seek his help, and ask his forgiveness. I bear witness that there is no God but Allah, and that Muhammad is his servant and messenger," Rahman began, then flipped open his Qur'an.

"I want to read from Surah four, Ayat seventy five. It says..." he began to recite the Qur'an in Arabic, his deep baritone caressing each syllable and his articulation punctuating the guttural sentences.

"Wa Maa la-kum la tuqaatiluna fi sabili-llahi. Wal-Mustadifina min ar-rijali Wan Nisaai Wal Wildan. Al-Latheena yaqulu-na Rabba-na Akhrij-na Min Hadihil. Paryati Zalimu Ahlu-ha Wa Hab la-na Min Ladun-ka Nasiraa."

Then he repeated the prayer in English.

"And what is wrong with you that you fight not in the cause of Allah and for those who are weak, ill-treated and oppressed amongst themselves, both men, women and children, whose cry is: Lord rescue us from this town whose people are oppressors and raise for us, from you, one who will protect and raise for us, one who will help."

He closed the Qur'an and paused to let the words sink in.

"This was a cry for liberation. Is this cry still not heard today? All around us, in every ghetto in America, brothers and sisters are crying and yet the call continues to go unanswered. We in this room come from every part of the U.S. The north, west, south and east, the inner cities, boondocks and back country roads. We know that the ghetto is everywhere. People in society use this prayer every day, with or without understanding. But instead of calling on God, they call on the numbers man, the dope man, the liquor store, the strip club, or the corner bar. They call on anyone, anywhere, and anyway they can to escape the oppression being inflicted upon them."

Many of the brothers nodded their heads in agreement.

"But what is oppression? Is it just racist cops, politicians and judges? Isn't debt oppression? The type of debt that keeps us tied to two and three jobs tryin' to come out of it? Isn't the game oppression? It leaves a brother with only two options — jail or death. It's a vicious cycle and where does it get us? Where are we now?" Rahman's voice boomed.

"Where we are now? Here. It gets us here. It gets our women in strip clubs. It gets our kids in group homes. Why do you think there are fences around the Projects tall as the fences around maximum security prisons? In prison, fences mean they don't want you to get out. So, can it mean anything different around the Projects? Oppression. The white man knew exactly what he was doing when he built the prisons and the projects. But Islam is the liberator. Not the nation of Islam, not the 5% of Islam, not Moorish Science or nationalistic ideologies, but Islam. Sunni Islam, pure and simple."

Rahman paced in front of the brothers with his hands clasped behind his back.

"Now some will tell you that Islam doesn't liberate. Islam enslaves. Look at the Arabs on the east coast of Africa. They were doing the same thing the Europeans were doing on the west coast of Africa! To them I say, know the difference between liberator and conqueror. Many start out as liberators but become conquerors, and the Arabs were no different. This is when we lost our glory as Muslims. But I challenge you to find any religion that has liberated any country in the history of the world. Christianity? That is only a facade for Roman imperialism. Buddhism? No. Judaism? Stop playin'," Rahman smiled and a few laughed quietly.

"But Islam? Yes, yes and yes again. This is history. So this is what we must take home to our families. Islam. Not as conquerors but as liberators. Teach them what they can do and they won't need for what they don't have. Lead by example, not by rhetoric, and they too shall follow. As-Salaamu Alaikum."

After Jum'ah, Akbar and Rahman walked the yard.

"That was a beautiful khutbah, nephew. I taught you well," Akbar joked, Rahman smiled.

"All praises are due to Allah."

"Indeed. But, ah... you didn't plan on speakin' on that particular topic today did you, Ock?" Akbar inquired knowingly.

Rahman answered him with his eyes.

"I noticed you weren't using your index cards. So, I figured you were free-styling," Akbar surmised, then added, "Got anything to do with that Don Diva magazine?"

Rahman looked around the yard, formulating a response.

The other inmates were recreational under the Pennsylvania sun, balling and lifting weights like they didn't have a care in the world.

"Something like that," Rahman replied.

Akbar nodded. "That's why I showed it to you. So you'd know what's waitin' for you when you touch down."

"If I touch."

Akbar shrugged.

"Allah is the best of planners, but He's already set the stage for your return. How you gonna handle this Angel thing?"

They lapped the yard several times before Rahman wanted to rest. They stopped and sat down.

"What you mean, how? You know what we planned. Nothing will get in the way of that, Insha Allah."

"Insha Allah," Akbar repeated, then added, "Look, Rah. I've been watchin' you for three years. Watchin' you grow in Islam and watchin' how your character has changed. You're a beautiful brother, but nephew, that gangsta is still in you."

Rahman wanted to defend himself, but Akbar continued.

"I'm not saying you frontin' or you ain't sincere. But we were born and trained to be what them streets made us. You, a gangsta. Me, I'm a grand master, but that's a personal jihad within myself. Like you said today, the liberator or the conqueror. The liberator is Rahman, but the conqueror is One-eyed Roc, the cold-blooded killer and big money getter."

Rahman let Akbar's words sink in before responding. "I hear you, Ock, but believe me, I'm ready."

"Are you?" Akbar shot back. "Because what we're plannin' to do is serious. It ain't no game. People gonna pay the price."

"I know that."

"Well, what if one of those people is Angel? If you had to pull the trigger, could you look her in the face and pull it?"

Rahman's eyes locked with Akbar's. It was a thought that had crossed his mind but one he didn't want to face.

"Every Saul wants to be Paul," Akbar philosophized. "You know how many cats get locked up then wanna change the world? Crackheads wanna open up rehabs, trick niggas wanna respect black women, and killers wanna stop the violence. But one by one, they fail. They fail because when they see they can't change the world, they join it. And I see it in you, Ock. You want to change Angel, don't you? You think she'll listen to you? Roll wit' you on this?" Akbar questioned.

"Insha Allah," Rahman replied, not looking at Akbar.

"And Young World, too? You brought him in. What if you have to take him out?"

Akbar's questions ripped away Rahman's delusions one by one. Everyone he had ever loved, ran the streets with, got money with, even killed with, and would've died for, could easily become his enemy. Not because they had changed, but because he had.

He tried to tell himself that Angel and Young World would roll with him. After all, the plan wasn't only to clean up the community but make millions doing it. His plan was economic as well as social, political and spiritual. But he knew deep down that he was fooling himself if he thought they'd just walk away from the addiction of street life, especially if their hearts were still truly in it.

And if they didn't walk away, what was he prepared to do?

"Make no mistake, nephew. You've switched sides, not them. So think like a gangsta, but act like a Muslim. To beat a gangsta you got to know the mind of one. Because the question ain't can you do them, but..." Akbar leaned closer to Rahman's ear,

"Would they hesitate to do you?" Akbar stood up slowly and left Rahman with "As-Salaamu Alaikum, nephew. We'll talk later. Insha Allah."

Rahman watched his mentor casually stroll off and disappear in the crowd.

"Yo, nigga, I'm tellin' you, that shit is followin' us," Young World said as he glanced in the rear-view mirror of his CL 55. He had been constantly checking his rear-view until he was sure that someone was tailing him.

"Fuck you talkin' 'bout, followin' us? Ain't nobody followin' us. Nigga, you skitzin'," responded Duke, World's right hand man and the only survivor of his original team.

Duke hit the blunt and tried to pass it to World who waved it off and made a right hand turn. He didn't want to smoke and cloud his already paranoid brain cells until he was sure what was behind him.

"Watch, I told you, yo! That's the fourth corner in a row they took after us. Paranoid, hell! Niggas think we slippin' as it is!" Duke took a quick peep over his shoulder, weighing Young World's theory. He reached under his seat and pulled out a Mac 11 machine gun, locked and loaded.

"It's probably Roll and them niggas he fuck wit'. Fuck this. At the next light, I'm wettin' they whole shit. Fuck they think, shit is sweet?"

"Naw, naw, chill. I got this," World answered.

He suddenly hit the accelerator and the CL's AMG engine blurred like mercury as they jetted down the street. Whoever and whatever was behind them was left eight car lengths back as Young World whipped a quick right then a fishtailed left, slinging Duke in his seat.

"Fuck you runnin' for?" Duke growled.

Young World didn't respond. Instead he quickly pulled into a darkened driveway and dropped the headlights. He then pulled out a .45 from his waist, looking over his shoulder.

A few seconds later, the black BMW drove by. Young World backed out, engine kitten-silent. He had flipped the script and was now tailing them.

"At the light, I'ma cut 'em off, see who these niggas are, and if they flinch..."

Duke nodded "say no more". As they approached the stop light, Young World hit the gas and swerved around the BMW. Before the occupants of the BMW knew what was happening, Young World skidded up in front of them at a nose angle. Duke threw up the door and hopped out in one furious motion and threw the nozzle of the Mac in the face of the driver. The four passengers of the BMW screamed and ducked.

"Yo, Ock! It's Lana and some broads!" Duke hollered over his shoulder as he lowered the gun.

"What the fuck is you doin'?" yelled World through the open passenger door. "You tryin' to get killed or something?"

The girls finally uncovered their eyes and looked up, visibly shaken and teary-eyed.

"I'm sorry, World. I'm so, so sorry. God, you scared me. I'm sorry," Lana whined from the driver's seat.

"Naw, you was gonna be sorry. Now, you just crazy. I thought I told you I'd be back later?" World questioned, upset that Lana was out of position, especially in front of his man.

"It... it... I'm sorry, baby, but I thought... Peaches said..." Lana stammered before World cut her off.

"Peaches said what? Fuck that yellow bitch got to do with you followin' me?"

"Yellow, who!" Peaches shouted from the rear passenger seat after she got some of her sass back. "Nigga, please. Don't even go there, aiight!" Peaches said, rolling her eyes for extra emphasis.

"Whatever, bitch. Mind your business. Lana, you listenin' to Peaches now?"

"She told me she saw Tawanna from Hillside in your car last week, and she said that's where you was goin'," Lana explained, getting more teary-eyed by the minute, not only from fright, but from embarrassment for getting caught trying to follow him.

Duke laughed as Young World shook his head in aggravated amusement. He was on his way to a very important meeting with his connect, and all Lana could think about was some chickenhead he was fucking.

"You muthafuckas got way too much time on your hands. I ain't got time for this shit. Take your ass home and get all them crows out my car 'fore all y'all be walkin'!" World shouted.

Lana nodded, wiping her eyes. "I'm sorry, okay? I was silly I..."

World cut her off as Duke got back in the CL.

"Yeah yeah, I know. Just be naked when I get home," he said as he pulled off, giving her lonely, bitch-ass girlfriends something to talk about.

Young World turned the corner and sped off. Duke bust out laughing.

"Yo son, you is slippin'! You ain't even peep your own car was followin' us!"

"Everybody got black BM's, yo. How I'm supposed to know every BM in Newark?"

"Shorty must really got you on a leash, my nigga!"

"Fuck you," Young World replied with a chuckle. "That's how it is when a nigga know how to lay good dick, son. Shit, I should get outta the drug game and pimp hos for a living.

"Nigga, fuck around and be broke fucking with these hos out here," Duke joked, making them both laugh as they headed to Paramus, New Jersey.

Even though Young World was laughing, the situation was far from funny. It had been three years since Dutch's disappearance and already his empire had split into several factions. Young World was young, hungry and ruthless. However, he had stepped into the shoes of a man no one could ever fill.

Dutch had started with a team that had roots in every part of Newark, which made it easier to control. Young World's team came from Hawthorne and Prince Streets. So when Dutch disappeared, every team went for itself, and Young World had his hands full just keeping his territory under control.

Added to that was the fact that the police were seeing blood and weren't taking any prisoners. The police murder rate doubled while the criminal murder rate tripled. All together, the city was thrown into a frenzy. The Mayor empowered several new anti-drug teams to combat the threat, imposed curfews in certain areas, and kept the block so hot that where money once flowed, it now trickled. After 18 months, Young World lost major chunks of northern New Jersey. He had won the crown but getting down for it was another story.

Lana walked into the house and slammed the door. She felt like she had really played herself. It wasn't like her to second-guess Young World, so she couldn't for the life of her figure out why she had done it tonight. True, Peaches was one of her closest friends, but shit, World was her man.

Maybe Peaches want my man, her mind told her. But, she dismissed the thought as crazy.

Or was it?

Who wouldn't want Young World? He was rich, cool and fine. His baby-like dimples melted into the cinnamon texture of his masculine face, making his grins sexy and mischievous. He kept the crisp temper fade with waves that spun 360 degrees like the nigga on the Duke wave grease box. That, and he took good care of her.

Peaches, on the other hand, was a college drop-out turned secretary and didn't have a man. She had tried to get with Duke, but once he fucked her, he lost interest. Not to mention Peaches was always trying to put it in Lana's head that Young World was no good. She and Peaches had been friends since they were eleven. Two years later, Lana met Young World. They were just thirteen.

Back then, World was a corner hustler on Hawthorne, and she was a church girl from Peshine Avenue. Now at twenty-two, they had come a long way. She looked around the spacious living room of their West Orange ranch house. The interior would put half the MTV cribs to shame. The color scheme was a deep, creamy ivory accentuated with classic mahogany accents. The marble floor of the foyer opened up to a platform entrance that dropped three stair-steps to the living room. The Olympic-size swimming pool was visible through patio doors that stretched across the wall.

They had moved in eight months ago, and Young World had allowed Lana to have her way with the interior decorating. There was nothing Lana wanted for that World didn't make happen.

"Friend or no friend, ain't nobody gonna take this away from me," Lana whispered to herself.

Rationalizing, she figured if Peaches was right and World was fucking around with Tawanna, she didn't have the keys to a half-million dollar home. And, when it came to sex, Young World would never forget to be her lover. As a matter of fact, right before he left, she had been doing her aerobic workout. Lunging, bending, sweating, and twisting. He couldn't take his eyes off of her ass screaming through her tight stretch shorts. Lana found herself with her shorts around her ankles and bent over the arm of an Italian leather sofa as he gave her a real workout. Lana dropped her purse and keys on the marble coffee table on her way to their bedroom.

She entered the plush room and flipped on the answering machine. The first voice she heard was Young World's.

"Don't ever do that again, you hear me? Trust ain't never been an issue. So don't make it one."

The message ended.

Lana smiled to herself. Young World was right. She knew what he was going through out in the streets. He had the usual — the beefs, the police, the snitches, and those who wanted a piece of him. He had enough to worry about without his backbone getting weak, and she was definitely his backbone.

"I love you, boo," she chimed back to the recorded message. As she undressed for a shower, several messages rattled off, but the last one caught her attention.

"Young World, look this Angel. You don't know me like that, but I'm sure you know the name and what it's about. We need to talk. Call me 818-555-3879. Ask for Goldilocks. She got a message for you."

Angel? Lana thought as she flipped on her favorite Mary J CD and hopped into the shower.

She thought about a bath but was too lazy to clean the tub and run the water. Besides, she was in the mood to feel the pulsating pumps of the multi-jet sprayers. It was more relaxing, more sensual. Lana loved to feel the warm water cascade down her 5'5", 130 pound, well-toned frame. The spray felt like World's tongue all over her. The pulsating waters made her Jones come down for real. All she could think of was World in the shower with her, holding her tight and keeping her close.

Young World was her first and only lover, so what she knew of love he had taught her. He knew all of her secrets. She knew all of his weaknesses. Together, they had explored each other and learned life as one.

Lana turned off the shower and began to dry herself off, going back out the bedroom. Mary J's 'Seven Days' had just begun to play as Lana stepped onto a carpet so soft it felt like walking on a cloud. She turned up the temperature on their water bed then went to get some panties when she remembered World's last words and decided to leave them in the drawer. She stretched across the bed and lit up the half blunt that sat in the ashtray. Life was good.

The euphoria of the weed mellowed her out. Lana glanced at the clock. 12:27 a.m. She sighed as she snuggled into the silk Gucci sheets bunched up in all the right places and zoned into relaxation. She inhaled the purple haze. Young World was out taking care of business and she knew there was no telling when he'd get back. So until he did, she'd have to entertain herself. Her hands slid lower down her pelvis.

The iron gates of the sixteen bedroom, twenty-two bath mansion swung open slowly to admit Young World's CL 55 onto the private property. The driveway led to a bridge that crossed a man-made lake framing the front of the mansion like a medieval moat. The lights along the lake shimmered in the mirror of the water as the short bridge led him to a driveway that ended at the front door. The mansion was built to suit Greco Roman tastes. Four spiral ivory columns supported the curved alabaster awning that led up the stairs to the first floor.

Duke looked at the spread lustfully. It was the exact type of place he saw himself in in a few years. After he finished his grind, he too would live like this. From one room, roach-infested tenements to rented condos to this. This was what the game was all about for Duke. He had never met the connect before and wondered if he was a Tony Montana-looking Cuban or suave Sosa-type muthafucka.

"Damn this muthafucka laced!" Duke exclaimed in a whisper full of awe, thinking of Jadakiss's words to 'Mansion by the Lake', and Young World silently agreed. Young World had only met the connect twice before but never at his home. It made the crib World had just purchased look like a double-wide in a redneck trailer park.

As Young World pulled up to the awning, two burly men in dark suits wearing earpiece communicators emerged from the shadows and approached the car.

Young World lowered his window before speaking to the dark suits, "Mr. Ceylon is expectin' us."

"We know," said the taller of the two who smirked. The CL wouldn't have gotten in if they weren't expected.

"Follow me," said the shorter one.

World and Duke got out of the car as the short guard led them to the door. Before letting them enter, he scanned them both with a hand-held metal detector. The erratic beeping blurted out sirens near Duke's waist. Duke handed the guard his gun and Young World did the same with his .45. Once relieved of their weapons, they were escorted into the mansion.

Inside, they were greeted by the sounds of a piano sonata that World thought was a record, but it was Ceylon sitting in his living room playing Mozart himself. As Duke and World entered, Ceylon kept his eyes closed and continued to play. The guards closed the door and left them alone with Ceylon.

Duke looked at the man behind the piano, eyes closed like he was meditating. He was nothing like Duke expected. Instead of a suave Spaniard, Ceylon was small, almost tiny, skinny and frail. He reminded Duke of a bookkeeper. His sharp aquiline nose gave away his ethnicity.

Ceylon was of Turkish origin, and although he was small, his power was huge. He was a diplomat, and the man he represented would make Frank Sosa look like a corner hustler. Ceylon himself was far from a drug dealer. His international influence merely made it easy for men like his clients to flood the streets of New York to Frankfurt with the deadly white poison.

Ceylon dined with presidents, dictators, world bankers and terrorists, and now here he was, meeting with two brash young thugs from the ghetto. Never underestimate the power of the streets. He had called Young World and asked to meet him personally, something he rarely did, and Young World knew why. World knew he wasn't moving a fifth of what he used to move, and Ceylon's patience was running thin. How thin, World didn't know. He made World wish he still had his burner on his waist, just in case.

Ceylon ended his sonata on the Steinway and sat stone still, eyes remaining closed, as the last vibration of notes dissipated into silence.

"Mr. Cey...,"

"Shhh," Ceylon softly whispered, putting a finger to his lips. "Music is like fine wine. It must be savored, and talk is bad for my digestion," he philosophized in a nasal Turkish accent. He sounded like a cross between Elijah Muhammad and Einstein.

Young World and Duke exchanged glances. After a few seconds, Ceylon rose from the piano bench and approached his guests.

"Mr. Young World and Duke, I presume," Ceylon greeted. Duke nodded.

"Pleasure to meet you, Mr. Ceylon," Duke replied extending a hand which Ceylon disdainfully regarded then totally ignored. He folded his arms behind his back and responded,
"It remains to be seen if it is a pleasure to meet or not."

Duke lowered his hand, gritting his teeth on the low. Ceylon turned to World.

"I would offer you a drink but you won't be staying long. I am a man who does not mince words and waste time, and you, Mr. World, are wasting my time."

World's ego stiffened and he wanted to answer him with some fly shit but checked his tongue.

"Mr. Ceylon, with all due respect, I'm doin' all I can but things are hectic right now. Wit' everybody snitchin', the Feds everywhere and the mob..." he tried to explain, but Ceylon smoothly cut him off.

"Excuses are never good reasons," Mr. Ceylon said with a patronizing smirk. He turned on his heels, went to the bar and poured himself a drink.

"I am fully aware of your current situation, painfully aware actually. You have lost major portions of your territory to rival factions and defections from your own camp. The mob, as you call them, has muscled you out of entire cities and you appear powerless to do anything about it."

Ceylon sipped his drink and approached Young World.

"Do you know how much product Dutch distributed weekly? No less than 2500 kilograms of heroin. While you, his chosen, so-called protégée, can barely muster 1300 or 1500 a month," Ceylon explained steadily eyeing World.

"I ain't Dutch," World stated as a matter of fac, returning his gaze.

"This, too, is obvious," Ceylon agreed before placing his drink on a table. "There are few men I have trusted, five..., no four, because I can't always include myself. Four, and I have known countless. Dutch is one of those four. Do you know why?" he asked as he looked Young World in the eye.

Young World didn't respond, so he continued.

"Because of the eye," he said, tapping his eyelid and turning away. "It never lies. To know a man is to know the truth as to what he will or won't do, and it all lies in the eye. I have searched many eyes and read them all. Except Dutch. Do you know what I saw in his eyes? Nothing except the reflection of myself."

"What do you see in mine?" World asked, wanting to know where he stood in all this.

"Fear, hate, confusion but most of all, determination to overcome all of that."

Young World didn't know if he had just been insulted or complimented so he thought carefully before he spoke.

"Look, Mr. Ceylon. I didn't come here to make excuses. Like I said, shit is hectic. They bleed, we bleed, then they bleed some more. That's how it goes on the streets 'cause not everybody got the luxury of sitting around playing piano."

Ceylon smirked at Young World's snideness. "This is very true... But, I wonder, Mr. World, if you know the difference between a goon and a gangster?"

"I suppose you gonna tell me."

"Every gangster starts out as a goon. He must because power is born of force. But when a man continues to use violence, it means he didn't use it right the first time. He is still a goon. His power is always in question, therefore it will one day be usurped. But a gangster, ahhh, a gangster is a man who makes his own rules and the rest are left to follow. His nod is his gun, a mere smile seals the deal, and his word is law."

Ceylon dropped his jaw then added, "Now, because I trusted Dutch, I trust his judgement. So therefore I am open to trust you because yours is the name he left. It is against my own judgement, but after all, that is what trust is about, no?"

World nodded. Duke wanted to speak but World was in charge so he played his position.

"Whatever I gotta do to rep my bloodline, I'll do. You got my word on that Mr. Ceylon," World vowed, meaning every word. "Just give me six months and..."

"Thirty days," Ceylon interrupted.

"Huh?"

"You have exactly thirty days to double your output. After that, you shall be cut off and cut out and please do not try to replace us with another supplier. It would be deemed disrespectful and treated as such," Ceylon smirked, unveiling his threat.

Thirty-days? This guy is crazy, World thought, but he held his composure and responded.

"Mr. Ceylon, I can't..."

Ceylon's nasal tone escalated a decibel. "Can't is not a word men of caliber use, unless, of course, it proceeds the word fail."

He turned away quickly and went back to sit at the piano.

"To your credit, I can see the potential Dutch saw in you. You do have determination and you do have zeal. You just lack the audacity it takes to be our mutual friend's successor. Good evening, gentlemen."

With that, Ceylon began to play his piano again, and as if on cue, the double doors swung open. The guards had been waiting to escort Young World and Duke out.

Duke was heated. He and World drove in tense silence. He pulled on his Newport forcefully, and it glowed fire-red to match his temper. The old man had dissed World to his face, threatened him like a schoolyard bully, and talked to him as if he was a child.

The old man must've thought they were illiterate, but Duke knew exactly what Ceylon meant. He had basically called World a dumb fuck and a coward, and World didn't even defend himself. In so many words, Ceylon had even threatened to take the streets they controlled. Niggas bled so they could eat and World let some old man tell him to his face that he'd take it.

Duke shook his head. Young World was getting soft. He had been suspecting it, and tonight confirmed it.

"What?" World asked, glancing at Duke. "You got somethin' to say?"

"Nothin', kid," Duke replied, then tossed his cigarette out the window.

"Naw Ock. Don't bite your tongue. You got something to say, say it," World insisted.

"Man... who the fuck does that nigga Ceylon think he be fuckin' talkin' to? I don't give a damn who he know or where he from. Ain't nobody takin' shit from us!" Duke exclaimed, in his mind replacing us with me.

Young World felt the same way, but what could he do? He knew Ceylon wasn't the kind of man you took to war with a gun. He was above street fights. To World and his young wolves, Ceylon was untouchable.

"So what do you suggest, huh? Go back, guns blazin' and then what? Wait for the muthafucka to send his army?" World tried to reason.

"We got an army, too. So fuck all that shit that nigga poppin'," Duke reminded him, then almost as an afterthought he added, "It ain't nothin' but a phone call unless you can't make the call."

Young World had reached a red light. "What the fuck that 'posed to mean, Duke?"

Duke was fed up with the way World was running things. "Just like I said, Ock. Shit that's been happenin' didn't even have to happen, but lately you been on some bullshit and I ain't wit' it."

"Bullshit like what? Ceylon? You think you coulda handled it better, huh?"

The light turned green but World was so busy defending himself that the drivers behind him started hitting their horns. Young World shot an evil look into the rear-view, then slowly pulled off.

"I ain't even talkin' about Ceylon. I'm talking 'bout the bullshit!"

"What bullshit?!"

"Roll!" Duke barked, and Young World got quiet.

Roll was of the team and rap group, Rock and Roll, until Craze broke them up with mind games. Rock stuck to producing music and got out of the game but Roll had become one of Young World's chief rivals. Roll's name had been ringing bells and he had a team spread out as thick as World's. The only difference was that Roll was steadily expanding and World was steadily contracting.

A team of four gunmen had robbed World's people in Atlantic City for over a million dollars in heroin and cash and killed two of World's top dogs.

World got word that it was Roll who had robbed him and stuck him for the million dollars. Roll didn't try to hide it either. It was a slap in the face, a provocation for World to go to war, yet Young World hadn't responded and that was over a month ago.

"Fuck Roll! I ain't forgot about that fat muthafucka! I got other shit to worry about. You heard Ceylon. We got thirty days to double our distribution or we cut off. I don't give a fuck how many guns we got. We get cut off, it's finished!" Young World spat heatedly.

"What you mean 'Fuck Roll'? It's because of shit like that why we losin' spots as it is! Muthafuckas think we soft. Fuck that! We go all out and take all these bitches to war! Ceylon, Roll, and whoever the fuck else! That's how we double distribution, and if we don't, we find another connect."

Duke had it all figured out and was ready to get down for his crown or die tryin'.

Young World shook his head. Duke was letting his emotions speak for him, but Young World knew better.

The last three years had taken a real toll on his team, he and Duke the only survivors from the original clique. Except for a few remaining Angel's Charlies, the rest of his organization was bound by the dollar, or fear, not by loyalty. And they were second-rate at best.

World felt trapped. It was like every time he solved one problem, two jumped up to take its place. He was like any other young black man on the streets, trying to win by someone else's rules, trying to play the game without understanding the nature of power. He forgot the lesson Dutch's game plan laid out. He loved Dutch for putting him in his present position. *But damn, why'd you have to die?* he thought.

"Look, yo," World began in a calm tone. "Ain't shit soft about World, son. I handle shit my way, period point blank. I'm the one gotta answer for this shit, and I'm in this to get paper. Niggas be on that ra ra shit, fuck 'em. I'll see 'em on my terms, on my time. Until then..." Young World looked at Duke, "You either wit' me or against me."

He gave Duke the ultimate ultimatum, but Duke wasn't prepared to go solo... yet.

"Whatever you say, Ock. Whatever you say."

Young World turned up the system and Scarface'd his way back to Newark. He pulled up to Sammy's Place off Broad Street where Duke had parked his Hummer.

"On the real, Duke. I feel where you comin' from, and I feel the same way. But I need you to trust me, aiight? Let me handle this my way," Young World said, throwing his car in park.

Duke shrugged and opened the door. "I got you, World."

"Duke, we been through too much together to fuck up now, yo."

Duke flashed a phony smile.

"Fuck you need a hug nigga. I said I got you," he chuckled and eased the tension between them. They shook hands.

"I'll call you later," said World.

"One," replied Duke.

"One."

World pulled off with ease, thinking everything was love, but it wasn't. Duke watched the tail-lights of the Mercedes disappear, then turned towards the door of Sammy's and went inside.

It was a small, sleazy joint but out of the way enough that Duke felt that he would see no one he knew. He had another important meeting, one Young World knew nothing about. He had a meeting with the mob.

Vinnie Z and his fat henchman sat in the rear of the bar at a secluded booth. Vinnie was all smiles the moment he saw Duke.

Vinnie was the stereotypical young, cocky Italian, always grabbing his balls and using hand gestures with his syllables. They had met when Vinnie tried to convince Young World that he needed the mob in his corner, not against him, but Young World refused. Duke, on the other hand, saw his opportunity and seized it, sending word to Vinnie that they should talk and this meeting was a result of that message.

As Duke approached, Vinnie stood to greet him, giving him a firm and vigorous handshake.

"Duke! Paisano! How you doin', eh? You look good. Mikey, it's Duke. Say hello to Duke," Vinnie ranted like Duke was a war buddy.

Jabba-like Mikey just grunted inaudibly. To Mikey, a nigger was a nigger, and he didn't want to be bothered. Vinnie felt the same way. He was just a better actor. He knew young black guys loved the Mafioso persona, so Vinnie laid it on thick.

"Sit down, Duke. What choo drinkin'?"

Duke sat down and unbuttoned his coat. "Naw, I'm good."

Vinnie sat back, shaking the ice in his glass. "Okay. Duke's good, so, ah, what's good with Duke?" Vinnie inquired.

Duke took out a cigarette, and Vinnie produced a lighter. "You tell me, Z."

"How's Young World?"

"He just left. You shoulda said something. I woulda told him to come on in," Duke answered sarcastically.

"If you don't mind my saying so, your friend is an asshole. I can't talk to him. You, I can talk to. You know why? Because you're a reasonable guy. You and I, we could have a good thing, eh?"

Duke blew cigarette smoke out his mouth before speaking.

"Maybe we can arrange a few things."

"Definitely, because a guy like you needs friends like me, eh? I give you a place to lay your hat. I talk to people, they talk to people, and we all sit down and eat, ba-da-bing?"

"Ba-da-boom," Duke smiled. "I just hope some of these people you talkin' to is judges and DAs 'cause niggas catchin' cases like snitches is sexually transmittin' 'em."

"Forget about it," Vinnie warned with a gesture of dismissal. "My guys are good guys, and we take care of our friends. You just gimme a call when it's a go on your end, capisci?" Vinnie grinned greedily.

He was itching to get his olive-oiled hands on Young World's territory and Duke was just the monkey to bring it to him. Dutch had run the Italians out of the Newark drug game and now Duke was ready to bring them back in and play puppet in their tangled strings. All Vinnie needed was a chance to implement his plan, and Young World was unwittingly about to give it to him.

Young World stood in the bedroom door and admired his

sleeping beauty. She lay wrapped to the waist in peach colored sheets that accentuated her ebony skin tone.

He loved her.

Lana was the perfect hustler's wife. She had been with him every step of the way, stashing money, holding work, and tucking pistols when necessary. Although it took him two years, Lana gave him her virginity. They had been inseparable ever since. Lana was his first love, the game was his second.

World loved being the man his position made him. And it wasn't just the money. It was the power and respect. a respect he knew he had to rep to maintain.

He walked over to the dresser and picked up a picture of him and Dutch at a Roy Jones fight. World admired Dutch's finesse. The smirk that framed his chocolate face told the world he knew he was that nigga. When Young World first met Dutch, he knew he was destined to be a legend and he wanted to be just like him, the way he bopped, his sharp Newark accent, his smooth style. But when Dutch peeped it, he checked him quick.

"I like you lil' nigga, word up. You a thoroughbred. You just been misled. I see you wanna be like me, but if you really wanna be like me, don't be like me. That's why I am who I am because ain't another muthafucka like Dutch."

Dutch wasn't his mentor. One-eyed Roc was. It was Roc who put him on, but Dutch would often come scoop him off the block and sharpen his game. World knew if Roc and Angel hadn't been locked up, he would've never had the opportunity he had now. So he looked at it as a fate he was destined to fulfill. But he needed answers, and he knew who had them.

Roc.

He needed to go see Roc.

World cursed himself for not thinking of it sooner, but things were so damned hectic. It was hard enough to catch some sleep let alone think straight.

Young World slid open the drawer and gazed at its contents. Dutch's dragon chain.

He lifted the heavy piece from the drawer and cradled it in his hand. The diamonds and rubies glistened and sparkled on the 24-karat gold nugget barrel link. Before Dutch, Kazami had worn the chain. Kazami, the wild African who everyone feared until Dutch murdered him and took the chain. Afterwards, Dutch locked down the streets. Ever since World had the chain, he had only worn it only occasionally. Now it was time to rep it to the fullest.

World kicked off his shoes, laid on the bed fully clothed behind Lana, and cradled her body to his. His touch instantly awoke her.

"Hey, baby. I missed you," she cooed sleepily.

"Go back to sleep, boo. It's late," World softly replied, his mind a million miles away.

"You hungry?" she asked, looking over her shoulder at him.

"Naw, I'm good."

They had been together too long for her not to recognize the troubled tone in his voice. She turned over and faced Young World, tucking her right hand under her head.

"Everything okay?" she questioned with concern.

He shrugged, "It is what it is."

"So, what is it?" she smiled, still probing.

World looked his love in the eyes, their faces only inches apart, and asked, "Do you think I've changed?"

"Changed?" Lana echoed with a wrinkled brow, "Changed how?"

"I don't know, just..."

"Is this about earlier? If it is, you were right. I trust you," she assured him, cutting him off from what he was about to say.

"Not like that," he began. "You think I'm gettin' soft?"

"Soft? Baby, you know I keep it all the way gangsta with you, but it's been so long since I've been around you like that to know," Lana replied, then added, "You locked me out of that part of your life."

"But you lay with me, therefore you know my weakness," World answered.

"Remember before Jazz died, y'all was beefin' with Chancellor?"

"Yeah."

"I heard you say to him that a gun may get you power but a gun can't keep you in power," Lana explained, using the jewel against him. He had heard it from Roc and now he better understood the difference between a gangsta and a goon. He had the goon part down. He just needed to learn the ways of a true gangsta. He smiled and gently kissed her forehead.

"I'm sayin', you my wifey or my godfather?" he joked.

Lana giggled and replied with the godfather rasp in her voice, "Just call me Vito Corleone."

They both laughed. Lana caressed his face.

"Just do what you have to do to come home to me every night. Shaheed, promise me you'll never let them take you away from me."

"I promise, baby. I love you, Lana."

"I love you, my World."

Duke slipped out of bed, stretched his arms wide, and embraced the morning sun. He had always been an early bird, a habit he acquired from his days on the block. Duke was the type of hustler who worked harder, not smarter. His strength lay in his endurance, not in his swiftness. A good trait for a soldier, but Duke wanted to be the general.

His mind went back to his conversation the night before with Young World. It had been a week since their meeting with Ceylon and Young World had been on his grind trying to meet the deadline. World had told Duke that he was going to see Roc, and of course, he was in charge during his absence.

"Yo, Duke, stay sucka-free," he added because he knew Duke's love for drama.

Duke was a live wire for gunplay, which was the main reason Young World had cliqued up with him back in the day. Once World's man Jazz had been murdered, it was only right that Duke fill the position. But Duke wasn't content being the man next to the man. He wanted to be that nigga.

He glanced down at the two naked white girls in his bed and his mouth twisted in a wicked grin as he remembered the lusty episode from last night. Duke had a thing for young girls and he found out that white women were real loose with black dick. The two sleeping seventeen-year-olds were no exception. He had pumped them full of "E" then pumped them full of his "D", and with his adrenaline pumping for what lay ahead, his bone hardened on the spot.

Both girls were blondes from their heads down to their pubic hairs, which turned Duke on. He slipped his fingers between the legs of the shorter of the two who had been sleeping on her stomach and slid inside of her forcefully, waking her up with one pounding thrust.

"Arrrrgghhh!" she groaned in shock, trying to squirm from under Duke's thug fuck. He pinned her wrists to the bed and spread her legs wider until she was spread eagle on her belly. All the moaning and shouting woke her friend from her slumber. She opened her eyes and caught the sight of Duke's long black dick sliding in and out of her friend and it made her horny.

"Oh Duke! Duuuuuke!" she groaned, loving the muscle Duke was running up in her.

He felt the build up in his balls and pulled out just in time to gag her friend's throat with his load.

"Good morning to you, too, Daddy," the shorter blonde cooed, rolling off her stomach, sore and satisfied.

Duke used her shirt to clean himself off."

"Y'all gotta get goin', yo. I got shit to do."

Duke headed for the bathroom to clean up. After his shower, he dressed in his favorite Carolina blue Roc-a-wear velour suit and Carolina blue Jordans. He headed for the kitchen and found that the girls were gone. He fixed himself breakfast like they usually did. They were at his beck and call, and because they lived in the same condominium complex, he had easy access to their favors.

Duke sat down to his omelette and turkey sausage and mentally planned his day. For him, it was the most important day of his life. His idea had been on the back burner for quite a while. So as soon as World said he was going out of town, Duke knew the time had come. He figured if he pulled it off as he planned, they could easily double distribution in one day.

He was going to have Roll killed.

Roll controlled major spots in New Jersey, and Duke believed if you killed the head the body would die. Besides, if Young World was afraid of an all-out war, this was the perfect solution.

If he could pull off the murder.

Roll wasn't someone to fuck with. He had been in the game for years, so he was sharp and always on point. He kept no pattern that could be used fatally against him, so he wasn't an easy target. But Duke felt confident in his plan. His greed told him that if he killed Roll, then all that was Roll's would be his. Then World would be dependent on him for the new spots. It would be leverage Duke could use in getting World to agree to the mob backing he finally had in his corner. From there, it was just a matter of time before he would push Young World aside and take his spot.

Everybody wants to be boss.

Duke checked his watch then picked up his cell phone and dialed his shooters. The phone rang several times before he heard the aggravated voice of an awakened killer.

"Who this?"

"Get yo' ass up nigga! We got work to do," Duke barked into the phone, flipping his plasma to ESPN to check the scores. Ty snapped up and rubbed his eyes, trying to revive himself.

"Oh, what up Duke, my bad son? I ain't..."

"Yo, is you ready?" asked Duke, cutting him off.

"No doubt."

"How the fuck is you ready and you asleep?" Duke fired back, catching Ty's dumb ass in a trick question.

"I meant I'm getting ready, yo. Gimme like 30 minutes, aiight?" Ty said, standing up with the phone cradled to his cheek while he put his pants on.

Duke didn't even bother to reply. He simply hung up the phone and grabbed his keys to meet Ty at the rendezvous spot.

Chapter Five

Free at last!

Angel stepped onto the Boeing 747 bound for San Francisco, California. She had been out twenty-four hours and anyone who's been locked up knows the first twenty-four hours are always the sweetest. The air smelled fresh, not stale like the recycled air inside the prison. The sun shined brighter and seemed to embrace her with welcoming warmth. Even the mundane sounds of car horns and the hustle and bustle of everyday life was music to the ears of a person who hadn't heard anything but the slamming of steel and the gravely shuffle on concrete. All that was behind her, and her lover, Goldilocks, had made sure that Angel stepped out in style.

Goldilocks had a stretch Benz limo waiting outside the federal women's prison in Alderson, West Virginia. But she didn't stop there. She had an outfit, shoes, and everything Angel needed waiting for her. Goldilocks knew Angel's taste for men's clothing and dressed her to look like one. When the female CO escorted Angel to the front door and took one look at Angel in the outfit, her face turned green with hate.

Angel smirked.

"Take a picture for Trina and Lil' Kim and let 'em know who

the baddest bitch really is!" Angel remarked, rubbing her wealth in the face of the heavyset low-wage earner.

"Hmph, you'll be back," said the CO.

But going back wasn't the plan for Angel. It was time for the jump off. She wasn't only going to take back what was hers. She was about to elevate the game to the next level. All who couldn't hang had best bow out.

"Welcome to Continental flight 1707 from Atlanta, Georgia to San Francisco, California. Enjoy your flight and don't hesitate to let us know if you need anything," the shapely stewardess announced with a friendly smile.

Angel eyed the woman, from her long sexy legs to her small slim waist and perky breasts, and couldn't help but smile. The flight attendant couldn't help but notice and returned Angel's smile with a grin of her own.

"Believe me, sweetie, You'll be the first to know if I need anything," Angel said, stressing anything.

"You do that," the flight attendant flirted back as she walked down the aisle. Angel watched her from behind.

Angel was exotically gorgeous. Her time in prison had only served to enhance her already voluptuous figure. She and Goldilocks had worked out religiously and had succeeded in sculpting Angel's 5'7" frame into a Beyoncé-type figure. Her panther slant, light brown eyes gave her the look of a dangerous beauty.

She relaxed as the plane taxied and took flight. The takeoff was always the worst. She had only been on a plane twice in her life and both times had been with Dutch. Her heart ached for him as she imagined him sitting next to her instead of the elderly white woman in pearls.

Relax, mami. We where we 'posed to be 'cause stars belong in the sky. That's what Dutch had said to her the last time they were on a plane. The whole crew had flown to St. Tropez, back when shit was sweet, when they were on top of the world, untouchable and together. Now he was gone, but her heart refused to accept it.

Dondé es, papi? her palpitating heart asked, and it was as if she could hear his reply. *Wherever you are, I am. They can't stop what they can't see. Never forget that. Now it's your turn. Rep the bloodline and show these muthafuckas real niggas don't die.*

Te quiero, her mind replied because she thought only in Spanish.

The flight to California took forever. The only thing that kept Angel amused was the cat and mouse game she played with the stewardess. Angel flirted and the stewardess blushed, so Angel flirted some more.

The flight attendant brought Angel a drink, which for Angel was the perfect opportunity to make a move. When the flight attendant handed her the plastic cup, Angel caught her hand and held it in hers. She looked at her nails.

"You need a manicure, boo."

The stewardess giggled nervously, "I plan on taking care of that when I get some time off."

"I got some things you can take care of when you get some time," said Angel, throwing it out there.

"I guess it depends on what types of things," the flight attendant replied as she slowly withdrew her hand.

Angel knew she had made her point. Before she got off the plane, she had the stewardess' number tucked away in her pocket.

Once she arrived in San Francisco, Angel cut through the

terminal in a confident stride and headed for the baggage claim area. Goldilocks was supposed to be waiting for her, and just as she promised, she was.

Goldilocks was leaning on the hood of a jet black 760i with a charcoal gray interior. She was casually dressed in a Juicy jogging suit, Nike sneakers and Fred sunglasses. With no makeup, she radiated beauty. Goldilocks was shorter than Angel and more petite. She was half-German and half-black. German, in her smoke gray eyes and high yellow skin, but black in her fat ass and sassy attitude.

She got the name Goldilocks because of her shoulder length dreads that were sun-kissed to a golden brown. She and Angel had met in prison while Goldilocks was doing a stint for bank robbery. She was bi-sexual and had been gay way before she met Angel. She was not only Angel's lover but her best friend, a first for Angel who had always swung with men and rolled dolo.

Goldilocks had gotten out a few months before Angel and had been counting the days until they would be reunited. As soon as she saw Angel come through the door, she hurried to her, threw her arms around her neck, and tongue-kissed her like Angel was a soldier coming home from war.

"I missed you! Oh my God! I can't believe you're finally here," Goldilocks whispered, caressing Angel's ear with her tongue.

People walking through the baggage area couldn't help but stare at the two women locked a passionate embrace. Even in San Francisco, passion that electric turned heads.

"Be easy ma before you start something we could be arrested for finishing," Angel smirked, wet with anticipation.

Goldilocks took Angel's hand and slid it inside her sweat pants down to her pussy. "It ain't like we ain't been there before," she teased.

"Yeah, and it's somewhere we ain't goin' no time soon," Angel replied as she removed Goldi's hand and smacked her on the ass with it. "Take me home."

Once they arrived at Goldilocks' apartment, the two girls wasted no time. Goldilocks stepped out of her sweatpants, revealing her firm, juicy ass to Angel's lustful eyes. She began to do striptease for Angel, removing her shirt and bra slowly. Her tits were the size of ripe grapefruits and had tiny red freckles around the nipples that Angel tickled with the tip of her pierced tongue.

"Damn, you got me so wet," Goldilocks moaned, rubbing her clit then sticking her finger in Angel's mouth so she could taste her sweet nectar. Angel undressed and stood over Goldilocks as she lay on the couch, spread-eagle. Angel then took Goldilocks' legs and placed them over her shoulders before going down on her.

Goldilocks arched her back to meet Angel's adventurous tongue that lapped greedily over her pulsating pussy, bringing her to a thunderous orgasm.

Then it was Goldi's turn.

"I got a surprise for you, boo," Goldilocks announced mischievously after Angel came in her mouth. She reached under the couch and produced a large nine-inch strap-on. She started to harness it around her waist, but Angel grabbed it from her.

"Nah, that's my job," Angel said, asserting her dominance and refusing to have a dick, fake or real, fuck her.

Angel strapped on the dildo and bent Goldilocks over the edge of the couch, plowing into her with the hard rubber as if it was real.

"Sssss-awwww," Goldi gasped, sucking in air through clenched teeth. Angel slid deeper inside her tight hole with the nine-incher.

"Ohh, Angel, Angel, Angel!" Goldilocks repeated like a hook in her favorite song. It was definitely good to have her lover home.

After they showered, they ate Chinese takeout and laid naked on Goldi's bed, basking in the glow of their reunion.

"If I told you I loved you, would you believe me?" Goldilocks asked, looking Angel in the eyes.

"Should I?" Angel countered.

"I wouldn't say it if I didn't mean it," Goldilocks replied solemnly. "You mean a lot to me, Angel. What we have, the world may not understand, but I do and I never want it to end."

"Nothin' last forever, ma," Angel said, remembering all that she had lost in life.

"But it can last for life."

Angel shrugged, "Love makes you do crazy things, G. And I don't need crazy right now. I need D.B.D."

"D.B.D?" Goldilocks questioned, not recognizing the term.

"Death before Dishonor."

Angel eyed Goldilocks' reaction. She knew Goldi didn't have the heart of a killer, but if she was planning on rolling with Angel, she'd have to do something.

"Death before dishonor," Goldilocks repeated the code like a bride saying 'I do'.

She tried to kiss Angel, but Angel stopped her with an index finger to the lips. She traced the outline of her bottom lip and across her chin to the flesh of her throat.

"Everything I'm about goes against everything you've ever

known," Angel explained, sliding her index finger and thumb down Goldi's gently heaving cleavage and circling her breasts. "And I gotta know. I gotta trust that the only thing that matters to you is me."

Goldilocks closed her eyes and licked her lips, enjoying the soft sensuality of Angel's touch.

"I gotta know that your body is mine."

"It is, I swear."

"Your mind," Angel continued, caressing Goldi to her navel. "Will you kill for me?"

"Yes, I'll do anything for you," Goldilocks responded.

Angel brought her face closer until they were sharing air.

"Will you die for me?"

Goldilocks blinked and focused on Angel as her fingers slipped inside her wetness. Goldi nodded slowly.

"Anything."

Angel smiled and kissed her.

"Then we need to go to church," Angel announced.

First Street Baptist Church.

Angel struck a match with one manicured hand and sparked her cigarette. She concentrated on the reddish orange flame before blowing it out. She inhaled deeply, threw her head back, and blew a stream of smoke into the cloudy morning sky. The Los Angeles streets were slick from rain the night before.

Angel looked at the face of the church that boasted the name 'Reverend Qwan Taylor' on its marquee. It had been almost four years since Qwan testified against Dutch, and Angel dreamed of making this trip ever since. She understood why Dutch let Qwan live. Qwan had always been a coward. He wasn't of the same caliber as the rest of the team. Angel had known it ever since she first laid eyes on him. He was a good car thief and an excellent driver, but that's where his talents ended.

When the Month of Murder kicked into full swing, Angel saw how jittery and nervous he was. Qwan just wasn't cut out for that shit, and Dutch knew it so he pardoned him. Angel understood Dutch's motives perfectly, but she didn't agree with them, not yet. Not until she had the chance to see for herself if Qwan had been truly vindicated.

Angel approached the front door taking a long drag of her Newport before throwing it to the ground. She knocked on the door. No one answered. She knocked again louder, and still no answer. Angel tried the knob, but it was locked.

"Shit," she cursed before stepping around the side of the building to the parking lot. The only vehicle in the lot was a sparkling new gray Lincoln Navigator parked near the rear door. She walked across the small parking lot and knocked on the back door. A few seconds passed before she heard footsteps behind the door. Angel took a deep breath and let it out slowly as the door opened. Qwan stood behind it.

Angel recognized him instantly even though he had gotten a little chubby and had grown a goatee. He was dressed tastefully in a blue double-breasted suit that was clearly tailored to fit.

Looks like God's been looking out for a nigga, she thought sarcastically.

"Hello Qwan. Long time no see, huh?"

Qwan looked puzzled for a minute. It had been almost fifteen years since he had seen Angel, and her blonde wig hid the jet black hair he was used to. Qwan's eyes quickly took in every curve that generously filled out the body hugging silk dress she wore so well. Even Angel had to look twice at her own reflection. She couldn't remember ever wearing a dress in her life, let alone a dress so clingy and revealing. *How do broads wear this shit,* she thought, hoping her breasts didn't pop out of the front.

He looked at her face again and recognized her under the sexy outfit and wig.

"Angel?" he asked breathlessly.

"Who else?" she smiled, flinging her arms open. "Ain't you got a hug for an old friend, Qwan?"

He hesitated but Angel didn't. She enveloped him in a tight embrace, making sure to press her hot body against him, sending fire through his sanctified loins.

Angel stepped back slowly to allow Qwan a good look at her.

"How...where have you...I haven't..."

His questions and comments stumbled over each other as he attempted to be speak them all at once. Yet the main question he wanted to ask was what was she doing there.

"Now this is what I call a nice surprise," he said, admiring her from head to toe.

"Well, I moved out here temporarily, and you was on my mind. So, here I am," Angel replied.

"Come on in, Angel. Come on in," Qwan invited, stepping aside to usher her inside.

Angel brushed her breasts against him purposefully as she entered a small stairway that led to a plush office. The desk was black lacquer and the carpet was thick burgundy. A bookshelf took up three walls while the fourth held a large picture of a black Jesus and a golden crucifix. Under the picture was a long, beige leather couch.

Angel sat in the chair in front of the desk while Qwan perched on the edge of the desk.

"So... where did you move to?" Qwan inquired, hands

clasped in his lap.

"San Francisco. I met a few chicks in the pen that had a nice racket going on in the Bay, so I said what the hell, you know?" Angel explained, only half lying.

"Yes, I heard about that. I'm sorry I didn't write or anything, but with my duties here at the church... well, you know what they say, the Lord's work is never done."

"And from the looks of it, his workers get paid well. Is that your Navigator out there?"

Qwan cleared his throat nervously. "Yes. Well, I try to maintain a respectable persona. It's important that the congregation see the blessing God gives the faithful."

Angel nodded and looked around. An eerie pause played with the rhythm of the moment. Qwan broke the awkward silence.

"San Francisco's kinda far, but I know a few good churches I can recommend if you'd like."

Angel brushed blonde hair off her face. "You know me, Qwan. Ain't much changed. I'm still the same ol' Angel. Church is the last thing on my mind."

"Well, God is the changer of hearts."

"So I've heard," she sighed, tired of the small talk. "Listen Qwan, I think you know why I'm here."

"I have some idea."

"So why don't we talk about it, then? Why did you do it, Qwan? We was a family, La Familia. And family don't turn on family for nothin'."

Her eyes narrowed, but Qwan averted her gaze. He stood up and walked around the desk pensively. He sat down then and looked at Angel above tented hands.

"If I told you it was hard to do, Angel, I'd be lying. I don't feel any remorse. Maybe that's hard for you to understand but I pray I can make you. Do you remember the port?"

"Of course."

Qwan leaned forward in his chair.

"When I went to prison for that year, I took a long hard look at my life. I saw myself starting a vicious cycle that could only end in one of two places. Prison again and again or the grave-yard, and I didn't want either. One night, I prayed. I prayed like never before and I asked God to show me the way, to guide me, and he did. He guided me to His Son, my Lord and Savior, Jesus Christ."

Angel got the feeling he had recited this speech before, prob-ably to wayward youth, but she let the record play out.

"When I came home, it was like I forgot Him, forgot his Son, and I fell right back into Satan's trap. Dutch. You may not like what I'm about to say, but Dutch was a devil. He was evil. I just didn't know how evil until the night he and Chris murdered that girl's father in cold blood. Cold blood, Angel. We walked right into his home and took his life. For what? Because Dutch wanted to send a message?"

Qwan dropped his head, mumbling something inaudible.

I hope it's a prayer, Angel thought.

"You mean Simone's father?"

Qwan nodded with watery eyes. In his mind, he relived the moment.

"After that, I tried to get out, but I couldn't. I can't tell you why, but Satan had me. I... I was scared that Dutch would kill me, so I stayed. I stayed and I watched people die at his hands. I spent the blood money. I lavished in it. Until one night, one night I had a dream."

Qwan's eyes glazed over and his voice boomed like he was giving a sermon.

"I dreamt I was standing on the brink of fire. All I could hear were screams, agonizing screams, and I smelled burnt flesh. I saw myself standing over the pit. Then someone called my name. I turned around and it was Dutch. He said my soul was wanted in hell, and then an unseen force flung me into the pit. I woke up sweating and crying and I knew then, even if he killed me, I had to get out. I had to," Qwan said as he lowered his head.

Angel sat unmoved by Qwan's story. She had no pity and no remorse for what Qwan had done, no matter what he said. She stared at the top of his head until he raised it.

"But he didn't kill you, did he, Qwan? He let you walk away clean," Angel said, still not understanding why he turned state and testified.

"But I couldn't be clean, not as long as I carried the burden I carried, and the trial was my only chance to unload it."

Qwan stood and walked around the desk.

"When the DA first contacted me to testify against Dutch, I said no. I didn't want no part of it. But the more I thought, the more I knew it was my only chance to purge myself. How could a man of God refuse to denounce the devil to his face? How?" Qwan emphasized with his open palms.

"He wasn't a devil, Qwan, and you know it! Your fuckin' conscience just wants to make him your scapegoat! Dutch was your friend and you sold him out!" Angel spat.

"Friend? He was a conniving manipulator! A... a... deceiver and a cold blooded murderer and a bastard who didn't deserve to live! If you want to know the truth, I'm glad he's dead! I'm glad to be rid of him. Friend! He was never my friend," Qwan spewed before collapsing on the couch.

His spirit felt much lighter, having finally spoken his true feelings.

Angel didn't speak for a moment, and when she did, she began calmly.

"Do you think I'm a devil too, Qwan?"

"God is the best of judges."

"How about a friend? Are we still friends?"

Angel's tone made Qwan open his eyes and look at her.

"I don't have anything against you, Angel."

"Liar," she playfully giggled. "I think you do Qwan because, after all you said, you left out one thing."

"What's that?"

A smirk played on Angel's lips. "I think you were jealous," she stated simply.

Qwan eyed her incredulously. "Jealous of who, him?"

"Its okay to say his name, honey. He's gone, remember? Yes him. Dutch. You were jealous of my devotion to Dutch."

Qwan quivered with laughter, shaking his head, "That's absurd."

"Is it? I remember when you first saw the BMW I saved for Dutch. The hate in your eyes, wondering why I didn't save one for you, too."

Qwan didn't speak. He also remembered the BMW and the envy he felt, wishing he had one as well.

"And I remember how you used to watch me when you thought I wasn't looking. Do you remember that, Qwan?"

She was initiating the cat and mouse, a game she had mastered. Qwan looked at her curiously.

"I was young. We were young and of course I looked at you, you were pretty and..."

"Am I still?"

"Still what?"

"Pretty," Angel asked provocatively, standing up and crossing the room to sit on the couch next to him. Qwan watched her, growing more nervous by the moment.

"Why does that matter now?" he asked, but Angel ignored the question.

"I remember how you used to be around me. I could tell you wanted to say things then that you were afraid to say. Do you still want to say them?" Her tongue tickled the 'th' in them, seductively.

Qwan stood up quickly, knees trembling. "That was a long time ago."

"And I was a little girl then, but..." she said as she purposely uncrossed her legs so Qwan could see what was between them. "I'm a woman now, and I'm all alone in this cold world," she said as she got up and moved closer to him.

"Wh... what are you doing?" Qwan asked, wide-eyed.

"Whatever you want me to," she smiled as she caressed his face.

Qwan jerked away from her, "No! I... I don't want you to do anything besides leave," he retorted, attempting to sound firm, but his tremor gave him away.

"Really?" Angel giggled. "Your spirit is willing but your flesh is weak?" she remarked, referring to his tented trousers.

Qwan swallowed hard and adjusted his crotch, "Get out!" he yelled out of embarrassment that she could so easily arouse his weakness.

"Get out or... or..."

"Or what?" Angel taunted, "What will you do if I don't?"

He stormed over to the door and threw it open with a bang, "I'll throw you out myself!"

Angel groaned so sweetly it played up and down Qwan's

spine like a chill.

"We'll see," was all she replied as she slowly shook the spaghetti straps off her shoulders. Her dress fell to the floor, and she stood there, her pecan nakedness exposed to him.

Qwan gulped audibly. He feasted his eyes on her heavy round breasts and tight stomach that vee'd to her shaved pussy.

"Now, how can you throw me out of a church like this?" Angel smiled.

"P-p-please, Angel, please put your clothes back on," Qwan begged, trying to tear his eyes away from her thighs.

"You've waited fifteen years to see this. Well, here it is, baby, and it's all yours."

Angel took him by the hand.

"Don't," he whimpered, attempting no resistance as she placed his hands on her breasts. It was the closest Qwan had ever been to heaven. Dreams of Angel defined his young adulthood. His every boyhood fantasy was made of what his nerve endings were feeling now.

"Please..."

"Exactly. Let me please you."

Qwan pulled his hand away. "No, I can't do this."

"No? Well can you do this?" Angel folded her body into his and kissed him, sucking in his breath and giving him her succulent tongue to taste. To him, it was like strawberry cream, and he sucked her tongue like a lollipop. Angel led him over to the couch and laid him down. She positioned herself on top of him, gyrating her hips, bringing him to the verge of wettin' all over himself.

"What do you want, Qwan?" Angel whispered in his ear.

"I... I want..." Qwan lay with his eyes closed, torn between spirit and flesh, unable to answer.

"Tell me, baby. Tell me how much you want me, how much you've always wanted me," she urged, darting her tongue in and out his ear, all the while squeezing his manhood through his trousers. Qwan groaned with desire.

"Tell me," she demanded through clenched teeth.

The dam of his righteous resistance broke and flooded him with desire.

"Yes," he admitted, looking her in the face, eyes full of lust, "I've always wanted you, Angel. Stay with me. I'll make you Godly if you make me whole."

Qwan knew this was a test of faith, and he knew he had failed. He just didn't know that his failure would cost him his life. He was too far gone to see the ice form in Angel's eyes, frozen rigid marbles that tensed her body.

"Are you ready to give yourself to me?" he asked lustfully, taking her breast in his mouth.

She watched him sucking on her breast for a moment, totally detached, numb to any sensation except murder. She lifted his head with her hand and bent to lick him from his ear to his neck and around to the other side. He never saw the thin steel razor she flipped from her tongue and into her clenched teeth. He was too busy trying to palm her ass.

The razor slit his throat from ear to ear. He felt no pain but heard the gurgling sound of his blood spewing from his body.

He grabbed for his throat, eyes wide with frantic fear and amazement. He had come in his pants the very instant his life began to leak all over the burgundy carpet. Angel slowly rose and watched him suffer.

"Punta!" she hissed. "You hid behind God because you were afraid to be the devil," she accused and spit on his convulsing body. "Your repentance ain't accepted, Reverend. Forgiveness denied."

He tried to get up but was too weak. All he could do was fall face down in a pool of his own blood at Angel's red stiletto heels.

"Judas," was her single worded eulogy.

Angel slid her dress back on, not stopping to wipe the splattered blood from her body. She wore it like a badge of honor.

She walked out of the office and down the stairs, using the ends of her dress to open and close the door. She crossed the parking lot to Goldilocks was waiting patiently in a Jag.

As she got in the driver's side, she removed the blonde wig, unpinned her hair and shook it out to its full length. Goldilocks studied her. She had never seen this side of Angel before. Goldilocks wiped the small spots of blood from her lover's face with a napkin.

"Death before dishonor?" Goldilocks inquired directly.

"Amen," replied Angel.

They pulled off, girlish giggles floating in the air in their wake.

"We fucked up, yo. He got away."

Duke couldn't believe the words he was hearing on the other end of the phone.

"Fuck you mean 'got away'?" he barked back.

Ty was on the other end, too shaken to speak. He looked in the rearview mirror as he hit the turnpike, heading south.

"Roll, yo, he..."

Duke jumped up from his couch and shouted into the phone, "I know who muthafucka! Tell me how!"

The word 'how' scrambled his brain like a bad hit of EX. He

formulated the perfect plan. He had organized it meticulously, down to the last detail. It was simple, a piece of cake, but somehow, it had blown up in his face.

The plan was to use Ty and three others. They were supposed to meet Roll's people, which they did, in Branch Brook Park. Roll had three cats with him. Duke knew that they'd be frisked, so the plan was to make the deal, then have two shooters in a stolen car positioned outside the park tail Roll, nod him at a stop light, then take back the money and merchandise.

The deal went down as planned. Roll took the duffel-bagged million, and Ty took the weight. Then Ty made the call to the shooters.

"He out."

The shooters readied themselves. When they spotted Roll's BMW, they followed him, swerved up beside him at the red light, and opened fire.

They didn't count on the BMW being bulletproof, but it was. They could've been tossing grenades at the car and still not cracked the windshields. The talons bounced off the car like it was Superman's chest.

Roll ducked out of pure instinct but came up laughing at the feeble assassination attempt. The shooters did manage to damage the tires, but even they were designed to roll in the event of a blowout. The shooters attempted to give chase, but the blare of approaching sirens made them quickly detour.

When Ty got the word, he jumped dead in his rental and aimed it for the Turnpike. He knew he had fucked up. He knew there would be retaliation. He now had two of New Jersey's biggest drug lords on his ass, and he wasn't about to stick around for the fireworks.

"Where you at?" Duke asked, head spinning.

"On my way out to your spot," Ty lied, already heading in the opposite direction.

"Naw, naw. Meet me in Elizabeth. You know the spot," Duke ordered, already trying to figure out where he was gonna dump Ty's body.

"No doubt. One."

Ty hung up and tossed the cell in the empty passenger seat. Wasn't no way he was gonna meet Duke anywhere, especially since Duke had found out that Roll got away with his paper. It was a total failure, but for Duke it loomed even larger.

Once Roll found out who was behind the assassination attempt, war was inevitable. Young World had warned Duke from sparking, and Duke had violated. He knew World wouldn't like it and knew he had to prepare for two wars. One with Roll and the other with Young World. Either way, it was on, and Duke couldn't turn back the clock.

Roll was a big, fat, black, Biggie Smalls-type nigga, whose belly shook when he laughed. As he and his main man, Nitti, walked into his wife's hair salon, his belly bounced with hilarious cackles.

"What's so funny, Roland?" his wife, Renée, asked as she prepared to open the shop.

Roll took the duffel bag from Nitti and kissed her on the cheek.

"Somebody tried to kill me," he laughed.

"And that's funny?" she asked in a panic. She knew her man was crazy, but she thought he had finally lost it.

Roll relaxed in one of the salon chairs.

"It is when you send stupid muthafuckas to murk a nigga like Big Roll," he boasted.

Roll explained the scenario, and Renée sucked her teeth.

"It's not funny, Roland. I swear I wish you'd leave this shit alone because everybody won't always be stupid muthafuckas," she told him, then walked away mad that he took the attempt on his life so nonchalantly.

Nitti, Roll's sleepy-eyed silent killer, wasn't laughing either. "I guess I ain't gotta tell you who it was, do I?" Nitti asked.

Roll lit a Cuban cigar.

"Hell no! Who else could afford to just give away a million dollars, except me, and I damn sure ain't try and kill myself," Roll chuckled, but his insides were beginning to boil over. "I'll tell you this though," he said between puffs, "I was startin' to think World's bitch ass was goin' soft, yo. He was makin' it too easy to play him out of pocket."

Roll blew out a puff of smoke. The more he thought about it, his nervousness subsided and his anger grew.

"Send toy soldiers at a real nigga like Roll? I'ma bury that nigga! Him, that bitch-ass Duke, his dick-suckin' mother, and whoever else get in my way! I'ma take what shoulda' been mine from the jump!" Roll huffed then added, "And my next Bentley on World!" Roll exclaimed and held up the million-dollar duffel bag.

"You got exactly one hour, Muhammad," the blonde C.O. told Rahman as he took off the cuffs at the door of the booth.

Rahman didn't respond. Instead he looked over his shoulder at Young World on the other side of the Plexiglas.

Rahman gave him a wink, but he could tell Young World didn't like seeing him in a cage chained like an animal. When the officer left, he firmly locked the door with a thud. Rahman turned to the phone and picked it up with a smile.

"As-Salaamu Alaikum, Shahid," Rahman said calling World by his born name.

"Alaikum As-Salaamu, my brother," World replied. "What up wit' this thick ass Plexi and crazy heavy phones? You been wildin' on them niggas in there or what?"

"Naw. You know how these crackers play with a nigga's life. A nigga ain't suppose to speak. And if you outspoken, then you losin' some type of privilege. It ain't nothin' though."

Young World nodded.

"What was you protestin' for, more food?" World joked. "I saw that gut, Ock!"

Rahman threw his head back and laughed. "Yeah, I know. I ain't been workin' out like I should," he confessed, noticing the dragon chain World was wearing. Rahman could clearly see the world he had introduced his young protégée to, a world based on slavery. Enslavement of self, morally and principally, enslavement to materialism, totally. It was the prison of the game many entered but few ever escaped. Rahman turned his head away.

Young World sensed his annoyance but mistook it for a different kind of disappointment. World thought Roc was upset with the way he had been handling the family affairs, so he sought to explain himself.

"I'm sayin' yo, I know I ain't holdin' it down like you and Dutch, but shit is crazy for a nigga right now. I know you heard about it."

"First of all this is a federal penitentiary, Sha. I'm in here on drug and racketeering charges. My mail, my phone calls, my visits are all monitored and documented. You see that?" Rahman asked, pointing to the cameras in the corners of the room. "My whole life is an open book, and you come up in here with a murdered man's chain around your neck, an armful of bling, sayin' names like Dutch and y'all? You must wanna go to prison."

"Naw, naw, my bad, I wasn't..."

"Thinking?" Rahman finished the statement, then sighed. "If you gonna live that life, you always gotta think before you act."

Young World was back on familiar ground now that his mentor was keeping him sharp, which was exactly what he came for.

"I got you, my bad."

"So what was it I'm 'posed to be hearin'?" Rahman asked changing the subject.

Young World glanced at the camera before beginning. "Just things. I know dudes in here comin' at you saying I ain't cut for this shit or whatever."

"It's a lot of talk that I don't listen to these days," Rahman replied.

"Everybody wants to be gorillas and killas like they'd rather see blood than money. You know me, Roc, and you know how you raised me. Ice cold, and I done dealt with shit on those terms, but it ain't enough, yo. It's like, I'm missing somethin'. I'm missin' a lot. That's why I'm here."

Rahman had lost his focus on Young World's words after World said 'how you raised me'. It echoed in his mind several times before settling in his stomach like a ball of hot lead. He grimaced over the lessons he had instilled in Young World.

Fuck the 48 laws of power, Rahman remembered saying once, referring to the true hustler's handbook. *The 49th law is break every law except your own.*

They were lessons that all ran counter to the Islamic faith, which he now held so dearly. Rahman rubbed his head.

"So what you sayin', Sha?"

"How he do it?"

"He who?" Rahman replied, feigning ignorance.

Young World just looked at him as if to say, who else?

"The only man that knew that answer is dead," Rahman replied dryly.

"But, Ock, you know son like that. Y'all came up from the dirt together. You know the moves he made and why. I know you wasn't in his head, but you was there from the jump."

Rahman could tell Young World was desperately seeking the secrets of Dutch's success, secrets only he could provide, ones he'd never reveal, not because of the code of the streets but because of the code of Islam. He knew he had created a monster in Young World, one that would eventually destroy itself.

"Let me ask you something, Sha. What does your name mean?"

Young World was puzzled.

"What? Young World? You gave me that name, remember? You said I was the next generation, the Young World."

I know this nigga ain't forget, Young World wondered to himself.

"But the next generation of what?" Rahman asked. "How's your Abu? He still go to the Masjid on Branford?" asked Rahman, changing the subject once again.

"Yeah, I guess," World replied, not really feeling the small talk when there was more important business to discuss in the hour they had.

"How about you? You go?"

"Sometimes," World lied.

"When's the last time you been?" Rahman pressed.

Young World realized where the conversation was going so he

sarcastically retorted, "I don't know, yo. Whenever. I ain't bodyin' a nigga or a nigga tryin' to body me. I drop by."

Rahman sighed when he saw the steel in Young World's eyes. The door to his soul was locked shut.

"If I could tell you, I would tell you, but then what? Huh? What you gonna do then? Go out and try and be like him? Be like me? Which one you want, death or jail, because that's where it ends. Don't look at what we did to get it. Look at the inevitability of how we lost it!"

Rahman was adamant in his tone, but Young World was just as adamant in his resolve.

"Naw, Ock. I ain't tryin' to be nobody. I am somebody! I'm muthafuckin' Young World! Let me worry about tomorrow, I'm askin' you about today!" World exclaimed.

"Sound like you want me to hold your fuckin' hand," Rahman cursed, which was something he no longer did. He was angrier with himself than at Young World.

"Yo, Roc, what's up with you? I fly all the way down here to holla at you and you on some bullshit!" Young World barked.

"Naw, nigga. YOU on some bullshit. The life you livin' is bullshit, and you flew down here on some bullshit, that's bullshit, nigga!"

Young World cracked a smile of understanding. "Ohhh, I see now. I see what this is all about. They got you up in these muthafuckin' mountains and now you on some peace shit. Some Malcolm X-type shit, and you thought you could get me to turn the other cheek with you," World snidely surmised.

Rahman met his gaze. "Look, I'll probably be home sooner than you think, Insha Allah. And we got big plans, believe me. It's official. I want you to roll with me on this, but you gotta leave the game behind. You do that and I'll tell you what you need to know," Rahman explained, trying one last time to bring World over to his side.

World laughed in his face.

"While you safe in a cage, and I'm out fightin' wolves, you talkin' about some plan? Some prison dream?"

Rahman dropped his head. He understood Young World's dilemma. He was in too deep to just get out. His foolish man-hood telling him to get out now would be to run like a coward. He wouldn't just walk away from the level he had obtained.

But Rahman had his own dilemma. To tutor Young World would be to assist him in his dealings. In Islam, whoever takes part in devilishness is a devil himself. Yet, to turn him away would be to basically co-sign Young World's death warrant. Rahman was well aware of the latest developments in the streets. The Plexiglas was much more than just a security par-tition. It was a gaping void between the worlds of two opposing principles.

"Ain't nothin' I can do for you."

His simple answer was full of complex meanings, but to World, it was just that, a simple answer, an answer that meant Roc had simply turned his back and threw him to the wolves. Young World shot to his feet, exploding with rage.

"Nigga, you'sa bitch! A muthafuckin' coward hidin' behind a Kufi! You ain't no Muslim! You just a scared-ass nigga!"

Rahman silently seethed. He was a changed man, but a man nonetheless. He still possessed a killer's instinct, and had the Plexiglas not been between them, he probably would've flipped on World, violently. Not for the insults he was spewing, but to rid himself of the guilt for what he had created. He knew that once he returned home, Young World would become an issue that would have to be dealt with one way or another.

He stood up.

"The visit's over," Rahman announced, then hung up the phone. He turned to the door and knocked twice to signal the C.O.

"Fuck you, nigga! Fuck you! If you do come home bitch, I'll kill you myself! You hear me? Myself!"

Rahman felt each expletive hit his back like a slug as the C.O. opened the door and cuffed him.

"Did you have a nice visit?" the redneck asked slyly, but Rahman's eyes checked him so coldly, the officer dropped his head, red-faced.

Young World watched the door close, then turned and walked out.

Once he was back in Jersey, Young World prepared his mind to go all out. His anger still had the best of him and his emotions were controlling his intellect, but Roc had left him no other choice.

What I got to lose? his mind asked as he heard Dutch's advice.

A better opportunity.

He remembered Dutch saying that to him, dropping a jewel on his young mind about desperation.

Never think you have nothing to lose. Because then you move out of desperation. And desperation is the worst motivation for action.

But World couldn't help but feel desperate. Everywhere he turned there was treachery, deceit, cross-dealings and double-dealings. It was like Biggie said, the more money, the more problems. He had Ceylon threatening to cut him off, Roll gunning for his crown, and when he needed him the most, the man he looked up to like a father had turned his back, leaving him out in the cold.

Things had moved too fast for Young World, going from a block lieutenant to a Don damned near overnight, and he simply wasn't cut out for the responsibilities. His ego wouldn't let him accept it even though his heart was beginning to agree.

He pulled his pearl white Aston Martin convertible into the horseshoe driveway of his crib in West Orange. He turned off the car and sat back, taking in the landscape. The six bedroom, eight bathroom ranch-style house was the type of house he'd always dreamed of owning ever since his block hustling days — chasing dimes and nickels, day and night, grinding hard, showering every two or three days and sleeping in hoopties on lookouts. His only goal was to get money. He would hustle all night then take the money to Lana's mother's house, catching her before she went to school. Sometimes he'd talk her into playing hookie. They would go downtown to buy clothes or look at jewelry. Then they'd sit on her porch and watch bigger hustlers drive by in their Benz's and BMW's.

"I'm tellin' you, girl. That's gonna be us in a minute, word. We gonna have it all, baby," he'd tell her and she would reply, "I already got it all."

Now look at me, he thought. He had two homes, this being the larger of the two, complete with a swimming pool and full basketball court. His three-car garage held the $230,000. Aston Martin DB9, a $135,000. CL 55, and a $70,000. Cadillac Escalade, not to mention Lana's $120,000. 760li series BMW.

"You've come along way, son," he said to himself. But deep inside, he wondered if it was all worth it.

So what if Ceylon cut him off? In his three-year run, he had stacked NBA-type paper. What else did he have to prove? And to whom? Roll? Duke? Lana? Himself? Young World lay back against the headrest and rubbed his eyes with the palms of his hands.

Maybe it was time to get out, take Lana somewhere quiet and exotic. Logic and reason pointed him in that direction and he had almost convinced himself. Until he felt the weight on his chest.

The dragon chain.

His chest filled with foolish pride and impotent rage. He cursed himself for even thinking such thoughts.

"Fuck that! I ain't runnin' from these bitch-ass niggas!"

Dutch had left him the dragon to represent, and like a die-hard gangster, he planned on repping his jeweled flag to the death.

Young World entered the house with his mind set on his course of action. All he had to do was put Lana on point to his decision because she'd have to relocate.

"Lana!" he yelled loud enough to be heard all over the house.

He got no reply.

"Lana, you here?"

Young World noticed the TV showing her favorite fitness channel. The leotard-clad women were jumping and stretching to a muted beat. He smiled to himself. Lana had an hourglass figure and flawless skin which she attributed to her vegetarian diet and workout regime.

He turned off the TV and looked out to the patio where he saw Lana sitting at the edge of the pool. He started towards her then stopped in his tracks.

Lana. Suppose something were to happen to her? he thought.

The game he was playing wasn't only with his life but with hers as well. It had always been in the back of his mind and with the decision he was about to implement, he knew shit could get real ugly, real fast. God forbid if they came for him through her. Young World would never rest until he avenged her death, but revenge wouldn't bring her back. Again he questioned his stance, but his pride wouldn't let him reconsider.

He walked over poolside and heard Jaheem's CD playing in the background.

"Lana."

She jumped, slightly startled. "Oh hey, World," she smiled and stood up to hug him. She kissed him. "I didn't hear you come in."

"How could you with this bullshit blastin' like you in the Projects or somethin'," he snapped.

"You know it ain't that loud, boy. Quit trippin'."

"Did you hear me come in?"

"No."

"Then it WAS that loud. I coulda' been fuckin' anybody. I warned you about slippin'," he scolded.

Lana watched Young World go to the mini bar and pour himself half a glass of Remy Martin.

"What's wrong, Sha?" Lana asked.

"You! I tell you all the time, watch your..."

His words were silenced when Lana pulled out a .25 caliber pistol concealed in her bikini bottom.

"Happy now?" she smirked, then laid the gun on the bar.

"You still ain't hear me come in," he grumbled, downing the Remy in one gulp.

Lana studied her man. "What's really wrong, Shahid? You can't talk to me no more or somethin'?"

World looked into her face and his heart melted.

"Long trip," he said before sitting down on a chaise lounge.

"And I see you still on it," she quipped as she eased onto the edge of his chair.

Young World didn't reply. Instead, he stared into space for a few seconds, thinking.

"You movin'."

"What do you mean I'm movin'? Moving where? For what?" Lana asked with a frown.

"ATL."

"Why?"

"Because I said so."

Lana chuckled to hide her mounting annoyance. "Why don't you just say how high when you want me to jump?" she remarked snidely.

World knew he wasn't playing fair with her, but he had already made his decision and he wouldn't allow her to sway him.

"Do you trust me, Lana?" he asked sincerely.

"With my life," she replied without hesitation.

"Then don't ask questions about this, okay?"

Lana sighed hard and stood up. She had a lot to say but she held her tongue in check.

"Whatever," she said as she tossed her hair back nonchalantly and walked away.

"Lana!" He called her just like she knew he would. She had been with World long enough to know how to manipulate him when she wanted something. And she really didn't want him leaving her alone tonight.

"What, Sha?" she answered without turning around, her arms folded across her breasts.

Young World admired her delicious frame in the peach bikini she was wearing. It wasn't a thong, but her ass was so round, it might as well have been.

"These niggas want a war, so I'ma give it to 'em. I don't want you nowhere around when it pops off."

He broke down and explained, not knowing it had already popped off and war had already declared on him.

"What about you? Where you gonna be when it pops off?" she turned and asked.

"On the front line where I'm suppose to be," he declared like he was some kind of hero.

"Like I said, whatever," she replied, tears welling up in her eyes.

"Look, baby. I ain't running from nobody. I just can't. As much as I love you, I can't. If I did, then I'd be a target on every hungry nigga's plate! I ain't goin' out like that, ma. Word. You can't ask me to."

Lana loved him for his strength and confidence. But she was beginning to fear that those traits would become his weaknesses.

"Please, World. Don't..."

He couldn't explain his motives to her. It was what he felt he had to do. His hand was forced. There were no words. So he responded with a hard and passionate kiss, taking Lana's breath away, replacing it with his own. He attempted to console her with his embrace, soothe her with his caress, and fulfill her needs with his manhood.

In the background, Jaheem's 'Just in Case' was playing, and Young World indeed made love to her like it was the last time. The energy was so intense, Lana cried tears of passion as Young World filled her with his seed of life.

"I love you, My World. Please don't go, not tonight. Stay with me, okay?" With all his heart he wanted to, but he needed to laid and the sooner the better.

"I won't be gone long. As soon as I can, I'll be home."

"Promise me?"

"I promise."

Rahman laid on his back and looked at the bottom of the bunk over him. His celly was locked down in what everyone called the 'bing' or the 'hole'. In the hole you were locked down for 23 hours with one hour to take a shower and have recreation. So, Rahman had the cell to himself. All he could think about was the Don Diva article and Angel. She said she had won her appeal. He figured she had probably already touched ground by now. The interview didn't take place yesterday. Because his case was based on the same evidence as hers, it was certain that he'd go home soon, too. Or at least that's what his lawyer told him. He knew he had the perfect plan, but he couldn't help but wonder if he was ready for the streets again.

It was easy to be righteous in prison. But once freed, it was another story. Like a crackhead in jail, he could easily believe he had conquered his addiction. However, when faced again with the powerful substance, the sound of the sizzle, the sweet smell of its burn, and its mind-numbing effects, could any addict resist taking that welcome-back hit? It was just like that with the streets, and Rahman knew the game was just as addictive. It was like stealing. Half the niggas he knew didn't steal because they needed to. They stole because they liked the rush they got from stealing, the sneakiness in the take, and the thrill of getting away. Money is a high of its own. The art of the deal, the brrrap of the money counter flinging bills as it counts, the intoxicating effect of being 'that nigga' — rims spinning, jewels gleaming, the VIP status everywhere he goes, and oh my

God, the chicks on his dick!

Addiction. It's what Rahman feared. Not just the streets but HIM on the streets. Freedom was the ultimate test for a recovering addict of the game. But even worse was a nigga with options. And Rahman had plenty of them.

He heard a cart squeaking along the corridor and looked out of his cell. It was Donald from the library, collecting books.

"As-Salaamu Alaikum, Rahman."

"Alaikum As-Salaamu," Rahman replied.

"Here you go, brother," Donald said as he passed *The Tales of Huckleberry Fin* through the steel bars to Rahman.

"What I want that for?" asked Rahman, annoyed.

"Page 137 contains a valuable message, my brother," Donald said as Rahman relieved him of the book.

"Shakron."

"Afwan," Donald replied as he rolled his cart away.

Rahman opened the book to page 137 and found a folded piece of paper tucked in along the spine. He opened the slim piece of paper and read to himself:,

How you? I heard our young friend came to check you. You don't have to tell me how it went because I know the mind of a young gangsta. Remember, we already wore those shoes. Now you see firsthand what you're up against. Your freedom is near and the moment of truth is upon us. Everything is in your hands. Move wisely. You know I'm here for you. Everything I have is at your disposal if need be. Stay focused and keep Allah first.

As for our friend, he chose... now you must choose as well.

Salaam Alaikum, Akbar.

Young World guided the pearl white Aston Martin through

traffic like a missile. His theme music pumped out of the surround sound system, banging like a war drum.

What you think the game is for? he reminded himself.

World's destination was a strip club on 16th Avenue. He was part owner of the Eleganza. His many businesses included other strip clubs, but the Eleganza was the Newark's player's club of choice. The girls were top notch, no stretch marks, sagging bellies, or droopy titties allowed. You had to be a dime to even walk through the door. The girls were hand-picked after being interviewed, usually by one of the other partners. The interview was to strip naked and give a lap dance along with a sample of the goodies. World had interviewed some of the girls himself. He had sampled the goodies from most of them but hadn't gotten around to knocking off the rest. It was like being a jockey and walking into a barn full of stallions in every flavor and every shade of the rainbow. Only the biggest ballers, athletes, and entertainers could afford a table at the Eleganza.

Downstairs, ballers gambled for pots that easily exceeded fifty grand, game after game, night after night. It was always the same — alcohol, gambling and pussy. What more could a man ask for?

Young World placed his cell phone back in his pocket. It was the sixth time he had tried to phone Duke with no success. *Why this nigga not answering his phone?* He figured Duke was at the El, his home away from home. That's why he made it his first stop.

He entered the club and approached the bar, greeting the bartender.

"What up, Tank? What's good?"

"Same ol', same ol', Young. What up wit' you?" the big bartender asked back.

Young World glanced around the club. Five of the girls were working the floor. One of them, Tania, saw Young World and her heart leapt with lust. Not for him, but for the $5,000. Roll had offered her if she called him the moment he came in the club. Tania was Roll's cousin and she knew Roll was looking for him. She knew Roll had ordered a hit.

She watched World at the bar. *Where's his army? He just walkin' around like it ain't nothing,* Tania thought to herself as she slipped away from her lap dance and placed a call to Roll. It rang twice.

"Who this?" Roll's gruff voice rumbled through the phone.

"It's Tania."

"Tania who?" Roll barked, wondering how the ho got his private number.

"Your cousin, nigga! And guess who here?"

"Who?" Roll asked, not interested in playing twenty questions.

"World."

Roll sat straight up. "Where?" he asked with murderous anticipation.

"The Eleganza. He just walked in and he by himself," Tania said, ready to get her five thousand.

"Hold him! Whatever you gotta do, hold him. If you got to put that nigga's dick in your mouth and hold him with your teeth, do it!" he ordered and hung up.

"That nigga really think shit's sweet! He at the El right now, alone!" Roll said as he turned to his main man, Nitti.

That's all Nitti needed to hear. He and his driver Jay were out the door.

At the Eleganza, Tania sashayed across the floor and rubbed

her bare breasts up against Young World from behind. Young World turned around, annoyed.

"Bitch, get your titties off of me. Do I look like a trick to you? Ain't your ass supposed to be working?" he arrogantly spewed, turning away from her, back to Tank.

"But I need to talk to you, World. It's important," she insisted. *That's why you about to get fucked up muthafucka. See how you like it then,* she thought to herself.

"Talk to me for what?"

"Just let me holla at you before you leave, aiight?" she said, sucking her teeth.

"Yeah, whatever, if I remember."

"Shit, you won't never forget," she mumbled to herself as she walked away.

"Anyway, yo. What was you sayin', Tank?"

"Oh yeah, they tried to murder that nigga, Roll," gossiped Tank.

"Who was it?"

"I don't know," Tank said as he shrugged his shoulders. "All I heard was Roll was comin' out of Branch Brook and some guys caught him at the light. Lit his shit up and completely missed," Tank explained, cleaning a glass.

Young World shook his head.

"Musta been some lame-ass stick-up kids. Fuck was they shootin', sling shots?"

They both laughed.

"Must've been," Tank agreed.

Young World looked at his watch. "Where is this nigga at? Yo, Tank. Call Duke again. Fuck is this nigga doin'?"

Tank slid over to the phone and dialed Duke's cell as World had asked him too. He let it ring until the machine picked up and confirmed that the mailbox was full.

"He still not answerin'," said World before hanging up.

"Nigga probably laid up with them nasty-ass white girls he be fuckin'," Tank said and they both laughed.

World got up from his seat and started for the rear of the club just as Nitti was parking his car outside. World entered the bathroom and went inside a stall. The toilet wasn't sparkling clean, but it wasn't bus station filthy either. He made a mental note to cuss Tank out for not keeping it cleaner.

He rolled the toilet paper across the toilet seat, lowered his pants, laid his gun on the floor, then sat carefully on the seat, making sure he didn't knock any paper into the toilet. Young World searched his pants for a match so he could light a blunt while taking a shit.

World thought again about his plans and began organizing his mental notes. Whoever tried to knock off Roll fucked up his plans. Roll was probably taking extra precautions and would be harder to get at. At least that's what World thought. Regardless, as soon as Duke arrived, he planned on getting the ball rolling. The way he figured, he had the element of surprise on his side. But, in fact, he was the element about to be surprised.

Jay walked into the club, trying to focus in the smoky, cloudy room. He spotted Tania and took a seat at a secluded table. She quickly made her way over to him and straddled him for a lap dance.

"Where he at?" Jay asked with Tania's tits jiggling in his face.

"In the bathroom," she said, grinding and bouncing on top of him.

"Aiight. Nitti's at the back door. Let him in," Jay instructed, wondering if it was true what he heard she could do with a

Corona bottle.

"Y'all gonna take care of me, right?" Tania inquired, her green contacts looking like dangling money signs in her pupils.

"Just go let him in and we'll talk later," he said, meaning it. She slid off his lap and headed for the back door. Tania looked around before she cracked it and allowed Nitti to step in.

"He in the bathroom."

Nitti winked at her, then crept along the wall.

After this shit all over, I'ma marry Lana, have some kids, settle down, do the family thing. He imagined himself a father, teaching his son how to dribble or having tea with his daughter.

The weed made his thoughts funnier than they were, and he laughed out loud just as Nitti entered the bathroom. Nitti heard the laugh, checked under the doors and saw Young World's Timberlands. He smelled the haze in the air. After spotting the gun on the floor, Nitti smiled. He had truly caught World with his pants down.

Tank watched Tania and knew her trifling ass was up to something. He couldn't figure it out, but knew something wasn't right. He had seen her dancing and then stop to make her way to the back of the club where she had no business. Then he watched her reemerge seconds later, looking as if she had stole something. Tank moved to the other end of the bar, trying to see down the darkened hallway. He saw the bathroom door swing closed, but he didn't see Nitti enter it.

Then he got a good glimpse of Jay who was headed for the bathroom, too. Tank recognized Jay as one of Nitti's people and put two and two together. In the blink of an eye, he snatched the pump shotgun from under the bar and hopped the counter.

"Jay!" Tania screamed, but her voice was swallowed by the music. He saw her frantic facial expressions too late. By the time he knew to look, Tank was aiming the shotgun directly at him.

Jay didn't ask any questions. He tried to go for his pistol but a shotgun blast to the stomach folded him on impact. Tania and the other girls screamed and ducked, but Tank's only concern was Young World. He ran for the bathroom.

Inside the stall, World finished shitting and was about to wipe his ass when he heard the muffled shot in the club. His ears easily picked out the sound of gunfire from the bass of the music.

Nitti heard it, too, and knew he had no time to waste. He barged the stall door. Young World found himself staring down the barrel of a .45 silencer. The game was over and he had lost his crown. He'd never know Lana as his wife or the mother of his children. He'd never know life without the game. He'd never know life at all.

His last thought was of Lana. *Stay with me, World. Please.*

Two shots caught him in the forehead and two more imploded in his chest. He slumped against the wall as Nitti pumped four more into his body. The lit blunt fell from his hand. He was still breathing and his eyes were still open when he saw Nitti's gloved hand lift the dragon chain from his neck.

"You wasn't rockin' it right," Nitti smirked, putting the chain in his pocket.

Tank kicked the bathroom door open, his pump ready to blast. He saw no one, just one of the stall doors swinging open.

"World?"

Tank pushed the bathroom door against the wall to make sure no one was behind it. He looked under the stalls and saw blood and World's boots.

"World!" he yelled, running over to the open stall. He grimaced at the sight of World's bullet-ridden body and his pants around his knees. He never noticed Nitti who had been standing on the toilet in the next stall. Nitti knew whoever had the shotgun had come for World.

Just as Tank turned his eyes from World, Nitti leaned over the stall wall.

"And behind door number two..." Nitti joked as Tank's eyes widened in surprise.

He fired a bullet into his head and Tank slumped to the floor. Nitti exited the bathroom, leaving an unsolved double murder.

The news of Young World's death sent shockwaves through the streets and everyone scrambled into position to best exploit the situation. Teams under his control made new alliances or posse'd up to lay claim.

Duke was no exception.

After the failed hit on Roll, Duke took refuge with Vinnie Z in Hoboken, a town known for it's mob ties and strong Italian community.

"I can't believe the fuckin' guy died on the toilet," Vinnie Z joked. "Since when do gangstas die on toilets?"

"They don't," Duke replied, implying that Young World wasn't a gangsta in his book.

He showed no remorse for his slain friend and ex-boss. In truth, Duke was relieved by Young World's demise. He was glad to be out of Young World's shadow. He felt World had inherited a position he didn't earn or deserve and being left leaking on a toilet confirmed it. It was time to make the moves necessary to solidify his position, and Duke planned on wasting no time. He planned on sending many of Young World's team with him.

Vinnie handed him a glass of Henny and held his own up. "To the new boss of bosses, eh? Salud."

Vinnie toasted and they drank to new beginnings. Duke was now the nigga he'd been itching to be. All he lacked was Dutch's dragon, and he planned on taking it from Lana. He didn't realize that Nitti held the chain.

With the mob behind him and the streets at his feet, he felt like the new Dutch. The mob had been a front for Dutch, and Duke would only be a front for the mob.

The news of Young World's death reached Rahman, and he prayed an absentee Janazah prayer for him, a prayer for dead Muslims. Rahman was devastated because he felt responsible. He questioned himself and his decision not to assist Young World out of the bind he was in.

"To Allah we belong and to Allah we return," he whispered to himself, reciting a verse from the Qu'ran.

Lana was a mess. She refused to believe that her World was gone, no matter how many times it was explained to her. She waited for him to come home. She had yet to cry. Her mother and Peaches were worried sick.

"We going to see World?" Lana asked with childlike innocence.

Peaches looked at Lana's mother.

"Yes, baby. We're going to see Shaheed. But he's not the same," her mother answered.

"Why not?" Lana seemed to sing, head cocked to the side. "Is he sick? I hope he's not sick. I miss him so much."

Her mother tried to respond, but tears choked her. All she could do was pull her daughter to her bosom and hold her tight.

"Don't cry, mommy. We're going to see World. Aren't you happy?" Lana smiled.

"He... help her get ready, Peaches," Lana's mother said, shaking her head as she left the room.

The wake was held at Whigham's Funeral Home in Newark. It looked like the President had died and it was his funeral instead of a local drug dealer's. Young World was well respected by the street elite. The hustling community showed up in full force to prove it. Bentley's, Benz's, and multicolored SUV's double-parked in the streets for two blocks. Platinum, diamonds and furs seemed to be worn by everyone.

Inside, hustlers mingled and females flirted like it was club night. The life of a hustler was good but sometimes death was even better.

Angel and Goldilocks sat at the back of the room, both wearing full length chocolate brown minks and dark brown Gucci shades. The whispers of Angel's return burned up the grapevine but only a few had enough heart to approach her.

"I'm sayin', you come home and don't even holla at your peoples?" a hustler named DC playfully remarked as he approached Angel.

"You know how it is, DC. Only fools rush in," replied Angel.

"I hear that, ma. At least you could give a nigga a hug and introduce me to your friend," DC signified, eyeing Goldilocks' tantalizing frame peeking through her mink.

"The hug ain't a problem, but, ahhh, I don't think you're her type," Angel replied, squirmingout of the embrace.

"Why is that?"

"'Cause you ain't got a pussy," Goldilocks calmly answered, showing no expression at all.

"Damn, ma. My fault," he said before turning back to Angel.

"Fucked up how they did World and shit. I know them was your peoples, so I'd hate to be whoever did it," DC said, trying to see where she stood. But Angel wasn't ready to play her hold card yet.

"That's the game, DC. A bitch did too much time to need this drama in her life. I'm just here to pay my respects."

"That's gangsta," he replied, not believing a word of it. He knew Angel too well. Drama was the bitch's middle name.

"Well, holla at me if you need anything, aiight?" he said before breaking away.

Angel surveyed the room. A new generation of ballers and hustlers had cropped up in the short time she'd been gone. Many names had reached her, but no one impressed her in style or reputation. They were all just chasing the crumbs off the table Dutch left behind. He was more than a legend. He was a spirit that haunted the streets, and every gangsta would be forever judged by him.

Just wait. We 'bout to take it to the next level. Y'all mutha-fuckas ain't ready, Angel thought as she looked towards the rear door. She watched Duke make his entrance. He had two girls with him, one on each arm. Straight dimes that even made Angel look twice. Duke was outfitted in an all-white Armani suit and matching Gucci shoes. He had a gold tipped cane, and his diamonds twinkled and winked like they were stars in the night sky.

Angel watched Duke closely until he noticed her. Their eyes

met through the crowd. Duke acknowledged her with a nod and Angel did the same in return.

Duke walked up to the casket and peered down at Young World's body. They had done a lot of work on him to have an open casket. Young World was sewn together like a stuffed rag doll, but he was dipped. He was to be buried in a black silk Versace suit with all his jewels except the dragon which Duke believed Lana was holding. He turned away from the coffin to find Angel eyeing him. He knew who she was at first sight. He just hadn't been informed that she was back. *The bitch could change the game,* he thought and wondered if Angel would be a problem. He had every intention of taking over Young World's fragmented territory and hoped she wasn't back to get in his way. *For her sake, she better not be,* he thought.

Lana, her mother, and Peaches came in and scanned the room. People whispered as they watched Lana, the hustler's wife. Duke walked up the aisle and hugged her.

"Lana, I'm sorry, ma. I know how you must be feelin'. Sha was my man and I promise you we gonna ride for money. You ain't got to worry about that."

Peaches sucked her teeth and rolled her eyes. She could see straight through his facade. She wanted to flip on him, but for Lana's sake, she didn't.

"But, yo. I need to holla at you after the wake, aiight?"

"Don't worry, Duke. You can talk to Young World about it later."

Duke looked at Lana like she was crazy. *Shortie's fucked up for real. She looks good though,* he thought as he eyed her bangin' frame.

"Can we see my World now, mommy?" she asked like a child wanting to open her Christmas gifts early.

Her mother could only nod and lead her down the aisle to the casket.

"I'm so sorry, Lana."

"I'm here for you, girl."

"Be strong."

The words spoken to her by her friends had no impact. Lana approached the casket holding her mother's hand. She imagined that she was in church, wearing a Cinderella white gown, heading for the alter where Young World stood holding his hand out to her.

She peered into the softly cushioned casket at World's face and slowly the room began to spin around her. The veil that protected her from reality had been snatched away, leaving her heart naked to the truth. There would be no wedding, no sandy beach honeymoon, no church. World was dead.

Dead. The word echoed in her head and all she could do was stare. Lana's mind flashed back to the day they met, their first kiss, the first time they made love, the pain, the pleasure, the tears, the laughter. She remembered the last thing he said.

I promise.

Her body began to tremble. Her mother gripped her tighter.

"Steady, child. He's with God now. You must be strong," her mother said comfortingly.

Lana heard none of it. Her trembles became a bodily earthquake like the moment before a volcanic eruption. It started as a whimper.

"No... nooooo..." she moaned.

"Please, baby. It's going to be okay," her mother tried to console her.

"No, no it's not! It's not ever going to be okay. How can you say something like that? It's not okay! Nothing's okay!"

Her mother pulled her close, but Lana shoved her away. The mourners stopped talking and socializing and turned their heads toward the casket and Lana.

"You think you gonna take my World from me? You're not. It's not going to happen. It's not going to happen!" she screamed.

Her mother was embarrassed and covered her face with her hands to wipe her own tears. It was a mistake she would regret for the rest of her life because she took her eyes off Lana long enough for Lana to dig into her purse and pull out a .25 automatic. It was the .25 Young World always made her carry.

"You won't take my World from me!" she screamed hysterically, pointing the gun at anyone near the casket.

"Get away from him!" Lana yelled, aiming the gun at Peaches who jumped back.

"Lana, no! What are you doing?" Peaches begged through tears.

"Get away!"

Peaches grabbed Lana's mother and pulled her away, but she kept reaching out to Lana.

"Lana, give me the gun, baby. Please. He's gone now. He's with God!"

"I want him with me!" Lana bellowed, backing towards the coffin.

No one knew what was going to happen, but within seconds Lana had climbed into the casket, raised the gun to her temple, and fired a single shot into her brain. The gunshot reverberated through the stunned crowd. Her mother broke the silence with a scream.

"Somebody get an ambulance!" Peaches yelled.

Lana's bleeding head lay on Young World's neck. World, Lana, and their unborn seed were gone.

Angel stood outside the funeral home as the EMT workers wheeled Lana's white-sheeted body past her to the ambulance. People lined the sidewalk, stunned and amazed. It was one thing to stand by your man. It was another to ride and die for a nigga. No one could believe what Lana had done and everyone was talking about the tragic event that had unfolded in the funeral parlor.

Angel waited for Duke until he emerged from the building. When his eyes met Angel's, she subtlety beckoned him. He quickly crossed the span between them.

"Crazy night, huh?"

"Crazy world," she shrugged.

"Love makes a nigga do some crazy shit, right?"

"And what 'bout you?"

"Naw, how 'bout you?"

Angel grinned and blew out Newport smoke. "Kinda fucked up how World went out, yo."

"Word, and you can believe it ain't over. Niggas gonna bleed for this. We gonna rep son till the last man's standing."

"Come on, Duke. Who you think you talkin' to? I can see it in your eyes. Now World's out the way, you the man. What you care about some bitch-ass nigga that got nodded on the toilet," Angel asked, wiping her eye with the palm of her cigarette hand.

"You bein' real disrespectful to my man. Watch yo' fuckin' mouth," Duke warned, fronting like he really gave a fuck.

"Dig, Duke. If you wanna stand around and bullshit behind a fake-ass vendetta, then you wastin' my time. Don't worry, I ain't here to cause you no problems. I just want the bloodline represented right. So either you the man for the job or you ain't."

"Yeah, I'm the man. But what kind of job you got in mind?"

"Let's ride and discuss the possibilities," Angel suggested, throwing her cigarette in the street.

Duke glanced around, weighing the proposition. Angel was Dutch's main shortie. To have her come fresh out the joint and ride with him would let the streets know that his shit was official. But something about her vibe wasn't right. Angel read right through his hesitation.

"Nigga, it's cold out here in more ways than one. Them same niggas that got World see you the same way. But wit' me, you fuckin' wit' a vet, and niggas know it. The name Angel rings bells in these niggas' hearts. So what's it gonna be?"

She didn't wait for a reply. She waved her arm and Goldilocks pulled up in an '85 Cadillac Fleetwood. Angel approached the car and opened the back door.

"You rollin' or what?"

Duke walked over and got in the backseat. Angel closed his door, got in the front seat, and signaled for Goldilocks to pull off.

"I double-checked that account personally. The check deposited on October 4th did not clear the system because of insufficient funds. So when the customer checked his account and saw those as available, they actually hadn't cleared the account. They were merely posted on the account. Mr. Hamel doesn't seem to understand."

"Uhh huh," she added.

"Exactly. The check he deposited was no good and he should receive it in the mail within seven days once our system kicks it out."

"You're welcome," she added before she hung up the phone

and removed her Cartier frames. She pinched the bridge of her nose with her middle finger and thumb. Being a bank manager wasn't all it was cracked up to be. But she put up with it because she was ambitious and had her eyes on bigger and better.

It wasn't only about the money. It was mostly about the challenge of being a thirty-four-year-old black woman making her own way in the lily-white world of finance. For the last year and a half, she had dived headfirst into her career, trying to fill the void Dutch's death left in her heart. She relived their last time together and her aborted trip to the courtroom over and over. She went through the shoulda, coulda, woulda stages and finally left the what ifs for the reality of what was. Dutch was gone, and as painful as it had been, Nina had to continue with her life. Her career filled a missing void.

Until she met Dwight.

He was a mechanic and worked at a local body shop in town. She met him when her BMW needed body work after a minor fender bender. He was a regular Joe, not into the streets or the game or the fast life. Dwight was a hard-working man. He worked a seventy-two hour, six day work week and watched football on Sundays. He didn't feel intimidated because she earned more than him, nor did he try and exploit it and live off her. He viewed their relationship on equal terms and respected her independence.

All that, and he was fine.

Dwight wasn't tall or muscular, but he did have big, strong hands that Nina loved to hold. He had a brown complexion, clean-cut face, brown eyes with bushy eyebrows, and a charming smile that brightened even the cloudiest day.

Her day was going horribly, and she really needed to hear his voice. She picked up the phone but was interrupted by a knock on the door.

"Miss Martin," her secretary asked before entering.

"Come on in, Susan," Nina sighed, wishing the day was over.

"You have a visitor. It's Dwight," Susan teased.

Nina beamed and hung up the phone. Dwight always seemed to have perfect timing.

"Sure, Susan. Show him in."

Susan giggled as she closed the door behind her. A few seconds later, Dwight walked in and closed the door behind him. He had taken half a day off and was dressed casually instead of in his work clothes.

"Gimme all the money and nobody'll get hurt," he joked, aiming a finger gun at her.

Nina laughed.

"On second thought, forget the money. Fine as you are, I'm takin' you instead," he charmed as he sat on the edge of her desk.

"Yeah, right," Nina replied "Me over all the money in the bank? I don't think so."

"Well, maybe not all the money," he said with a grin as she playfully hit him. "So how's your day been? Lunch on me?" he offered.

"I wish. I've already got a lunch meeting scheduled at 2:30."

"So cancel it."

"If only it was that simple."

"It is," he answered, staring her down with his pretty browns. He made her wish it was that simple.

"Anyway, I just dropped by to check on you."

"So you're checkin' on me now?" Nina's eyebrows arched playfully.

"Damn right, 'cause a brother ain't takin' nothing for granted when he's got a woman like you."

"Excuuuuuuse me," she replied.

"You heard me," he said as he studied her, expressing a bit of his concern. "You okay, baby? You look tired."

"Long day, I guess," Nina shrugged.

"Long? It isn't even noon."

"I know. This day is going to take forever to end."

"Don't worry. I've got the remedy."

He walked around the desk and got on one knee in front of her then patted his knee. "Put your feet right here."

"Dwight, what are you up to?" she asked skeptically.

"What? I can't give my lady a foot massage without twenty-one questions? Feet please, right here. That's an order, not a request."

"Yes sir!" she said, saluting him jokingly.

Nina kicked off her tan leather pumps and placed her stockinged feet on his knee.

"That's what I'm talking about," he crooned, using his strong hands to knead and rub the palm of her right foot. "Why keep toes this pretty covered up?

"Dwight, I'm a bank manager. No one is interested in seeing my toes," she giggled.

He continued to soothe her spirit as he massaged her foot.

"This is all wrong."

"What?"

"These stockings. You're going to have to take them off."

"Excuse me?"

"Your stockings. I can't do this right with these stock..."

"Nuh uh! See, I knew you were up to something," she said, removing her feet from his knee.

Dwight lifted them back into place.

"No, no, for real. I can't massage your feet like I could through this material," he said lying through his pretty smile.

Nina eyed him but his gaze melted away her resolve.

"Foot massage, Dwight," she reminded him.

"Scout's honor, I'm telling the truth," he smiled, holding up the two-fingered Boy Scout sign.

"Mmm-hmm," she doubted, sliding her stockings down from under her blue skirt. "Your ass probably wasn't even a Scout."

Dwight chuckled as he slid the stockings all the way off. He began to work his magic, and Nina leaned back in her adjustable chair, relaxed, and closed her eyes. She definitely needed the attention. Her pumps were murder on her feet.

"Feel good?" he questioned.

"Mmm-hmm," she answered.

The feeling almost made her fall asleep, until she felt his tongue on her ankle, gently kissing along her calf muscle.

"See, I knew it," she protested, but it felt so damned good. His expert tongue found her most sensitive spots along her inner thigh and made her squirm in the chair. "Dwight, no! Not here," she said weakly.

"Okay, how about here?"

She felt his breath tickle her flesh. He ran his tongue tantalizingly lightly across her clit.

Nina gripped the arms of the chair. He leaned her back, parting her inner flesh with his thumbs and probed her orally. She couldn't believe this was happening in her office. She felt like Samantha in Sex and the City.

Nina couldn't take it anymore. She pulled his head up from between her legs and fumbled with his belt.

Dwight helped her by pushing his jeans down around his

ankles and entered her all at once. The moment had her on fire as Dwight filled her throbbing walls. He placed her legs on his shoulders and pounded her incessantly. It took all her will not to scream out and alert everyone in the bank of what she was doing in her office. It was a hot and intense quickie. Nina exploded followed by Dwight moments later. They lay slumped in the chair, huffing and puffing.

"Some foot massage," Nina quipped.

Dwight laughed. "Hey, I'm a mechanic. All we do is body work, baby."

For the rest of the day, Nina floated on cloud nine, beaming with happiness. The meeting was stress-free, and before she knew it, it was time to go home. She parked her burgundy BMW in front of her newly purchased home in the Jefferson Park section of Elizabeth. It was a modest-sized house that was just the right size for her needs.

She got out of the car just as two young children rode their bikes down the street. She could imagine herself coming home to her own children. Her blossoming emotions could easily place Dwight in the role of the man waiting for her.

She unlocked the door and let her keys fall into her purse. Her future family thoughts were interrupted when she opened the door and heard music playing. She stopped dead in her tracks and listened carefully. Music was coming from the living room. It wasn't loud, but it could be heard from the doorway. She entered the living room, realizing the song was Rolls Royce's 'I'm going down'.

Time on my hands, since you been away boy, I ain't got no plans...

Nina mentally reviewed her morning. She was sure she hadn't left the stereo on because she never played it in the morning. She liked her mornings quiet to help her prepare for the day. She did turn on the television but only to listen to the news and weather as she dressed.

No, she was sure she hadn't left the stereo on. But if she hadn't, who had? She lived alone. Despite the mystery, it was a nice surprise to come home to her favorite song. She caught herself singing along.

Sleep don't come easy... please believe me. Since you've been gone, everything's gone wrong.

The song brought back memories as she traveled back in time to the last time she heard it.

She had been with Dutch.

Nina would never forget the night they stopped at a light in downtown Newark. Dutch had a Cut Master Cee slow jams mix CD playing and Rolls Royce came on.

Nina reached over and turned it up.

"Damn, I haven't heard this in years!" she exclaimed.

"What you know about Rolls Royce, little girl?" Dutch teased.

"Little girl? Please!"

Then she went into her diva routine, singing the first verse word for word.

That's when they stopped at the red light. Dutch got out without a word and walked around to the passenger door. He opened it and extended his hand to her.

"Show me how much you like it then."

"What, dance? In the middle of the street? Dutch the light just turned green," Nina protested, feeling self-conscious about holding up traffic. But Dutch was persistent and wouldn't let her get away that easily.

"Fuck a light. These my streets, and I wanna see you dance in 'em," he replied, pulling her from the car.

He slid her arms around his neck, and they danced right then and there in the middle of the street.

The memory warmed her and depressed her all at the same time. She still missed him and the feelings Rolls Royce unearthed proved it.

What did I do wrong? What did I do wrong? Please forgive me baby... and come on home.

Nina sighed deeply and told herself, *Girl, we've been there before. Let's not go there again.* She knew that her inner voice was right. The song ended and she waited for the deejay to say HOT 97 or WBLS, but when another slow song came on, she frowned and approached the stereo.

Her heart froze in her chest after it skipped a beat.

A CD was playing. She looked closer and it was the same Cut Master Cee CD she once listened to with Dutch. *Where in the hell did this come from?* she wondered. Dutch owned that CD, not her.

An eerie feeling overcame her. She felt like she wasn't alone. Nina shut off the music and listened to the silence of the house.

Girl, you trippin', she told herself. *Did I have that CD in my collection and just forgot? Maybe I was playing the CD this morning.*

Nina shook off her thoughts and attributed the oversight to her hectic schedule. There were times she didn't know if she was coming or going. This must be one of them. She went to the phone and called Dwight, but got the answering machine.

"You so nasty," was the simple message she left, giggling like a schoolgirl with a crush. Nina decided to call Tamika because she didn't want to be alone with her thoughts. The phone rang twice before Tamika picked up.

"Who dis?"

"Who dis? Must you be so ghetto?"

Tamika sucked her teeth, "Like yo ass ain't from Pioneer Homes, bitch," Tamika shot back.

"What's up, Mika? What you doin' tonight?" Nina asked.

Tamika was curled up on her couch watching Jerry Springer. "Why, what's up?"

"I want you to go somewhere with me."

"Where?"

"A poetry reading at the Paradise Lounge."

"A poetry reading? You really on that boo-gee shit now, huh?" said Tamika, hoping Nina wasn't serious.

"Fuck you, Mika. Poetry readings ain't hardly boo-gee."

"Well, where's your broke-ass man? Why he don't take you?" Tamika quipped, referring to Dwight. She couldn't understand why Nina insisted on dating a mechanic. Dick was one thing, but Nina appeared to be getting caught up.

"My man ain't broke, okay? He has a job. What about yours? Oh, I forgot. You don't have one!" Nina teased as she squawked like Morris Day.

"No, dahlin'. I don't have one. I have many."

"Slut."

"Hater."

The two friends laughed.

"For real Mika. It'll be fun. There'll be a lot of cute guys there," Nina baited.

"Cute and broke, on some back-to-Africa shit. Give us free!" she said, mocking the brother from Amistad.

"Okay, okay. I got a deal. If you go with me, we'll go to the club, too."

"Now you talkin'. Gimme about an hour."

Nina hung up the phone and looked at her watch. The truth was she'd rather go with Dwight, but he didn't like poetry readings either. Nina really wanted to go and hear Monte Smith, an acclaimed spoken word lyricist. Even though she hated clubbin', she was willing to compromise.

Nina showered and changed into a wool cardigan and a pair of boot cut jeans, opting for the casual look so she wouldn't be mistaken for a hoochie once they got to the club.

She drove for five minutes to the South Park section of Elizabeth. Despite the proximity of the two neighborhoods, they were like night and day. The houses were two, three, and four family homes, dilapidated and neglected, not quite the Projects but close. Nina always wondered why Tamika chose to live surrounded by violence, drugs and despair.

Wearing her man-eating red Gucci tube-dress and black faux fur, Tamika sashayed up to the car and got in. Nina loved Tamika like a sister but sometimes felt that it was women like Tamika who gave sisters a bad name and left brothers with a bad taste in their mouth.

"Lets get this boo-gee shit over wit'. The rent's due, and I ain't wear this dress for nothing," Tamika huffed.

Nina shook her head.

"Instead of that rose you got, you shoulda got a 'for sale' sign tattooed on your ass," Nina commented, half-jokingly.

"I would have, but your mama beat me to it wit' her old ass. Drive, ho, and don't worry about my ass, okay?"

"Thank you ladies and gentlemen. Thank you," said the emcee

of Club Paradise over the soft applause of the small crowd. "That was my man, Slim Direction, deep brother. You can catch him Saturday at the Black Moon Café. Now this next brother, what can I say? You know him from Def Poetry Slam, but he was gracious enough not to forget us little people. Seriously though, the brother is an experience. I bring to the stage, Monte Smith. Show some love, people, show some love," chimed the emcee to the small cheering crowd.

Everyone except Tamika applauded. Nina nudged her with her elbow.

"Stop wit' your bony elbow," Tamika said, sipping her drink. Nina loved the atmosphere of Club Paradise. The mellow lighting matched the mellow mood. For her, poetry seemed to have a euphoric effect. There was nothing more relaxing for her than to kick off her shoes, sip an apple martini, and feel the deep thrust of powerful words massage her mind.

Monte Smith, a slim light-skinned brother, stepped to the mic. The applause died away then he began:

I don't know about you, but its funny to hear
Bush and Ridge on TV
Telling me to keep my eyes open
For the enemy at home.
If that's the case, I'll be watching the police.
They're the only enemy I got.

The crowd laughed softly.

It's been time to show
The propaganda machine. It'll
Remain impossible to reach us

As long as his story's in pieces
It doesn't make sense like Mary and Jesus

How many victims of police brutality
Do we have in the place to be?

Individuals silently acknowledged there were some in attendance.

Who remembers
Tompkins Square Park
Kent State
Or Howard Beach?
I debate.
We can't wait on man's laws to
Manifest justice for humanity's sake.
These past acts
Of protectin' and servin'
Prove the scales will remain unbalanced
Until the pigs find their rights
Burnin' in the same fire
That's cookin' ours in broad daylight.
I'm tellin' ya,
They'll bomb ya like MOVE in Philadelphia.

Monte stepped down from the slightly raised stage, mic in
hand.

Who remembers
Shaka Sankofa
The massacre at Waco

Talkin' blues?
Sorry Bob.
Slave driver caught in the fire and threw it back
With plenty of matches, pipes and crack
All wrapped up in a CIA party pack
With a little tag attached
Reading die blacks.

Nina's mind pictured her brother, Trick, and then Dutch. Caught up in a game designed for their failure.

So to all the rich fraternities and sororities
Soon to be judges and DA's
Stop booking reggae bands at your keg parties.
It's a slap in the face of the starving.
For real
Think about that the next time you're
'jamming' 'til the game is through.
Off the record smoking herb with the band
But in five years you'll be responsible
For building more death camps
To imprison the youth.

Thank you.

The crowd erupted with applause, except for Tamika, again.

"Whack! The shit ain't even rhyme," she criticized.

Monte caught her disapproving body language. Her style of dress expressed her state of mind so Monte crossed the room to address it.

"I see we have some very beautiful sisters in attendance. Give yourself a hand."

It was the first time Tamika clapped all night.

"And you, you are definitely beautiful."

Tamika blushed.

Then Monte recited:

Hey beautiful.
I was just looking for someone to screw
When I first met you
And your pre-abused blues.
And I mean...
Blue like the bruise underneath the black tattoo
Of a past lover's name
Who came to show you shame and solitude
Rhymes with pain and attitude
And believe me I do strain to understand you
When you scream
LEAVE ME THE FUCK ALONE!

The crowd laughed hard, but Tamika subtly shifted in her chair because his words had killed her softly, singing her life with his words.

Monte winked then walked away.

"Don't lie, you were feelin' that one," Nina said, nudging her friend once again with her elbow.

"At least it rhymed," Tamika replied, trying to brush it off.

Next, it was time for Nina to fulfill her end of the deal.

Brick City was the club, formerly known as Zanzibar, the infamous Newark nightclub that made Tony Humphrey and Chef Pettibone famous.

Nina hated clubs, but Tamika wouldn't let her back out.

The spot was unusually packed for a Thursday, which only made it worse for Nina. She hated the loud blaring music, the bumping and touching people did to make their way through the crowd, and the way men thought every woman was an easy fuck for the night.

Now it was Nina with an attitude while Tamika was amped.

"Hell, yeah! Now this is what I'm talkin' about. Look at these niggas going up in there. Girrrrrrl, hurry up and park!" Tamika urged.

Nina maneuvered through the tight parking lot full of luxury automobiles equipped with so many amenities it made her BMW look like a Hyundai.

"Girl, how are we going to get in? Look at that line!" Nina remarked, referring to the line of people that went around the corner of the building. "It's too cold to be standing out here."

"Please! You think I'm about to stand out in Jack Frost? I don't think so," she said, snapping her fingers and making a S in the air.

"Well, how we getting in then?" Nina asked with her eyes bulging.

"It's called Cavalli, Roberto Cavalli. Honey, with this dress I'm wearing... it's like a VIP pass. My ass is a pass," she said, laughing to herself as she looked in the rear-view mirror and applied some lipstick. "Shit, I rhyme better than them fake-ass Def Poetry Jam niggas you had me up there listening to. I shoulda been up there on the stage. Maybe that's what I need to do."

"You need to get some help," Nina said, finally finding a parking space.

Nearing the entrance, Nina looked at all the people on line

and frowned. Why was everybody dressed like it was 1987? Everyone was dressed in Dapper Dan, Gucci, Fendi and MCM velour suits mingled with beef and broccoli Tims, Guess jean suits with leather pockets, Adidas sneakers, and Kangols. One nigga even had an 8 ball jacket on. *Where the hell did he find that,* Nina wanted to know. The outfits were accessorized with dookie ropes, door-knocker earrings, and Cazel frames. They wore sheepskins, shearlings, and bombers instead of leathers and furs. Nina and Tamika couldn't believe their eyes.

"Damn, Mika. Where the hell you bring me?" Nina asked.

Tamika looked at herself. Suddenly, her dress had lost all its flair. But dress or no dress, she was still a brown skinned stallion, thick like Luke dancers.

She led Nina to the door where two huge bouncers stood.

"What's goin' on y'all?" Tamika questioned.

"It's a private welcome home for Angel," he informed.

"Well, if it's private, why are all these people standing on line?" Nina wanted to know.

"Just that. They're standing on line," he replied with a chuckle. Then added. "But how can I turn away such lovely ladies?" he flirted

He was obviously referring to Tamika because Nina's was a simple beauty. He removed the velvet rope and ushered the two of them in, sparking curses from the haters on the line.

Once inside, Nina looked at all the banners that read, 'Welcome home, Angel!'

"Who the hell is Angel?"

Tamika shrugged and grabbed two glasses of champagne off a passing waiter's tray. "Damn if I know. But drinks is on her tonight," she chimed and handed Nina a glass.

The theme was definitely the 80's and Biz Markee was DJ'n it up in the proper fashion, spinning all the joints from back in the day. Nina had to admit it was fun, hearing all the hip hop classics she hadn't heard since high school. She even danced a few times, doing the wop, the Biz Mark, and, of course, the cabbage patch.

Angel and Goldilocks were moving in and out of the crowd, mingling, greeting old faces, and being introduced to new ones. Angel had on a pink suede Adidas suit with pink shell toes and bamboo earrings while Goldilocks had on Jordache Jeans, a silk shirt, and a pair of stiletos.

Angel had thrown the party for herself, but the festivities had a double meaning. She wanted a full view of all the players who moved New Jersey. Everyone had shown up except Roll. She had no idea he wasn't coming, so she continued to wait patiently. In the meantime, she let go a little bit and fed into the nostalgia, wildin' out on the dance floor, a bottle of Remy XO in one hand and a bottle of Cristal in the other.

Until she saw her. She looked through the crowd of happy partying faces and spotted Nina.

Nina noticed Angel staring at her and knew the face from somewhere, she just couldn't remember where. Angel knew exactly who Nina was because she couldn't stand her.

Why you so on this bitch all of a sudden, Angel asked after pulling Dutch to the side.

What, you my mother now? You thinkin' wit' my dick? he replied, trademark smile making Angel's blood boil.

Somebody need to. You don't know this bitch. She could be anybody, fuckin' Feds, fuckin' anybody! Remember Simone, don't you? Angel asked, warning him to be cautious.

How can I forget? Dutch said, looking down at the dragon chain dangling around his neck. Then he walked away.

From then on, Angel hated Nina, and she was glad when they finally broke up and Dutch stopped seeing her.

She probably here lookin' for another Dutch to suck off, Angel figured before turning back to Goldilocks.

Nina saw the Puerto Rican girl grillin' her.

She's probably drunk or gay, thought Nina who was ready to go home.

"Mika, we gotta go," Nina said, hoping Tamika was ready.

She sucked her teeth.

"Come on Nina, chill out. The party's just startin'. Shit, it's getting hot in here, take off all my clothes," Tamika sang with the music.

"Well, you can stay butt-naked if you want, but my black ass is 'bout to be out. I'm goin' home," Nina said, dead serious.

"And how I'm 'posed to get home?"

"Back seat of my jeep," Nina joked, rapping the hook of LL's classic.

"I got yo' back seat bitch."

"You ready?"

"Do I have a choice?"

They made their way through the parking lot pimps, nearing the car when a red Bentley Continental GT pulled up with a Maybach following it's lead. Niggas turned their heads twice at the cars as they brushed through the streets.

Tamika gasped with lust.

"See? Just when we leavin'," she pouted, wishing she didn't have to leave the party so early.

But something else caught Nina's eye. She could've sworn the fat man driving the Bentley wore the dragon chain Dutch used to wear. It was a quick glance, but the image of the coiled serpent stuck in her brain. Nina stretched her neck to see, but the car passed and the driver was no longer in sight.

She shook it off, thinking her mind was playing tricks on her again. She figured wrong. The dragon was draped over Roll's fat, sweaty neck. Nitti had delivered it to him after he murdered Young World. Roll wasn't wearing the chain out of respect. He was wearing it out of disrespect. He was arrogantly letting niggas know he was behind Young World's demise. He had the chain, and if anybody didn't like it, too fucking bad.

Roll, Nitti and the two guys in the Maybach made their way to the entrance. They weren't dressed in the 80's fashion because they didn't come to party. They came to make a statement. And the dragon did exactly that, bouncing off Roll's fat belly as he approached the entrance. The two bouncers instantly removed the velvet rope and admitted him and his crew.

When Roll reached the floor, all eyes fell first on him, then on the dragon. People whispered as he passed, openly greeting him or moving aside to let him pass by. When Angel finally spotted him, her blood began to boil upon seeing the dragon gleaming against his sweater. It was the dragon she should be wearing. *Who the hell do this fat muhfucker think he is?* she asked herself, taking a look as she unconsciously flipped the razor over in her mouth. But she controlled her emotions. *It's just a matter of time, papi,* she told herself. Roll looked at her and smirked. She was heated and wearing her emotions on her sleeve. *That's the problem with most broads,* Roll thought. They didn't need to be in the game because they were too emotional.

Angel fought hard, trying not to let him see her emotions, but it just didn't work. Roll knew Angel was treacherous, but her return could benefit his team if she played fair. If she didn't, curtains. For Roll, it was that simple.

Angel held out her hand and shook Roll's.

"What's the deal, Roll? Long time no see," Angel smiled.

"Ain't nothing," Roll replied, referring to Angel's and Goldilocks' outfits. "I woulda dressed for the occasion, but ah... I ain't come to party."

Time was money to Roll, and he didn't waste either.

"Duke wanted me to holla at you. Now that World is gone, he don't want no beef, and he hoped you and I could squash it," she finished, trying to keep her eyes off the dragon.

Roll rubbed his chain. "Well, where Duke at?"

"He chillin'."

"Chillin'?" Roll echoed.

"Let's go somewhere and talk. Follow me," Angel said as she and Goldilocks turned to walk away.

Roll looked at Nitti. They were strapped, and Roll felt shit was legit so they followed Angel to a storage room in the back of the club. It was empty except for a six-foot long meat locker. The sounds of the music bounced around the hollow room as Angel faced Roll.

"If Duke was here, he'd want you to know he didn't want no problems. He inherited World's territory but hopefully not his beef. He wants you to forget the past."

Roll looked at Nitti, amused.

"Forget the past, huh? What's in it for me?"

"A merger. World's spots with yours. You keep your connect and seventy percent of the profit," Angel proposed.

Roll momentarily avoided answering, thinking of the thirty percent she had offered.

"Where is Duke, anyway? He shook or somethin'? He lettin' bitches speak for him now?"

Goldilocks tensed but Angel laughed. "I told you, yo," she

began then opened the meat locker. "Duke's chillin."

Duke was really chilling. He lay on a bed of chipped ice, wearing Angel's trademark, a slit throat. His blood tinged the ice pink around his head. Rolls' eyes widened momentarily, then relaxed to normal. It was unexpected, but not a surprise.

"Duke ordered the hit on you, Roll, not Young World. World ain't know shit about it. He was in Atlanta when Duke put that lame shit down. He was movin' on you and World because he was the only one who could've benefited from a war."

Roll nodded. "Regardless, ma. World had it comin'. If it was his doin', he got what he deserved, and if he didn't, then he couldn't control his people. Either way, it's still on World," Roll replied, and Angel acknowledged his point.

"Well, they both gone now. So now what?"

"I'm sayin', Duke gone but what about this shit I'm hearin' about him fuckin' with some spaghetti heads in Hoboken? They chillin' too?"

Angel closed the meat locker and leaned against it. "A bunch of fuckin' nobodies. They ain't even in the mob. They wish they was down with the mob. Duke was their meal ticket, and they were his middlemen. The mob was charging Duke for protection. And now that Duke's gone, they'll go back to jackin' airport trunks."

Roll was impressed. Angel was still on top of her game. She was beautiful, but she wasn't to be fucked with. The deal was sweet, almost too sweet.

"So what you sayin', ma?"

"I think we'd make better friends than enemies," Angel smiled wickedly.

Mmm hmm. Keep your friends close and your enemies even closer, Roll thought to himself, then looked down and glanced at his watch.

"I think me and you should hang out sometime. Get to know one another," Roll suggested. His tone said he was interested but not yet convinced.

"Time is money, papi."

"Then we'll spend some of both," Roll responded as he and his people turned for the door.

"Roll," Angel called out. He turned around at the door. "I like your chain."

Roll chuckled and left with his entourage.

"Fat muthafucka," Angel hissed to herself.

RAHMAN

Chapter Six

Daddy!" the three tiny voices cried in unison.

Rahman kneeled down to receive his three children, Ali 6, Aminah 5, and Anisa 3, as they ran to embrace their father. They smothered him with a collective hug then he scooped them up in his big arms.

He was free.

He stood with the ominous structure of the federal courthouse in downtown Newark behind him. Rahman had won his appeal and was walking away a free man. He didn't want his family in the courthouse and opted instead for them to await the decision outside.

"Mr. Rahman Muhammad, you are free to go," the judge stated. It was a dream come true. Night after night he had dreamt those very words. Yet to hear the judge actually speak them brought tears to his eyes.

Free.

Rahman stepped down the courthouse steps like a slave unsure of his emancipation. For three years he had been told when to eat, sleep, get up, wash his ass, and move. To have his rights restored was truly a divine blessing. He vowed never to forget his ordeal and all he had endured.

Rahman smothered his babies with tears and kisses, "As-Salaamu Alaikum!"

"Alaikum As-Salaamu!" his children cried.

"Welcome home, Abu!" Ali told him, happy to have his daddy back.

Rahman looked up at his beautiful wife standing by their forest green Escalade. Ayesha was dressed in a flowing powder blue dress that covered her to the ankle. Her kemar was the same blue, and she wore a veil that covered her face but showed her eyes. The veil wasn't necessary in Islam, but she had worn the veil for three years because her husband was imprisoned and away from her and their family. It was her own vigil and her way of representing him. Now that he was home, she stripped it away to embrace him with her smile.

He put the children down and pulled Ayesha to him.

"You know we're not suppose to be out here in public like this," she said, wanting to hold him in her arms on the spot but knowing they should wait to be in private before hugging and kissing.

"Ayesha, after these past three years, you can't ask me to wait," he said, holding her close and hugging her.

"You are my peace," she whispered in his ear while rubbing her face on his.

Ayesha had maintained a perfect Muslim household. For Rahman's entire incarceration, she religiously made the journey, first to Lewisburg then to Atlanta, twice a month, flying with her brother and her children. She endured the nasty attitude of racist CO's, the violation of her privacy by female CO's, and the harassment of the federal prison system to bring her man all her love each time. Not just for him, but for herself as well. Rahman was truly her peace, and after dealing with the trials and tribulations of day-to-day life, she needed her man's strength and warmth. To have him again in her arms was almost too much to bear. So great was the miracle, so much all at once, all she could do was cry tears of happiness, relief, and most of all love.

"Don't cry, ma. It's over. We never gon' be apart. I'm here, and I'll never leave you again," he said, kissing her face all over.

"What's wrong with Ummi, Abu?" Aminah, the curious one, questioned. Rahman smiled, kissed Ayesha on the forehead, and said, "Ummi's fine, Minah. She's just happy daddy's home."

Rahman went to the Masjid first as most Muslims do, or should do, when returning home from a journey. He prayed his return prayer and when he finished, he got up to a rousing chorus of Takbir and Allah Akbar. The other Muslims who attended his Masjid knew he was on his way home, but to actually see him made them excited. He had been in touch with many of them while locked away. He had helped a lot of families and the Masjid by building a children's school and paying for roofing and plumbing repairs.

"All praise is due to Allah! My man's home!" Salahudeen shouted as he hugged Rahman. Salahudeen was an ex-kickboxer. He used to travel in the same circles with Akbar's people and would serve as Rahman's right hand.

Salahudeen was followed by Hanif and Mustafa, both reformed gangsters now in the independent oil fragrance business. They all greeted Rahman.

"See how Ock do us? Don't even tell nobody he out so a brother could be prepared," Hanif commented.

"A Muslim is always prepared," noted Rahman.

"No doubt, no doubt! This is true," Hanif agreed. "But are you prepared to put this thing of ours in motion?"

"Insha Allah," Rahman said to Mustafa.

"Aiight, dig. Let's go up to my spot. I already talked to..." Salahudeen began to explain because he was always about business.

Rahman laughed.

"Whoa, Ock. Slow your roll. I ain't been home yet! My family's in the car waiting for me."

"My bad, my bad. Your wife does have rights over you," Salahudeen.

"Three years worth of rights," Hanif joked.

"Exactly! You might not see me for another three years, either messin' with Ayesha."

The brothers laughed together knowing what it was like to be finally be home from a prison stay.

"Just gimme a week," Rahman told them. They all agreed and dispersed.

On his way out the door, Rahman spotted Hakim coming in. Hakim was an older brother with salt and pepper hair. He was also Young World's father. Rahman felt apprehensive as the man approached him, but he had no intention of avoiding him.

"It's good to see you home," Hakim said politely as he firmly shook Rahman's hand.

"It's good to be home," Rahman replied. "You look good." The brief silence between them was awkward.

Hakim smiled knowingly. "Ahkee, believe me. I don't blame you for Shaheed. By Allah, I don't. It was the life he chose to lead," Hakim explained softly. He knew Rahman's part.

"I know but..."

Hakim placed a warm hand on Rahman's shoulder, and

although he was five inches shorter, the respect Rahman had for him made them look at each other as if they were eye to eye.

"Allah knows best. All I ask is that you stand firm, okay? These streets are man-eaters, black man-eaters. Stand firm and that'll convince me that you are sincere."

Rahman took the lesson with him out the door.

For the next seven days, Rahman's family was in heaven. The children had their daddy back and Ayesha had her husband home. He spent his days playing with the children and his nights with Ayesha. He was finally able to lead his family in prayer, something he had neglected to do during his life in the game and something he had longed to do when he was in prison.

The return was bittersweet. Sweet because he was where he had prayed to be night after night. Bitter because he had missed so much.

Anisa, his baby girl, was born the night he was arrested by the Feds. He had missed the first three years of her life, footsteps to words. Ali and Aminah were only two and three years old when he left, and although still young, he had missed seeing them develop.

Rahman knew he couldn't make up for lost time, but he planned on making the most of every moment.

"Is it over?" Ayesha asked him one morning after prayer.

They stood together watching the sunrise from their bedroom balcony. Rahman stood behind her with his arms wrapped around her and hers wrapped around him.

"You ain't gonna pass out again are you?" Rahman joked. She elbowed him in the stomach. "Ow!"

"Then stop playin' and answer my question."

Rahman understood what she was asking. She wanted to know if he was through with the game. She knew of his plans, but she also knew the man her husband was and the man he was struggling to become.

"Yeah, boo. Its over."

She turned to look him in the eye. "No... I mean over. Over. All of it. Is this plan of yours gonna become another game? Another thing to take you away from me?" Ayesha questioned, searching his eyes for the answers.

Rahman caressed his wife's cheek.

"Nothing can take me from you."

"You once told me you couldn't be a gangsta and a Muslim at the same time."

"I remember."

"Well, which do you chose now?"

Rahman looked away towards the rising sun.

"Muslim."

"But this thing you got going on, these big plans. They will take you right back to the same streets and the same world," Ayesha warned, hoping he had carefully considered what he was doing before making a final decision. She turned his face to hers.

"Rahman, I know you want to do right and I know you want to help as many as you can. But baby, please don't do anything that's going to jeopardize our family. I don't know what I would do if they took you away from me again."

Tears trekked down her cheek and onto Rahman's chest as he held her tight.

"I can't survive another bid. Please. I can't do this thing called life by myself because you want those streets. You can't keep asking me to," she said, angry at the past three years without him.

"I won't," his mouth said, but it was a statement he knew his heart couldn't follow.

"To get rich or die tryin' is the motto of fools and clowns," Rahman bellowed to the crowd around him.

He was in Salahudeen's martial arts studio on South Orange Avenue. He was surrounded by more than fifty street vendors. Hanif and Mustafa were there. Rahman paced the floor slowly, looking from face to face like a general addressing his army.

"Why? It's simple... you can't take it with you."

A few heads laughed.

"No! You get power or die tryin' because either way, you make a change. Power brings riches but riches don't always bring power."

He let his jewel sink in before continuing.

"The oil fragrance business has always been a good hustle. On every corner in every major city there's a Muslim pushin' 'em. But up until now, it's only been nickels and dimes. You know why? No organization. If we organized it efficiently, we would be talking millions of dollars nationwide. Who ain't tryin' to touch that?"

"Holla back!"

"The man's a genius!"

Rahman grinned.

"Okay then. This is why you're here. We about to lock down the oil fragrance trade across the east coast, starting today in Newark. And whoever rolls wit' us, I can guarantee to double your profit margin, Insha Allah."

"Then let's double up!"

"I'm prepared to give each of you five thousand dollars to purchase oils for your businesses. The conditions, however, are that you will order from one supplier, once a month and at the same time, regardless of inventory. You will also order a mini-mum amount and spend a minimum amount of money every month regardless of inventory. Once we increase volume, our prices will be reduced and our profit margins will increase."

"Takbir!"

"Allah Akbar!"

"Didn't I say the man's a genius?!"

The voices rose into a cacophony of enthusiasm. Rahman signaled for them to quiet down.

"Hold up a minute. Let me finish. Now, each of you will remain independent but central control remains with Salahudeen. What he says is law. Period. Any objections?"

He looked around, but no one spoke.

"Same thing with clothes. One supplier, same stipulations. Any objections?"

Silence once again filled the air.

Rahman signaled to Hanif and Mustafa to begin passing out the five thousand dollar envelopes to each man.

"I hope y'all accept cash because my money don't agree with the Kufar's banks," he announced, but no one minded.

Once they were passed out, Rahman continued.

"You all are proud shareholders in our vendor franchise. But one last thing. If anyone buys from another supplier or in any way violates our agreement, we'll expect our five grand back on the spot. If you don't have it, forfeit your corner. We move as one, so there's only two sides and your either with us or against us." Rahman's imposing stature gave his last words their need-ed emphasis.

The meeting ended and the men filed out, all except for Rahman's team.

"Phew! I never gave away two hundred grand so quickly, yo,"

Hanif commented, tossing the empty bag aside.

"In six months, our investment will easily triple based on the volume Newark does daily," Rahman informed them. He had done the calculations and configurations and had it all figured out.

"Mustafa, I hope your peoples can handle this kind of weight."

"Can they? They got barrels and barrels of oils, shipped straight from Arabia," Mustafa said.

Rahman turned to Salahudeen.

"What's next?"

"I talked to them guys on 18th Avenue. They willin' to sell the block for a buck-fifty."

"A hundred and fifty grand?" Rahman asked, rubbing his beard as he thought for second. "Alright, cool. Make it happen, and Sal?"

Salahudeen looked at him.

"Please tell them dudes business is business. Once the block is ours, not one rock touches 18th avenue, alright?" Rahman warned.

Salahudeen winked.

"Come on, Ock. Who gonna try and cross One-eyed Roc?" Salahudeen joked. Rahman chuckled.

"Okay, now it's party time. Salahudeen call the brothers. We goin' to a strip club."

Hanif's eyes grew as wide as dinner plates.

"Yo, Ock. I know you been gone awhile but a strip club?"

"It's a Muslim party, yo," Rahman told the huge muscle-bound bouncer at the door. They were outside the Diamond Club. The parking lot was packed with niggas coming to get their freak on along with the 35 Muslims, give or take a few, who stood shoulder to shoulder, keeping order. The bouncer looked at the solemn-faced brothers then back at Salahudeen and Rahman as another bouncer hurried to the door. Both of the men looked like black Arnold Schwarzeneggers.

"What the fuck? Y'all on some bullshit! Get the fuck outta here before I lose my patience," the first bouncer barked, standing toe-to-toe with Rahman. Rahman took a step closer to the bouncer, tensing his muscles, ready for action.

"18th Avenue is under new management, brother. Now, let me in to see Freddie. Tell him One-eyed Roc is here."

The second bouncer recognized the name instantly.

"Ay, yo, Roc. We don't want no problems. We just tryin' to do our jobs."

"Well do 'em and go talk to Freddie before I lose my patience," Rahman retorted calmly.

The second bouncer disappeared inside the doorway while the other bouncer continued to glare at Roc. He could feel the bulge of his nine in it's holster and he was itching for a reason to pull it out.

The second bouncer came back and tapped the first on the shoulder. "It's cool, Joe. Freddie said let 'em in."

Rahman and Salahudeen moved to enter, but the man put his hand on Salahudeen's chest. His intention was to stop him and scan him for weapons, but he didn't get a chance to speak. He heard so many guns lock and load, the metallic clicks echoed through the parking lot like the breaking of a thousand twigs. Upset, but not stupid, the bouncer slowly removed his hand from Sal's chest, and Salahudeen and Rahman entered the club.

As they walked through the double doors, Rahman looked

around at all the women. They were dancing on stages, on tables, on laps, upside down, on their knees. He shook his head as the bodyguard escorted them to Freddie's office. Rahman didn't stop and knock. He turned the knob and let himself in.

"Roc baby! How you doin', son?" Freddie chimed nervously.

Freddie was a tall, lanky, light-skinned brother. He stood up and rounded his desk, adjusting his Cartier frames. He held out his hand to Rahman, but Rahman didn't take it. Instead, Rahman said, "You're closed."

The bodyguard had already informed Freddie of what was going on. Freddie knew Roc and he knew what Roc was capable of. He didn't want any part of the gangsta.

"Closed?" Freddie echoed. "What's the problem, Roc? What I do? How you gonna come up in my..."

That was all he was able to get out before Roc open-handed him so hard his glasses flew off his face and smashed against the wall. Freddie fell back against the desk. The bodyguard tried to make a move on Roc, but Salahudeen delivered a vicious blow to his kidneys. The bodyguard doubled over but quickly recovered and charged Salahudeen like a bull. Sal was only six feet tall and 175 pounds at best. But what the bodyguard didn't know was that Sal was a lethal weapon. Salahudeen sidestepped the oncoming assault and followed it with an leg sweep that sent the bodyguard crashing headfirst into the door. He then grabbed the man's dazed head and rammed his knee up into his face, twice. Blood covered Salahudeen's pant leg as he released the unconscious body to slump to the floor. Meanwhile, Rahman had snatched Freddie off the desk by the throat and pinned him to the wall, trembling with rage.

"You heard me, nigga! I said closed! Out of business! Ain't

gonna be no strip club on 18th Avenue. Either pack up or DIE!"

Freddie was terrified. He couldn't understand what was going on. All he could think was that Roc wanted the business for himself, or maybe he was on some extortion quest. Freddie was willing to pay.

"Come on Roc, man. Is it money, man? You wanna piece of my hustle?" Freddie asked with his mouth bloody.

"Hustle! Hustle? Nigga, you ain't no hustler, you a pimp! A hustler, I respect. But a pimp, I'll kill in front of his mama! Get out and if you even breathe something to the police, I'll murder you and your family. Understood?" Rahman asked, throwing Freddie against a file cabinet. It crashed to the floor. Freddie quickly got up and staggered out the door.

"Clear the club and bring the girls in the back," Rahman told Salahudeen. The Muslims moved into the club in an orderly fashion. Salahudeen grabbed the mic from the DJ.

"The Diamond Club is officially closed for good. All y'all trick-ass niggas get out and all y'all females, if you want a thousand dollars, get dressed and meet us in the dressing room."

Niggas yelled obscenities and threats, but a room filled with gun-toting Muslims helped move things along at a rapid pace.

While the brothers cleared the club, Salahudeen and Rahman entered the dressing room where all fifteen strippers waited patiently to learn what it was they had to do for a thousand dollars. As soon as money was mentioned, they hurried and covered themselves, either dressing in their clothes or a robe. Only two girls remained as they were, bare-breasted and wearing thongs.

Any man would've been sexually aroused by a room full of exotic dancers. But the Muslims weren't. They were enraged. Enraged in what the ghetto had done to the sisters sitting there with their falsely arched eyebrows, falsely tinted eyes, and dangling hair weaves. They looked like mannequins, mere shells of their beautiful black selves. Salahudeen gave them all a thousand dollars, and Rahman handed a robe to the two girls with exposed breasts.

"Cover yourself, ma. Ain't no tricks back here," he said turning to another female in a web-like dress that barely covered her ass. "And you, put some clothes on."

"I got some clothes on," she retorted with an attitude. To her, there was nothing wrong with the way she was dressed.

"Sal, show her the door, please," he said extending another $100, which she took from his hand. She looked at the $1,100 she was holding and realized her mouth had gotten her into trouble.

"Ay, yo. I'm sor..."

"Sal, the door," Rahman repeated and turned his back to her.

She sucked her teeth and stormed out. The other girls without robes or coats quickly covered themselves. They certainly weren't tryin' to piss the nigga off, especially since he was so free with his money. They definitely wouldn't make the same mistake. Besides, if they could take their clothes off for tens and twenties, they could damn sure put them on for gees and cees.

"Is this what you want?" Rahman's voice boomed, waving more money in the air. "Is this what your dignity is worth? They pay you to take it off so you can sell your soul to the highest bidder? You call that independence?" he asked, looking around the room, shaking his head in disgust. He looked at one of the girls, who couldn't have been more that eighteen or twenty.

"Why you a stripper?"

"Cause I'm grown," she snapped with attitude.

Turning to a Puerto Rican girl sitting in the corner, he asked, "What's your name?"

"Mona."

"Why you strip?"

"Bills. A checkout girl at Pathmark don't pay 'em," she replied.

"I can dig it," Rahman agreed. He turned his attention to a tall red bone.

"How much you make a week?"

"Two gees," she said, lying through her teeth.

"Tops, fifteen hundred," he surmised, recognizing game. "Now back to Miss Grownie Pants," he said to the young girl. "You like bein' a stripper? You like niggas treatin' you like a piece of meat? A slut?"

"I ain't no slut," she spat. "I'm an exotic dancer, and no, I don't like it. But I got two babies that tell me I ain't got no choice."

"What if I offered you a job?"

"What kind of job?" Miss Grownie Pants asked skeptically.

"One that doesn't involve sex, drugs or disrespect. Jobs for beautiful black queens and bonita latinas," he said, smiling at Mona. "Making double what you make at the club."

"Hol' up," the tall red bone spoke up. "What's wrong with being a dancer? My body is my asset, just like an athlete's. I like to dance. I like..."

"Then go dance, mami," he said, throwing a hundred dollars in her lap.

Red bone rolled her eyes and tucked the money in her ample bosom on the way out the door.

"Anybody want to go with her?"

Nobody made a sound.

"You work for me, you work by my rules. Rule number one, don't question me and play your position. I promise you, I'll never ask you to do anything illegal or immoral. I'm a Muslim concerned with my nation. It's my duty to provide. I'm not here to judge you. You wanna be a boy toy, there's the door. But if you want to hold your head high because of who you are, then trust me."

He looked from face to face. He could tell the women were used to being abused and tricked by so-called players and bitch-ass niggas. They had never met a sincere man who truly wanted to help them. His honesty, even more than the $1,000. he had given them, made the women listen to him further.

In the next month and a half, Rahman expanded his circle of control to three more blocks, buying them to be drug free. His oil enterprise flourished and cash began to flow. The strippers had all been employed. Some had been hired to cook and care for the elderly in the neighborhood while others were hired as childcare for working mothers. The word spread about the jobs the Muslim brothers were offering, and Rahman ended up hiring fifteen more girls all out of his own pocket.

Even Miss Grownie Pants was won over by his strength and commitment to the community. He didn't deal with the women directly, but Miss Grownie Pants always watched him, admiring the big man she had nicknamed Sugar Bear. She liked the way the Muslims carried themselves with high regard and respect for one another and their wives. She was curious about the lifestyle she had heard so much about so she started asking questions.

One day, Rahman was walking down the street and heard a soft voice.

"As-Salaamu Alaikum."

He turned around to find Miss Grownie Pants dressed in a loose fitting jogging suit and kemar.

"Miss Grownie Pants?" he asked with surprise.

"My name is not Miss Grownie Pants. It's Sonia. But, you can call me Jamillah," she said, smiling from ear to ear. It almost brought tears to his eyes. Every dime he had spent was worth that one moment.

"Al-hum-dil-li-lah," he said to her before parting ways.

Everything was going smoothly. The money was slow but steady, and the community was thriving. It had become safe for small children to play outside. The streets were calm. Even the elderly were out on their stoops. People seemed happier. The small-time hustlers who once occupied the neighborhood's corners weren't making any noise. They knew who they were dealing with. The community knew him as Rahman, but the streets remembered him as Dutch's vicious lieutenant.

But the real test lay ahead.

For now, Rahman was satisfied. He felt humble but powerful, quiet but strong. He felt like Dutch.

In an ironic way, Rahman owed his plan to Dutch. He'd never forget the day they all met to discuss the murder of Kazami. Rahman remembered his reluctance and apprehension to take such a bold step. Dutch's words made him realize his own power.

It ain't what can we do, it's what can't we do.

That was the attitude of men who made things happen instead of waiting for things to happen to them. Those words had given birth to Rahman's plans to rid the black community of the poison that plagued it.

Poverty.

It wasn't drugs or crime that were to blame. It was poverty and desperation. Rahman figured if Dutch could infest the city with his strategy, then he could clean it up with his own.

"There go my baby!"

He heard a female's voice shouting as he stood on the corner talking to a few young hustlers. He turned around to find Angel.

"What's up, boooooo?" she sang as she climbed out of the drop top Jag. She was dressed in cuffed D&G jeans and a crisp white v-neck tee shirt. Her hair was pinned back by Dior sunglasses, and she walked with a confident strut.

"I know, I know Muslims can't hug she devilz," she joked, slurring the words. "But you know I wanna wrap myself around yo' big ass!"

Rahman chuckled, uncertain of what to say.

"Look at you! You got all fat," she said, poking his stomach.

"How you, ma? What's good?" he asked, hoping she couldn't tell he had been caught off guard by her presence.

Rahman had heard about Angel teaming up with Roll, and his old dark side wondered why she was dealing with a sucka like him, especially after he found out Roll had Young World killed. Roll's blocks were definitely on his hit list.

"I'm good. But word up, papi. I am so mad wit you. I can't believe you been out all this time and you ain't even holla!" Angel said, shaking her head in disbelief. "I just can't believe that!"

"I'm sayin', I been kinda caught..."

"Caught nothin'. Don't front, nigga. You been gone three years, and Ayesha had that ass on lock!"

They both laughed.

The truth was he had been avoiding her and avoiding what a

meeting with her meant. He didn't know, but Angel had been doing the same thing. She heard about Roc's community actions. She remembered all his letters from prison. But she thought it was just the bars talking. She didn't think he would actually come home and put it down.

The time had come for two old friends to have a meeting of the minds.

"On the real, though. It's good to see you. What you up to now? Let's go get something to eat. And don't worry, I don't eat pork either," she said with a smile.

Rahman glanced at his watch.

"Yeah, we can do that. Gimme about twenty minutes."

"Aiight, cool. Meet me at Applebees."

"Insha Allah."

Rahman arrived at the restaurant first. The sun was setting and his eyes stayed glued to the window. The Applebees happened to be across the street from University Hospital, the hospital where he was shot by the Feds.

Freeze!

The bullet didn't freeze him. It jolted his inebriated mind into a painful sizzle. The bullet wound burned his flesh. He lay on the hard asphalt, blood gushing from his wound, looking up at the night stars wondering, *Is this the end?*

"Kinda ironic, huh?"

He heard Angel's voice, and it brought him out of inner thoughts.

"Ironic?" he repeated.

"We're both back where it all ended," Angel said, sliding into the booth across from him. "And where it all begins," she added, getting comfortable.

"For who?"

"For us. Me and you, Roc. We grand champions in this game, and it's time to put it down like true thoroughbreds."

"And Roll? He a true thoroughbred, too?" Rahman smirked.

Angel sucked her teeth then sipped her water. "He's a pawn. A fuckin' fat, black, fake-ass Biggie lookin' pawn. He thinks I'm givin' when I'm really takin'. I got him so twisted, he don't know if he comin' or goin'," she boasted nonchalantly, then added sincerely.

"But, this thing ain't right without you, bro."

"Would you like to order?" the waitress politely asked.

"Just coffee," Rahman replied.

"And you?"

"Same thing," Angel told the waitress, watching as she walked away.

"Come on, Angel. You know where I'm at. You been hearin' about me just like I been hearin' about you. You know what I'm doin' and it ain't a game, it ain't a joke, and it ain't a front for somethin' else," he explained.

Angel lit up a cigarette, trying to conceal it from view.

"It may not be a joke Roc, but you can't be serious. Muthafuckas been gettin' high since the beginning of time and ain't shit gonna change that, no matter how many blocks you buy, or strip clubs you... strip," she said, hitting her cigarette and blowing the smoke under the table. "You tellin' me THAT ain't gangsta? You fuckin' gorilla'd him!" Angel laughed.

The waitress returned with their coffee.

"Thank you, sister," Rahman said.

"You're very welcome," the waitress smiled, then walked away. Angel watched her again. Rahman stirred his coffee.

"I can't stand a pimp, Angel. They ain't nothin' but leeches preying on our women. He had it comin', and it wasn't about bein' gangsta."

"Okay. You want certain blocks drug-free, cool. I feel you. I respect what you're doin', for real. But somebody, somewhere is gonna see it and somebody gonna buy it. Why not use that money and put it to good use?" she suggested.

"Blood money."

"This is America, Roc. It's all blood money. But look at what you can do with that blood money. I'm talkin' controllin' it all — boy, girl, E and smoke, brick to bottle," Angel said.

But Rahman shot right back. "I'm talkin' 'bout the same thing except it's legal. We control every dollar, not just drug money, but a piece of every dollar in the community. Off all alone, we bring in over three hundred grand every six months."

"Three hundred?" she said, her voice rising, but she caught herself. "Three hundred grand! Roc, we used to piss that. I still piss that," Angel said as she realized he was definitely thinking on a smaller level than he once used to. She smashed her cigarette under her boot.

"My little three to you is a start for me."

"Then we right back where we were when we came in, a start. Me and you. I help you lock down the legal shit and you ride wit' me on this thing of mine and together we got every angle covered."

He sighed deeply. They were at a stalemate. They both had the same plan for different reasons and neither could convince the other to abandon theirs.

"Angel, it's time to take the game to another level."

"Exactly."

"Not that game, the real game. That game you playin' only keeps us trapped at the bottom of the barrel," he said trying to reason with her.

"Listen, it was good seeing you, but..."

He stood up and Angel smiled at him.

"I love you, nigga. And I don't care what you say. One-eyed Roc is somewhere in that belly of yours. I'ma make him come out if it's the last thing I do."

"As-Salaamu Alaikum."

"Siempre."

Rahman backed out in his Cadillac Deville, watching Angel through the plate glass window of the restaurant. Their eyes spoke a language of their own and the words of Nas echoed in his mind. *Love changes, a thug changes, and best friends become strangers.*

Angel meant what she said and was determined to bring out the One-eyed Roc she once knew. She just hoped he came out for her and not against her, because if that happened, things could get very ugly.

He took the longer way back home, driving slowly in deep contemplation. The visit with Angel had been planned. She wanted to feel him out, see what he was doing, hear what he had to say, and see if he was serious. Now that she knew, what would be her next move?

He had purposefully avoided the hottest drug blocks run by the bigger dealers. Sooner or later, however, he'd have to deal with them, whoever they were, even Angel. He knew what she was capable of because he had taught her. In Dutch's organization, he had been the problem-solver. Now that he had become a problem for her, he wondered if she would try and use his own tactics against him?

One-eyed Roc is somewhere in that belly...

Her words struck a chord within him because she was right. He felt it that night at the strip club, the way his temper took control, the assault on Freddie. He was on a mission and was prepared to use any means necessary to accomplish it. He prayed he wouldn't have to be Roc to do so.

Rahman checked his rear-view mirror several times and made the unnecessary wrong turns until he was certain he wasn't being followed. He took the same precautions every night and believed he wasn't being followed.

Or so he thought.

He pulled up to his spacious but modest home. It wasn't far from Newark and offered a peacefulness that Newark couldn't provide. The house was a two-story, five-bedroom brick structure with a large basement that he used for study and prayer.

Rahman entered his home and smiled at the sounds of Ayesha being mommy.

"Ali! Where is your other shoe and why is this one on the wrong foot?"

"Aminah got it!" Ali squealed.

"Aminah!"

Rahman went into the living room and greeted his family, but Ayesha detected a problem.

"Ali, go get your shoes, boy, and put them on," Ayesha ordered.

"Okay, mommy," he replied, hobbling off in search of his sister with his other shoe.

Ayesha laced her fingers around Rahman's neck.

"You wanna talk about it?"

"Talk about what?" Rahman responded, not realizing his face had betrayed his mental state.

Ayesha smirked knowingly. "That knot in your brow."

"What knot? I'm smilin'," he said, putting on a happy face.

"Every smilin' face ain't a happy face."

"Being home makes me happy."

She saw that he was being evasive, so she changed the subject.

"Are you hungry? I made hamburgers for the kids, but I could whip you up something."

"A burger would be fine. In fact, let me serve you tonight, my queen," he said and scooped her up in his arms and carried her into the kitchen.

"And to what do I owe this honor?" she asked, although she wasn't surprised. Rahman was a wonderful husband who never forgot the little things.

He sat her at the kitchen table.

"It's the way of the Prophet, peace be upon him. He helped his wives with household chores, right?"

"True... which reminds me, the dishes need washing too," she giggled.

Rahman took four burgers out of the skillet and put them on buns. He sat down with Ayesha, breaking off a piece of burger and placing it gently in her mouth.

"Oh, I know what this is," Ayesha chewed.

"What is it?"

"You must know I saw your little girlfriend today."

Rahman chuckled because he knew whom she was referring to, Miss Grownie Pants. He also knew Miss Grownie Pants had a crush on him. He guessed his wife knew it, too.

"My little girlfriend? I have no girlfriends, only a wife. But I'm sure you think you know something, so please tell me," he answered as Ayesha placed a piece of burger in his mouth.

"'Oh, tell Rahman thank you so much. The kids loved the toys and they thank him so much. He's a beautiful brother,'" Ayesha mocked in a high pitch voice. "Then she had the nerve to ask, *'Can't a Muslim man have more than one wife?'"* Ayesha snapped.

"Can't they though? You let her know, right?" he asked jokingly, laughing at his wife's stunned expression.

"Don't play with me, Rah. Please! I don't want to have to hurt you," Ayesha warned, narrowing her almond-shaped eyes into evil slits.

"Yo, the presents weren't given to that girl by me. They were donated. You know that. Brother Shamzadeen passed out presents to all the single Muslim mothers. Besides, I ain't even seen that girl. But guess who I did see?" he asked, changing the subject to something relevant.

"Who?" Ayesha asked curiously.

"Angel."

Ayesha glared at him. She knew what Angel was about, and she knew exactly what his seeing her meant.

"And?"

"And what? You know the rest 'cause you know Angel and you know me," he said, shaking his head. "She down wit' some kid named Roll. Roll's the same dude who murdered Shaheed, or so the streets say. I don't know," he sighed.

"So, what are you going to do about it?" Ayesha inquired with concern because she, too, could see the storm brewing.

"I'll cross that bridge when I come to it."

"You already there, honey. You already there."

Rahman checked his watch.

"It's time for prayer. Go on and get the babies ready."

Ayesha let it go, trusting her husband to do the right thing and trusting in Allah to show him the way.

"Look at this muthafucka here! They can't fuck wit' Marbury. That's right, give it to 'em!" Roll exclaimed as Marbury dunked the basketball and scored two points for the Knicks.

He along with his wife, Renée, and Goldilocks sat in the luxurious skybox overlooking the arena at Madison Square Garden. It was outfitted with the amenities of wealth, courtesy of Gutter Records, a label his man owned, thanks to Roll. Roll had invested a lot of money in Gutter Records so his man gave him the skybox as a gift of appreciation.

Roll picked up a Cuban and lit it.

"I should buy a basketball team," he said to no one.

Angel walked in and slammed the door. She went straight to the bar and poured herself a glass of Hennessey.

Roll glanced over his shoulder. "How'd it go?"

Angel eyed him over the rim of her tinted glasses. "That nigga really on that Muslim shit hard!"

Roll was amused. He thought prison had really broken Roc and mistook his change of allegiance for weakness.

"He'll come around, though," Angel assured him.

"I think it's good what he's doing. It's about time somebody tried to do something to help the community and the poor," Renée declared.

Roll looked at her as if she was crazy. "The fuckin' community, the fuckin' poor?" he snorted, "Bitch, since you so concerned, why don't you donate some of those rocks you wearin' on your fingers or that Benz you drivin'? Better yet, give the hood your shoppin' money. Why don't you do something since you think this nigga is so great," Roll suggested.

"Look, you don't have to get smart. I was just sayin' that it's a good thing the man tryin' to do something to help the black community."

"Renée, shut up," Roll said, getting up. He walked over to the bar and sat next to Angel.

"So what's the deal? He really tryin' to clean up Newark? 'Cause if he come to my spots wit' that bullshit, he can forget it."

"I said he'll come around."

"And what if he don't? Then what? I'll tell you what. He's gonna be a problem. Shit, he already is," Roll spat, dropping his ashes into an ashtray on the countertop.

"I'll take care of it," Angel answered half-heartedly.

"Yeah, you gonna have to, 'cause if you don't, I will," Roll declared, then walked back to his seat to watch the game.

Angel couldn't stand taking orders from Roll. He was obnoxious, fat, lazy, and arrogant for no reason. He had too many weaknesses, but it wasn't time to reveal her hand, so she swallowed her tongue.

The blaring air horn sounded the end of the quarter. It was half-time.

"Roll, you worry too much. Look at you. You on top of the world, papi! And all the little people is scrambling for your crumbs."

"I don't worry. I prepare. That's why I am who I am."

"Well, tonight, I want to enjoy who you are," Angel replied in a seductive tone that annoyed Renée.

Angel flipped on the stereo and popped in a reggae mix CD. The banging percussion instruments filled the skybox.

"Goldi, let's give Roll a real half-time show."

Goldilocks didn't hesitate. She smirked at Roll, stood up and joined Angel on the floor. She began kissing her mouth deeply, gyrating her hips inside her lambskin skirt, ass facing Roll. Renée and Roll looked on in amazement as Angel pulled up Goldilocks' skirt to reveal a pink thong and pretty ass. She palmed Goldilocks and spread her cheeks for Roll to see Goldi's pink and wet lower lips.

"Oh hell no, bitch!" Renée shouted. "What the fuck do you think you doin'?"

Roll grabbed her hand and sat her back down. "Damn, Renée. Chill! She only dancin'," Roll smirked as Renée boiled.

Goldilocks dropped into a squat and spread her legs in front of Roll. Her arms were back up around Angel' neck. Angel fingered Goldilocks' pussy, making her tremble and bite her tongue.

"It's all about you, Roll," Angel crooned as she slowly removed Goldilocks' top until Goldilocks was completely naked.

"Ain't she sexy, Roll? Ain't my bitch sexy?" Angel asked.

Renée shot Roll an evil look. "Roland, I don't appreciate this shit. I really don't."

"Shhh!" Roll snapped.

Goldilocks continued to dance and seductively wiggled her finger to beckon Roll.

"Dance, hell! You freaky bitches wanna fuck my man!" Renée protested.

"Aww, honey. You got it all wrong," Angel assured her. "We don't wanna fuck Roll. We wanna fuck you," Angel said as she pulled off her shirt and Goldilocks pulled down her pants.

Roll was totally fucked up. He had wanted to fuck Angel for years, ever since he had first seen her. But he knew she was a dyke. But now, here she was, naked, in a skybox, conjuring up an orgy with his wife and her girlfriend. He was confused trying to figure out where he would fit in.

Does she mean she only wants Renée or does she want the both of us, he wondered.

"Me?!" Renee squealed, taken totally by surprise.

"What up, Nee?" Roll grinned lustfully. "You wit' it?"

"Hell no, I ain't wit' it! And I can't believe you'd ask me some shit like that! I'm your wife, Roland, not them nickel bitches you be fuckin'!" she screamed at him.

Angel and Goldilocks, both completely naked, slowly approached Renée.

"Even more so why we should be able to do anything together. You my wife!" he screamed back using reverse psychology. He was determined not to miss his chance. He couldn't wait to stick his dick up in Angel and her girlfriend ,and if the only way he could do it was through his wife, then she needed to get her ass in motion. "I do everything you ask me to, when you ask me to. Why you can't do this for me? I want you to," he said, convincing himself as he attempted to convince her.

Renée loved Roland and his money. It was true that he did everything under the sun for her and her children, even the ones that weren't his.

Maybe if we do it together, he won't cheat on me. He'll cheat with me, she rationalized as she imagined Angel and Goldilocks up in her house with her man when she wasn't home. *He's gonna fuck 'em regardless. He wants to fuck them. I could do it for him,* she thought.

"Don't worry, baby. We won't hurt you," Angel purred as she parted Renée's thick caramel thighs. Renée's skirt creeped up her thighs as Angel bent over between her legs.

"Please, Roland," Renée begged.

"Go 'head, yo," he drooled, completely aroused.

Angel and Goldilocks each placed one of Renée's legs over

their shoulders and began to double-tongue her apprehensions away. Two caressing tongues worked together for one common purpose.

Roll was too stupid to realize what the freak show would cost him.

Renée's eyes rolled back into her head, and she mumbled incoherently. Angel sat up, straddled her lap, kissed her mouth deeply, and pinched her hard nipples teasingly while Goldilocks licked and sucked her pussy. Renée never came so hard, or so quickly, in her life.

"Ohh God!" she gasped as Angel pulled her to the floor on top of her. Roll couldn't take seeing the three gorgeous bodies wrapped around each other.

"She's all yours now," Angel said, offering him his wife. Roll responded quickly, his dick rock hard. He dropped his pants and boxers to the floor and entered his wife doggie-style, keeping his eyes on Angel as he fucked his wife. For Roll, it was as if he was finally living out his fantasy with Angel and plowed into Renée even harder.

"Yes, Roland! Yes!" Renée screamed, gripping the carpet so hard she ripped off a nail.

"It's all about you, Roll," Angel repeated, feeling Goldilocks tongue across her nipple. "It's all about you," she repeated, licking her tongue at him before twirling it into Renée's mouth. Roll exploded inside his wife, all the while fantasizing it was Angel taking his dick.

Angel had used his mind and another woman's body to rock Roll to sleep. It was only a matter of time before she'd be in complete control.

"You love him don't you."

"Yeah."

Goldilocks and Angel lay in bed during the wee hours of the morning. Angel thought Goldilocks was asleep, but she wasn't. She was well aware of Angel's movements at all the times. She knew Angel was looking at the picture of her and Dutch at her twenty-first birthday party. It was something Angel did every night, almost like a prayer, and Goldilocks had gotten used to it.

Goldilocks rolled over onto her back.

"Let me see."

Angel handed her the photo. Goldilocks had seen it a thousand times before, but she liked to admire Dutch's features. He was definitely fine. His charisma seemed to ooze from the photo. She understood why Angel smiled every time she looked at him.

"You look so happy here," Goldilocks remarked. "How can I make you happy like that?"

Angel looked at her lover with appreciation. Goldi was definitely riding with her to the end. She took the picture back, glanced at it, then replied, "When I was eight years old, my father raped me," Angel stated flatly. "He called me his little angel, bounced me on his knee, kissed me, kissed me again, then slide his hand between my legs," she said her voice cracking with rage and resentment. "It wasn't just once, either. It was a lot and my mother, nada. She did nothing. She let him. She knew. She had to know. I know she knew what was happening to me, but she never helped me. She turned a deaf ear, a blind eye, and every week from when I was eight until I ran away from home at thirteen, he raped me. Sometimes it was two and three times a week. He would tell mama he was putting me to bed and going to read me a bedtime story and not to disturb us during reading time. She would be in the next room.

I thought that if I didn't look like a cute little girl, he'd leave me alone. So, I started dressing like a boy. I figured he'd leave me alone if I looked like a boy. But it didn't work. He still looked at me with that sinister lust in his eyes."

Goldilocks laid her head on Angel's chest and let Angel play with her locks.

"Every man I met, they always had that same lustful look in their eyes. I saw it in every one of them, and it always made me feel disgusting. My father made me feel disgusting. Dirty, ashamed, and I'm eight years old again, ya know?" Angel explained, trying to hold back all the emotions from the memories flooding back to her.

"Except for Dutch. He never looked at me like that. You know what I saw when I looked into his eyes?"

"What?"

"Aristocracy, beauty and arrogance. They're the only words that perfectly describe what I saw in him. He was the type of nigga you either fucked or feared, wanted to die for or despised and wished dead. He was the only man who ever saw me."

Goldilocks understood perfectly. She, too, knew how it felt to be judged solely on looks and nothing else. She clearly understood how beauty could sometimes be a curse.

"Do you think he's still alive?" Goldilocks asked, finally finding the opportune moment.

Angel paused and bit her bottom lip pensively. "I don't know. But I just can't believe he's dead."

"If he came back, would you be with him?"

"I'll always ride with Dutch. But be with him like that? Naw, never. With you, always."

Goldilocks smiled and kissed her softly.

"Besides, me and Dutch aren't meant to be like that. I would never tell him my true feelings anyway."

"Why not?"

"Because I, too, am an aristocrat. Besides, his heart belongs to someone ealse already."

"Who?"

Close your eyes...

She did.

Imagine yourself in the place you most want to be and when you get there, imagine you see me.

She could feel the warmth of the pristine white sand beneath her bare feet, smell the fresh blue water, feel the mist hitting her face, and touch the warm frothy water running between her legs.

Now... open your mouth... just... a little... a little more.

She parted her succulent lips ever so slightly, just enough to let her tongue out or his in. He traced her lips gently with his thumb, causing her to quiver with anticipation.

I thought you... you were gone.

Did you really think I'd leave you?

The feathery touch of his fingertips across her cheek, down the nape of her neck, between her breasts and to her bellybutton made her squirm. His kisses sent fire to every nerve ending in her body, from head to toe, releasing all of her pent-up emotions.

Pleasure.

Pain.

Joy.

Pain.

Ecstasy.

Pain.

Pain...

Where did you go?

She rode the rhythm of his tongue like a wave that engulfed her, threatening to carry her away. Then just like that...

He was gone.

"No!" she gasped and sat straight up in her bed, sweating and breathing hard. "But I lov..." Nina caught herself before she cried out.

Dwight rolled over.

"You okay, baby?" he asked groggily, still half sleep as he reached for her shoulder.

"Yeah, yeah, I'm fine," she answered as he rolled over too tired and sleepy to realize the distress she was in or what she had murmured before she woke him up.

In a cold sweat, thighs and panties soaked, she hugged herself and tried to shake off the feeling as she climbed out of bed and went to the bathroom. It was the third night in a row she had dreamed about Dutch, and she had had enough. Nina had to know the truth. *Was he really dead? Was he somewhere out there, waiting for her, wanting her, dreaming of her, like she was of him?*

She ran her fingers under the cold water and through her hair. Her life, after being so peaceful and tranquil for three years, had suddenly become one big question mark. It had all started with the flowers.

"You're not going to believe this," Nina's assistant said, sticking her head through the cracked doorway.

It was ten in the morning and Nina was already swamped.

"If it's a call, take a message. If it's a meeting, reschedule it. And if it's a question, the answer is no," Nina rattled, feeling grouchy.

"Oh, I don't think you'll say no to this. In here gentlemen," her assistant ordered.

Nina's jaw dropped. Three delivery men carried in dozens of beautiful bouquets of flowers from roses to gardenias, lilies to orchids. Money had obviously not been a factor when the order had been placed with the florist.

"What is this? Am I opening up a floral boutique?" she asked in amazement. When all was said and done, over thirty floral arrangements in different crystal vases filled her office. The aroma of the freshly cut loveliness scented her office like an exotic potpourri. Her secretary wondered how she would be able to come and go with the flowers occupying every inch of space.

"Someone really loves you," she said wistfully, wishing she had someone special to send her flowers.

One of the delivery men returned with the last multi-colored bouquet of what she thought were roses. When he handed them to her, Nina noticed they weren't roses at all, but silk panties in various soft colors, balled up and cupped like roses and placed on artificial stems.

She took the bouquet of panties and thanked the delivery-men with a $20. tip. Then she picked up the attached card, opened it and read: *Who else?*

That was what she wanted to know! *Who would send so many flowers?* The question galloped through her mind like a stampede of horses. *Dwight? He couldn't afford all of them. He didn't make that much money in a month!*

Dwight loved to surprise her, but he did so in simple, thoughtful ways. And always in person. He was hooked on how she thanked him. In fact, he surprised her all the time just for his 'thank you'.

Nina had dated casually before Dwight, and some of the men had been extremely wealthy. But none of them would ever do this. None had been that serious about her. Besides, they were months in her past.

No. Whoever sent the flowers was a man sure of his place in her heart. Therefore, there would be no need for a signature.

There was only one man in her life who fit that description.

Who else?

It had been over a month since the CD incident, and Nina had all but forgotten it. She explained it away even though it didn't make sense. She refused to acknowledge what her heart yearned to accept. Now, standing in her own Garden of Eden, the thoughts she had suppressed sprang from her subconscious and filled her mind with endless possibilities.

We've just found the body of Bernard James, she silently recalled when his death was announced. She had been on her way to the courthouse when she heard the news. Her body went limp as she heard the words. *Bernard James, Jr. has been pronounced dead. His body has been recovered.*

Nina thought of him and of what they shared and of what they would never share. It all died with him that day.

So who else?

"No," she told herself, refusing to let her emotions take her back to that dismal place in time. Nina had learned to live without hope. She had learned to fulfill her own expectations. She was a woman who wanted to believe, but life had proven that believing was too painful. She had accepted her fate and no amount of flowers would ever change it.

I have to get rid of these. What if Dwight comes in here and sees them and they aren't from him? But what if they are? she thought.

Instinct took over. She resolved to get rid of the evidence. Hope, in the form of bouquets was like a dead body lying cold in the middle of her office. She had once killed it. Now she had to dump the body.

She called her secretary and told her that every desk, every teller station and every office was to have a bouquet. She kept only three for herself. Her office was back to its normal drab in less than an hour and hope's body was safely buried around the bank. The bouquet of silk panties she stuffed in a drawer mainly because she couldn't find an appropriate place to put them.

Nina had always been honest with Dwight because he deserved it. And she never had nothing to hide. Now she wasn't so sure. *Why did I give all my flowers away? Who else, yeah, who else would send me a thousand flowers?* She couldn't help but ponder.

Dwight loved her. He loved her body, every inch of her. He loved having sex with her. It was so much better with Nina than it had been with anyone before her. She was beginning to open up with him, beginning to be more sexually expressive and eager and willing to please him anyway he asked her to. But he mistook her eagerness in bed thinking it was about him, when in fact, Nina was pretending that it Dutch she was fucking. Thinking of Dutch made her climax with ease. All she had to do was let him into her mind. If she was really there with Dwight, she'd be there all night trying. She told herself she wasn't cheating. Dwight had her body. A dead man had her mind. How was that cheating?

"Girl, you are cheating if you are fuckin' a nigga and thinking about somebody else's dick runnin' up in you. Say what

163

you want, you know it's true," Tamika stated matter-of-factly before licking the rim of a walnut caramel ice cream cone.

"Whatever. You're not cheating unless you're fuckin' someone else, period. It shouldn't have anything to do with who you think about."

"Well, do you be thinkin' about the other person when you cum or are you connected to the person you actually fucking?" Tamika asked, trying get Nina to be precise.

Nina sat back and just smiled. An answer to Tamika's question would only make Tamika right and Nina didn't want her to be.

"Ohh, you are a nasty slut!" Tamika exclaimed excitedly, "I fuckin' knew it. I knew it! You freaky heffer! I knew it! Who is it? Somebody at the bank? Somebody you just met? Girl who is you really sleepin' wit'? Tell me!" Tamika rattled.

"It's nobody," Nina lied. "It was just a question, gee willikers!" she shrugged and spooned out another bite of Haagan Daaz into her mouth.

"Bitch, don't give me the gee willikers routine. Just answer the question. Who do you be mind fuckin' while Dwight bangin' you out!"

"Shut up!" Nina giggled, kicking Tamika playfully.

"No for real, for real! It's cheatin'!"

"How?" Nina challenged.

"Because how would you feel if Dwight told you the same shit like that?"

Nina didn't respond.

"Well, as they say, if you can't be with the one you love, love the one you wit', right?" Tamika replied with ghetto-ified philosophy that led Nina right back to where she started.

And then it happened.

It was her 26th birthday. She and Dwight planned a quiet evening at home instead of suffering the hustle and bustle of the city. A nice quiet evening of dining courtesy of Mo Beys in Harlem. A bottle of Merlot and two tall white candles were neatly centered on the tablecloth.

The doorbell rang.

"I got it," Nina chirped as she slid off the kitchen stool.

She padded to the door in her bare feet and a tee shirt of Dwight's that swallowed her like a dress.

"Who is it?" she asked, peering through the frosted glass of her front door.

Standing on her porch was an older white man in a chauffer's uniform. Behind him was the creamiest stretch white Rolls Royce she had ever laid her eyes on. She was expecting a delivery boy from Mo Beys.

"Celeste Martin?" the man asked, using her middle name instead of her first.

"Y... yes," she replied nervously.

"Your limousine is ready," he said, looking at her doubtfully.

Limousine? Who sent a limousine? Dwight? He's over there ready to eat Mo Beys. Then she thought of the flowers and the card.

"Who sent you?" she questioned, looking at the driver strangely.

"Are you sure you're Celeste Martin?" he probed, stepping back to check her house number. "According to the reservation, you requested our services."

Dwight had come to the door when he heard a man's voice. He looked out at the limousine and whistled.

"Damn, boo! You just full of surprises, huh?" Dwight smiled

from ear to ear.

"Yeah, full of surprises," Nina said, not having a clue and not wanting Dwight to ask too many questions.

"Well, Miss Martin. Are you ready?"

It was the same question she had asked herself.

"I'll be ready shortly," she said politely before closing the door.

After quickly showering and dressing in a backless black dress and Gucci slingback heels, they drove to Dwight's to get his best suit. Then they slipped into the luxurious Rolls Royce and glided off into the night.

The surprise had been meticulously planned. The driver had an itinerary. First, they were driven across the water to Manhattan where they were taken to Cipriani's for dinner. Their next stop was Broadway for the play "A Raisin in the Sun" where they had balcony seats.

After the play, they were escorted to Hue, a cozy little spot in the Village. The entire downstairs had been reserved for Nina. All the tables and chairs had been removed except for one in the middle of the room with a bottle of Louis the XIII waiting. They were shown their seats then left alone. A man played the piano softly as a woman in a blue sequined dress sang Nina Simone.

I loves you Porgy
Don't let him take me
Don't let him handle me
And drive me mad
If you can keep me, I wants to stay here
With you forever and I'd be glad

I loves you Porgy

Don't let him take me
Don't let him handle me
With his hot hand
If you can keep me, I wants to stay here
With you forever
I got my man

Someday, I know he's comin' back
To call me...
He's gonna handle me and hold me so
It's gonna be like dyin', Porgy,
Deep inside me,
But when he calls I know I have to go.

"May I have this dance, birthday girl?" Dwight proposed, reaching out his hand to her.

Why can't he be Dutch?

The evening was so charming and so elegant, she wished terribly that the man dancing with her was the man she longed to be with. When she took Dwight's hand, she pretended it was Dutch's. When she reached around his neck, taking step after step with him, she continued to dream. *If only it was him.* The entire evening was a dream. For Nina, it really was Dutch who had placed his hand on her knee as they drove through the city streets in the glistening limousine. It was Dutch who tickled the inside of her palm during the play. And it was Dutch who scooped delicious spoonfuls of tiramisu into her mouth at Cipriani's.

"Tonight has been the greatest night of my life, Nina. I can't remember the last time I've enjoyed myself as much as I have tonight. Never have I known a woman who could compare to you, Nina. And if I had one wish, it would be that you would be my wife."

Dwight.

His words were the words she had waited to hear her entire adult life. Tears welled in her eyes, tears Dwight mistook for happiness. But Nina cried because the words weren't spoken by the man she loved but by Dwight.

Dwight unexpectedly dropped down on one knee and slid a two carat round diamond ring on her finger. Again he mistook her tears for tears of joy and assumed that she had accepted his proposal.

Nina didn't know what to say. How could she say no? How could she say yes? She glanced at the engagement ring.

"I love you, Nina. Happy birthday."

She sat on the edge of the bed, unable to sleep. She looked at the alarm clock. The digital display read 3:06 a.m. She looked at the engagement ring in the dark. She had had enough.

Nina slid on her slippers and shuffled down the stairs to the den. She flipped on the light switch and took a seat at her desk. She placed her Rolodex in front of her and began flipping through the cards. *Please don't let me have thrown her number away.* She flipped through the Rolodex until she reached the M's.

Mitchell. Moore. Morgan. Murphy.

Delores Murphy, Dutch's mother.

Nina grabbed the cordless phone from its base and took a deep breath. She looked at the phone. *Should I call her? She's going to think I'm crazy.* She dialed the number anyway, hoping that the number had been changed or even disconnected. She glanced at the clock, noticing the time. *It's 3:22 in the morning.*

Maybe I should wait to call at a decent hour. It was inconsiderate and rude to ring anybody's phone at that hour and she knew it, but the thumping in her chest wouldn't allow her heart to wait. She dialed the number and listened as the phone rang.

"Hello?" a woman answered.

She didn't sound at all irritated or groggy, especially considering it was the middle of the night. Her voice was casual like she was wide awake and waiting for Nina's call.

"Hello?" Delores Murphy repeated.

What should I say. Maybe this was all wrong. Maybe I shouldn't have called her. This is crazy! I'm calling a stranger in the middle of the night about a dead man. She'll probably get upset. I don't want to upset her, Nina thought.

"Miss Murphy?"

"Yes, who is this?" Delores asked, somewhat confused.

"My name is Nina, Nina Martin. You don't know me but, um, I really need to talk to you," Nina sighed.

"About?" Delores replied, already knowing exactly who Nina was and what her phone call was about.

"Well, you see, I'm a... well, I was a friend of Bernard's."

"I see."

There was a long pause as Delores tried to figure out exactly what the girl wanted. Nina simply wanted to hang up, run back upstairs, jump in her bed and hide under the covers, but she had to know.

"Miss Murphy?"

"I'm still here."

"I don't know how to say this, but a lot of things have been happening around me and..." Nina's voice trailed off.

"When would you like to meet?" Delores asked invitingly, figuring Nina needed someone to talk to.

"Now," Nina blurted.

Poor girl, she can't even sleep. What did Bernard do to her? Delores wondered.

Delores laughed softly. "It's going on four in the morning. You want some breakfast?"

"I'm not really hungry, ma'am."

Nina scribbled down the directions to Delores' house then made her way upstairs. Reality hit her as she saw Dwight laying in her bed, sound asleep, mouth open and snoring with each breath. Nina quietly tiptoed to her closet and threw on a pair of jogging pants.

Downstairs in the kitchen, she grabbed her bag and her keys and looked at the piece of paper she had written the directions on.

Ivy Hill, she thought to herself as she made her way out the front door.

"Come on in Miss Martin," Delores said, greeting Nina with a friendly smile as she ushered her into the living room.

Nina looked around the spacious penthouse. She could see that Dutch had showered his mother with every luxurious amenity possible.

"Can I get you anything, tea or maybe some coffee?" Delores offered as she sized Nina up.

Delores could see what her son saw in the young woman. Even without makeup, Nina had a flawless beauty. She was demure with a quiet strength and obviously educated but not removed from where she came from.

"Yes, please. Tea would be fine."

Nina saw immediately that Dutch had his mother's eyes and complexion. His height and smile, however, must have come from his father. Delores herself was aging with timeless beauty. She looked good for her age. Time had been good to her. Delores had jet black hair, and her face showed no signs of aging, no wrinkles, no blemishes, no crow's feet.

Delores poured Nina a cup of tea and placed it in front of her.

"Thank you," Nina said, reaching for the sugar.

"Oh, you're welcome," Delores replied.

"Miss Murphy, I want to thank you for letting me come over in the middle of the night like this. I really needed to talk to someone. Actually, I really needed to talk to you," Nina said, nervously stirring her tea.

Delores gently placed her hand on Nina's to comfort her.

"It's fine. Really. I don't get much sleep at night these days. I just hope I can help you. You say you were a friend of my son's?"

"Yes ma'am. We dated for a while," Nina said, nodding her head.

"Oh, I see." *I know she not here to tell me I'm a grandmother or nothing crazy like that,* Delores hoped but secretly wishing for a grandson that looked like her own son. But Nina's eyes told her a different story.

"I know that this may be hard for you... But what happened in the courtroom three years ago?"

"Happened? I'm not sure I understand," Delores interrupted.

Nina searched for a way to convey what she was feeling and why she had come.

"Miss Murphy, for three years I've tried to put Bernard and what he meant to me out of my mind. I had deep feelings for him, but I couldn't accept his lifestyle. I couldn't accept who he was until it was too late."

Nina noticed that she was stirring her tea again, so she let go of the spoon.

"By then he was gone, and anything we could have had was gone with him. I accepted that and tried to go on with my life. I did go on with my life, but in many ways, never completely," Nina took a deep breath. "Until things started happening."

"What do you mean, things started happening? What kind of things?" Delores questioned with furrowed brows.

"I know this is going to sound crazy. But little things of great significance. If I told you, you would probably think I was crazy."

"No, I wouldn't," Delores said sincerely, wanting to know the things Nina was talking about.

"Well, one night, I came home from work and music was playing from my stereo. At first I thought it was the radio but realized it was a CD that I didn't own. I never figured out how it was playing, but it was, and it was playing a song that we shared. Then flowers were sent to my office. Not just any flowers, but hundreds of exotic flowers that no one I know could have possibly afforded. Then tonight, a limo was sent to me for my birthday. The driver claimed I ordered it, but I didn't. I don't know who did, but whoever it was ordered the limo in my middle name. No one knows my middle name, and... I just can't think straight anymore. But I can't stop thinking."

"I take it that Bernard knew your middle name and you think it was Bernard who sent the limo and the flowers and somehow got in your house and played a CD that the two of you used to listen to?"

"I know it sounds crazy, and you probably think anybody could've done those things, but I know in my heart, I swear, that those things are signs, Miss Murphy. Signs."

"Signs of what?" Delores asked. *The girl must be crazy. Let me get her out my house.*

"I don't know. That's why I'm here. That's why I had to see you. I thought that maybe you knew something. If anybody knows, I figured it would be you."

"Knows what? If my son is still alive?"

"Yes, exactly. That's exactly what I was thinking, Miss Murphy. I know he's in a lot of trouble, especially if he's alive, and you wouldn't be able to tell anyone. I realize you don't even know me. But, I swear Miss Murphy. I just need to know. If he's alive, ask him why he's doing this to me because he's driving me crazy." Nina shook her head in despair.

Delores looked at Nina and watched her body language as she spoke about her son. She didn't know Nina. For all Delores knew, Nina could have been anyone trying to get information about her son.

If she thinks I know something, why would she think I would tell her? Delores asked herself. Delores never spoke of her suspicions to anyone and certainly wasn't about to start today. She felt bad for Nina. She reminded her of herself. She knew despair, she knew pain, she knew heartache. His name was Bernard James, Sr., and he was her son's father. She had lost her love a long time ago and also refused to let go.

"Please, Miss Murphy. I know you know something," Nina pleaded.

"And that ring, did Bernard send you that, too?" Delores inquired.

Nina glanced down at the lie she wore on her left ring finger and moved her hand from above the table to under it.

Delores stood up slowly.

"Nina, I can only tell you what you already know. Bernard is dead. This I can assure you because I cremated his body myself. Go on with your life and forget my son."

Delores wouldn't dare tell Nina anything else. She wasn't about to share her private thoughts with a complete stranger. Besides, if her son had wanted someone to know something, he would have said it himself. As his mother, she never said a word to anyone about him, and she wasn't about to start now.

"Go on with my life? How? I can't. I'm at a crossroad, a major crossroad, and I can't cross," she pleaded with Delores not to end their conversation. But she knew it was already over.

"What about all these unexplainable events?"

"He's dead, Ms. Martin. Please let yourself out."

Their eyes met for a split second before Delores turned and left the kitchen. Nina was trembling so violently, she had to brace herself against the table. She began to sob. Her tears splattered onto the table as they rolled off her cheeks.

She had come to learn the truth and in a way she had. Delores was hiding something. Nina could feel it. It was in the woman's eyes, and Nina saw right through her. *What was she trying to hide? She could hardly look at me when she spoke to me. Yes, his mother is definitely hiding something. But what? Maybe he is alive, maybe.*

Nina felt it, and deep down, she believed.

PUSSY CONTROL

Chapter Seven

*I*t's time to get money," Dutch told his crew one night, signaling the end of the 'Month of Murder'.

He along with Craze, Angel, Roc and Zoom met in Dutch's loft apartment on the outskirts of Newark.

"Everybody remotely close to Kazami is dead, thanks to Roc and Zoom," Dutch laughed, Kazami's chain swinging from his neck. "The rest of these niggas, we don't even need a murder game for."

"Don't need it?" Zoom questioned. "Fuck you think nigga's just gonna bow down?"

"Word up," Craze agreed. "I say we keep these niggas duckin' and runnin' until they bow down."

Dutch shook his head. "We ain't gotta gun 'em, just out think 'em. And since most niggas think wit' their dicks, we control that, we control them." Dutch turned to Angel. "It's your turn, baby girl. Whoever these niggas wanna fuck or bein' fucked by, I want you to tuck them under your wing. Use what you are to get us what we want. Lick 'em, trick 'em, spend cheese on 'em. Whatever you gotta do to get 'em on our team, do it," he explained.

"Then what?" Angel asked.

*"Then we lay on 'em to slip because they all do. If they movin'
against us, we'll know because their bitches will tell us. Niggas
won't even know they sleepin' with the enemy. Control the
pussy and you control the game."*

Angel understood and set out to master her craft.

"Look at this nigga," Angel giggled, referring to the driver of
the Pepsi blue Escalade sitting on twenty-four inch spinners.

He was smiling down at them in Angel's new cherry red Viper
drop top with black interior and red piping.

"Damn you doin' it, papi," Angel flirted, emphasizing the
Spanish in her accent.

The nigga's chest swelled, and he hung his wrist out the window flashing a platinum Piaget skeleton watch.

"Not as hard as you in them shorts. You doin' it," he said as
he eyed Angel's thighs and fat pussy through her daisy dukes.

"Watch this," Angel whispered to Goldilocks. She bent over,
kissed Goldi on the mouth and played with her pussy.

Angel looked up. "I'd rather be doin' you, papi. Me and my
boo here. What you think, huh? Can you handle two bad bitches?" Angel teased as Goldilocks rolled her tongue like a snake's.
The driver boned instantly.

The light turned green but neither car moved.

"Damn, ma! Slow down! You don't bullshit, do you?"

"There ain't nothing slow about me. Follow me if you can,"
Angel said with a smile, then darted off down the street.

"Pussy runs the game, Goldi, Don't ever forget that," she
said, laughing at the Escalade in her rear view mirror. "This
dude don't know us from jack, but look at him, followin' us like
a little lost puppy."

Angel made a left and the Escalade followed, continuing the

pursuit.

"Ask a broke nigga who took him out the game. Ask a crack-head cat who turned him out. Ask a nigga in any prison in America who half the time ain't worried about his spot or who's gettin' his cake. You know what he's worried about? He's worried about who's fuckin' his baby mama!"

Angel and Goldilocks laughed as Angel switched lanes.

"Is that what that thing with Leslie is all about?" Goldilocks questioned.

"Exactly. I remember the night Dutch broke it down to me. But the difference with us is we gonna take it to the next level. We ain't goin' after these niggas 'cause that's what they expect. We goin' after their bitches. Trust me, we're about to lock this shit down, boo. Lock it shit down, and Roll gonna give it to us!" Angel said, laughing.

"What about him?" Goldilocks asked as she gestured to the Escalade.

"Man, when we finished toyin' with this weak-ass nigga, we'll be sittin' right where we wanna be," Angel replied, taking a quick right, using the skills she mastered as a car thief. She swung a left and timed the next light on the yellow. Safely, she made it through but the Escalade wasn't as fortunate. A cab rammed into the driver's side in the middle of the intersection.

Angel glanced at Goldilocks, "Any questions?"

Angel wasted no time putting her game down. She concentrated on Leslie, and it wasn't long before Leslie had a secret fetish and her name was Angel. It was so bad, it got to the point that Leslie couldn't get through the day without calling Angel, and if Angel didn't answer, oh boy! Leslie called and called until she heard Angel's voice. The promise of a rendevous, the promise of her between her legs licking and sucking her pussy, completely opened her up. Leslie couldn't handle the sex. But not only did Angel get in her panties, she got in her head and meticulously picked at her brain.

Leslie owned four hair salons. Roc had sponsored them and all catered to the Who's Who of the upper hustling class. Leslie knew everybody's business. She knew who was fucking who, who was creeping with who, and who wanted to get crept on. She knew which chicks liked men, who went both ways, and who vacillated. Baby mamas, wives and mistresses confided all to Leslie, and Leslie told all Angel during the quiet of their intimacy. Thanks to Leslie, everyone became pawns in Angel's plans.

Angel was a hustler, a real hustler, and if she couldn't fuck you and suck you to get what she wanted then she'd break the fuckin' bank. She would always find a way to get at you.

"Damn, Angel! You know I don't get down like you, but, damn! If I ever do, you gonna be the first bitch I call," Jackie said. She was a fine red bone Angel wanted to fuck real bad. So bad, she bought her the Jacob heart.

"Thank you!" Jackie exclaimed, holding the heart in her hand.

"That's for you, baby. It's just between us, for our friendship. When you're ready, you know what to do," Angel said. "And if you need me, I'm here for you. Just call me."

It wasn't long before Angel's investment paid off. Jackie called her one day, half hysterical.

"Calm down, baby. What is it?" Angel asked tenderly, reaching for her Sean John boxers as she put her finger up to her lip and gestured to Goldi to be quiet.

"It's Devon," Jackie hissed under her breath. "He got

popped."

"Whaaat?! When?"

"About a week ago. Now he wants me to help him set some nigga up so he ain't gotta do no time. And he wants me to join the *Help Yourself* program. Angel, what am I going to do?"

Angel smiled and blew a kiss through the phone.

"You're gonna pack and get ready for Hawaii," Angel told her and hung up the phone.

Three days later, Devon was found in a dumpster in the Projects in Patterson, courtesy of Nitti. Roll was impressed by the way Angel always stayed one step ahead of the game even if he couldn't figure out how she did it. If only he knew the pussy she was getting, it might have given him an inkling. But he had no clue.

None of the hustlers understood Angel's game. They were too busy wrapped up in their own lustful greed and trying to fuck her instead of trying to figure her out. They didn't realize that Angel was sucking, both literally and figuratively, the loyalty from their women right in front of their lustful eyes.

"These niggas don't give a fuck about you, boo," Angel whispered in the ear of a chick named Trina. She was Rich's baby mama and one of Roll's chief bosses in East Orange.

She and Trina were lying next to each other in Trina's bed.

"But Rich takes good care of me and his son," Trina stated naively.

Angel brushed the hair from her face and massaged Trina's sweaty stomach. "Don't I take good care of you, too?"

"Yes."

"And I would never do anything to hurt Rich, but... I need you to promise me something. You'll never let Rich do anything to hurt me, okay?" Angel said in between laps with her skilled tongue. Angel really was a clit lickin' captain and could get a bitch to do anything she wanted.

"He... he won't," Trina gasped, gripping the sheets.

"Stick with me baby girl and you'll always be taken care of. Even when Rich is long gone."

Angel sucked and fucked the cream of the crop. She had all the most powerful husters' female companions on her side. She even got to the chicks the niggas had on the side. And once she felt her position with these different women was solid, she turned her attention to the street soldiers, the ones with the money.

"Them young niggas out here is fuckin' up, papi. I'ma show 'em how to grind and make sure our paper stays straight," Angel announced to Roll.

Roll was all for it. To have the legendary Angel out on the block for him, handling his business, made him look like a true kingpin, a real Dutch kind of guy. He didn't realize that Angel was toying with his mind, his ego and his dick.

Angel strapped up her Tims, put some sweats on over her long johns, grabbed her Canadian Goose Helliarctic, and went back to the corner to hustle bundles of heroin. She wanted to hand-pick her army from Roll's payroll. So carefully, she watched the young wolves in their prime and selected the best of them. Then she took them under her wing. Gradually, she won their trust. To them, she was a made bitch, a legend. Seeing her out on the block with them, sleeping in hallways, ducking 5-O and busting her gun made them feel like big niggas.

"This is how you stay on top of your game. Stay hungry. All the Benzes and bottles of Cris don't mean shit 'cause when a nigga gets too big to walk the same streets that made him, he's out of touch with his own fate. And no matter what happens, if he can't go back to where he started, how can he ever make shit happen again? Muthafuckas catch cases puttin' weak niggas between them and the streets. You got to be the streets," Angel said, schooling her wolves. They listened like she was teaching Hustle 101.

A young Puerto Rican cat from her old stomping grounds on Dayton Street was especially attentive. She nicknamed him Capo because she told him that was what he was gonna be.

"Never forget the grind, Capo. Never forget the streets. You hear me? And always throw back. Don't wait until you're Big Willie to throw back. Pay rent, give a dollar or two, buy some groceries. Create loyalty around you and you'll die fat and rich in Miami somewhere."

Capo soaked it up like he was a sponge.

Angel's plan moved steadily ahead until she got a call from Roll.

"Hey, yo. You need to holla at your man 'cause he about to make me see him!"

Her man was Rahman, better known on the streets as One-eyed Rock, and the reason Roll was threatening to go to him was Miss Grownie Pants.

Miss Grownie Pants, Sonia, Jamillah, got off the bus near her apartment on Somerset Avenue. She had just come home from her job at the abused womens' shelter to find a 5-series BMW parked outside her building. As she got closer, her heart skipped a beat when she realized who was leaning on the car, her baby's father, Jerome. He had been locked up for the last three years.

Before he went away, their time together produced two children. Once he got knocked, though, she basically turned her back on him. She stopped writing after a few months and lost her phone because he ran the bill up so high she couldn't pay it. Once the calls and the writing stopped, so did the contact and the relationship.

Jerome, for the most part, had carried himself while in prison, and over the course of his incarceration, his anger for Sonia festered. He felt his entire hustle had meant nothing to her. Didn't she know what jail was? Didn't she understand his sacrifice? To Jerome, his choices were between death and jail and he took the chances for his family, for her and for their two children. In his mind, she had become a fuckin' slut who didn't write or bring his kids to visit.

Jerome had anxiously awaited his release so he could see her face to face. He wanted to punch her in the eye. So his first stop after his release was to visit her. For Jerome, it was payback time. He planned to sex her then beat her, or beat her then sex her. He hadn't made up his mind. But either way, he was going to stomp on her head when he had the chance.

Jamillah wanted to turn around and wait until he left but she knew Jerome and she knew he'd come back again until he saw her. *What should I do?* she asked herself, her usual quick pace coming to a sudden halt at the sight of him. *I wonder if he's mad at me? I bet he wants to see the kids.*

It was broad daylight and the streets were packed with summer activity. Jamillah decided it was best to get the confrontation over with.

She took a deep breath and kept her pace. When Jerome finally recognized her, his eyes widened in surprise.

Sonia, a Muslim? he thought to himself. *Is she the same girl who always wore tight clothing that showed her frame and body parts? The last I heard she was strippin' and trickin' for change! Can't be!*

Jerome looked at her. She was covered properly with a niqab from head to toe, and she wore a baby blue khimar over her head. Jerome couldn't believe it but it didn't make him respect her. In fact it made him even angrier, thinking the man in her life had converted her.

"Ohh, so you a Muslim now?" Jerome snickered, stepping in her path. "No more strippin' and trickin', huh?"

"Hello, Jerome," Jamillah replied. "I see they let you out," she added as if she wished otherwise.

"Damn right I'm out and back on already," he responded, gesturing to his BMW. "I just copped the five but gimme a month and it'll be a quarter to eight," he boasted.

"Mm-hmm," she said, uninterested. "Well, the kids aren't here. They're in Linden at my mama's house. So come back..."

He cut her off. "Come back? Why can't we go get 'em now? I know they wanna see daddy. We can go shoppin', get somethin' to eat," he offered, trying to get her in the car.

"No, that's alright. I'll pick them up tomorrow. Just give me your number and I'll call you."

"Why can't I have your number? What, your man might answer the phone? Fuck dat nigga!"

"I ain't got no man! But if you must know, I don't want you callin' my house," Jamillah said, sucking her teeth. "You want to see your kids, fine. Tell me when and I'll have them ready. Other than that, we really ain't got nothin' to discuss."

Jamillah tried to turn away but Jerome grabbed her arm.

"Get off me!" she hissed, snatching her arm away.

"Oh, so it's fuck me now, huh? You think you gonna just shit on me like that?"

"Jerome, you went to jail and I was left behind with two babies. I was livin' in a shelter until my mama took me in. I had to work and I been trying to get myself together in school and I don't care what you or anyone else thinks of me. You shit on me when you left me and your children alone with nothing. I'm finally here and I'm not going backwards."

"Bitch, you ain't fuckin' nowhere! You still here. And fuck that, bitch! I went to jail bustin' my ass for you and my kids. Don't fuckin' play with me," he said, tightening his grip. "Bitch, I fuckin' took care of your shiesty ass. And this is what the fuck I get back?"

Jamillah saw the fire dancing in his eyes and it scared her. She knew it was time to go.

"Look, Jerome. Ain't nobody tryin' to shit on nobody, okay? I have a new life now and I'm tryin' to be a better person for myself and my children."

"So you think you better than me now? You broke, trick-ass bitch. You better than me?" he ranted.

Jamillah tried to move out of his way but she was too slow and caught a heavy backhand to the face that sent her spinning to the ground.

"Jerome, please!" she cried, balled up in a fetal position. "Leave me alone!"

"This my word, bitch! When I get back, I want to see my kids. You hearin' me? Call the police, call Bin Laden, call Allah. I don't give a fuck! But if you ain't here wit' my fuckin' kids when I get back, I'ma break yo' muthafuckin' jaw!" Jerome shouted, then punctuated his threat by kicking her in the back. He jumped in his BMW and pulled off.

Jamillah struggled to her feet, holding her swollen face, and headed straight for the phone.

"But how you be a Muslim?" the young boy asked Rahman.

"You don't become a Muslim. You just recognize who you already are. We are all born pure. Ain't no such thing as original sin. We are born in a sinless state — it's our environment that makes us other than who we are..." His words trailed off when he saw Jamillah emerge from a cab holding a pink towel full of ice to her face. In two strides, he caught up to her.

"Jamillah, what happened?"

Jamillah sobbed, trying to speak through her fear and apprehension. She knew Jerome was coming back, and she didn't want to get Rahman involved in her personal problems. But her mind told her there was no other way.

"Jamillah," Rahman repeated more firmly.

"My... my... my children's father!" she cried. "He just came home from prison and came to my house. He said he was comin' back!"

Rahman gently removed the towel from her face, and his entire body caught fire. The right side of her beautiful face was swollen and bruised.

"What's his name?" Rahman whispered menacingly through clenched teeth.

When Jamillah looked into his face, she saw no trace of the man she called Sugar Bear. She saw someone she had never seen before.

"Jerome. Jerome Mills," she said, wiping her teary eyes.

He gestured to the corner boys he was talking with to come over.

"Take this sister into the store and call Khadijah to take her to the hospital."

"Rahman, please be careful. Jerome is crazy!" Jamillah sobbed, but it was like warning a bear about a rabbit.

Rahman opened his cell and called Salahudeen.

"Sal! Who is Jerome Mills? Jerome Mills?"

"I don't know. But if he got a name, it won't be hard to find out," Sal answered.

"Find out who he is and where he is then meet me at the store, aiight?" Rahman ordered.

"Insha Allah," Salahudeen answered, grabbing his glock 9 and tucking it in his waist. He could tell by Rahman's voice there was a problem. The Muslims were like a ghetto Internet. Once the word went out, it crisscrossed the city like radar until Jerome's whereabouts were pinpointed.

Rahman, Salahudeen and six Muslim shooters converged on the small housing project like a SWAT team.

They approached the building. When Rahman was close enough to strike, he barked, "Jerome!"

Out of instinct, Jerome snapped his head out the window and gave away both who and where he was. Rahman grabbed him by the collar and a handful of pants and dumped him face-first onto the hard concrete.

The other gamblers didn't know what was going on so they moved for their concealed pistols. Before they knew it, however, six weapons aimed were at them. Salahudeen stepped forward and disarmed them.

Rahman snapped. "You wanna beat on a woman, nigga?" he growled, bashing Jerome's head into the concrete repeatedly until he lost several teeth and his consciousness. He then slapped him awake.

"You touch Sonia again, and I'll kill you. You hear me?" Rahman threatened, kicking Jerome in the ribs and groin until Jerome spit up blood.

Blood.

It was the first time in years Rahman saw blood, and his addiction to it made his instincts reach for his gun and aim it at Jerome's head.

"Rah, no!" Salahudeen yelled and grabbed Rahman's wrist.

The jerk made the bullet strike the ground inches from Jerome's skull.

"Ock, chill! Justice has been served, yo!" Sal urged, trying to get Rahman out of the zone he was in. "Chill, man. This is not the place for that!"

"Then call an ambulance," Rahman spat as he walked away from the scene.

"I want the block! The whole chunk, Sal, the whole chunk!" Rahman's voice filled Salahudeen's martial arts school.

He and Salahudeen had just come back from Lil' Bricks.

"Listen, Ock. Calm down. I know you're upset, but you gotta calm down. We've already got Jamillah moved. She's stayin' with Khadijah for now."

Rahman furiously paced the floor. He felt sick with guilt. He knew he had overdone it and he realized how close he had come to going back to his old ways, the ways of the street.

"And what about him? You think it's over? I shoulda murdered him right there!" Rahman replied.

Salahudeen shook his head.

"For what? He's a nobody. He used to get a little paper in Irvington, but he ain't major and none of his people are either. After he gets out that coma he's in... if he gets out his coma... he won't be comin' back no time soon. It's under control."

But Rahman was still furious. Everything was going beautifully on the streets he had cleaned up and he wanted more. Jerome had given him a reason to take it.

"Sal, I feel you. But a Muslimah was attacked. Regardless of who or why, it won't happen again," he vowed.

"But this ain't how we planned it, Ock. We planned to take the little blocks until we surrounded the hot spots. If we control the perimeter, it's easier to control the center. You know that. Hell, you taught me!" Sal protested.

He, too, wanted to rid the streets of Newark of the drug element but he thought it best to stick to the plan. Rahman was apparently changing the game in the ninth inning.

"A hundred thousand."

"A hundred thousand what?"

Rahman smirked and clasped his hands behind his back.

"One hundred thousand dollars for Irving Turner to High Street, north-south, and West Kinney to Elizabeth Avenue, east-west."

"A hundred?" Salahudeen gasped, clasping his hands again. "Rah, they make that in a day! You know they ain't gonna take that. We might as well say twelve dollars and a Snapple!" Salahudeen shook his head. "Is our whole plan worth one slap, one bruise, Ock?" he tried to reason.

"Death or success, my brother. Never forget that. One slap, one disrespect, one violation upsets the plan. We have to stop things like that from happening. I want all the niggas to know that if one of us is touched, then we touch ten of theirs. You touch ten of ours, we touch a hundred of..."

"But is that justice?" Salahudeen interupted.

"It's an example, Sal," Rahman shot back before turning for the door. With one hand on the knob, he added, "A hundred ,Sal. Not a dime more. They don't accept my offer..." Rahman grinned, "Can't say we didn't try. As-Salaamu Alaikum."

"Alaikum As-Salaamu."

Not long after Salahudeen put the word out on the streets to Roll's people, Roll got word. He called Angel.

"Ay, yo! You need to holla at your man 'cause he about to make me see him!"

Angel drove to Roll's mortgage company in Paramus.

"Didn't I tell you that muthafucka was gonna be a problem?" Roll growled as soon as Angel stepped through his office door.

"You heard what the nigga said? A hundred thousand for Irving Turner! Fuck! I wouldn't take a million from his bitch-ass."

Angel sat on the edge of his desk and lit a Newport. "What happened?"

"Fuck you mean, what happened? The nigga feelin' himself! He think 'cause he can muscle them petty niggas off them piss-ant blocks, he ready to fuck wit' the thoroughbreds!" Roll huffed hard.

"He IS a thoroughbred," Angel reminded Roll.

"Was. Was. He was a thoroughbred," Roll retorted. "He on some Mother Theresa shit now!"

Angel shrugged. "So I'll talk to him."

"You already tried that. Now, I'ma holla at his bitch-ass!"

Angel leaned forward towards Roll. "That was about family. This is about business. Let me talk to Roc. One last time, okay?" Angel proposed, but her eyes said it was an order.

Roll eyed her. He knew that for her business with Roc was personal. But she had proven to be one hell of an addition to his team. Angel was invaluable to him now. Despite all his gun talk, he knew Roc's caliber and he knew niggas like that didn't just change over night.

"One last time," he emphasized, holding up a chubby finger. "One time. After that, I handle it."

"Tan bien."

"Hello Angel."

"What's up, Roc? Long time, right?" she asked as she stepped out of the Viper.

"Yeah, long time," Rahman replied, cold and hard. "You said you wanted to talk? So let's talk," Rahman said, looking at Angel seriously.

She had asked him to meet her at Port Newark, the same port they had robbed so many years before. She walked up to him and threw her arms around his neck, hugging him playfully, then let go.

"All this gangsta shit between us, nigga... you need a hug," Angel snickered.

He tried to hold his composure but being in her presence always strangely comforted him. He cracked a smile.

"Where's Roll? What, he too scared to meet me so he sent you instead?"

"Naw. Nobody sent me. I wanted to see you. What Roll wanted was to send bullets through your Kufi for trying to play him," Angel explained.

"Ain't no play about it. There's a hundred grand in the trunk of the car." He gestured to the old Buick he was driving. "Tell Roll he can take it or try and send them shots."

Angel aimed her finger like a gun. "Bang bang."

"Angel... I'm serious."

"And you think I ain't? You want shots, there you go. That's what you want anyway, ain't it?" she asked, but he remained silent. She continued. "You want Roll to give you a reason to do what you've been wanting to do!" Angel accused. "You want a war."

"What I want is that poison out of the community. What I want is a safe environment to raise kids in. What I want is…"

"Power," Angel concluded quietly. "You want power, Roc. You wanna be in control."

"Allah is in control," Rahman countered.

Angel shook her head. "Yeah, you got a cause. But who don't? You just like me, just like Dutch. You wanna control the streets," she surmised, turning to look out at the boats on the dock. "You think I don't want the same things? What muthafucka in his right mind wants to risk his life every day, runnin' from a case, a stick-up or a hit? What muthafucka don't want the good life for their kids, huh? But for most of us, this is how we get it! You gotta go through hell to get to heaven. Have you forgot that or are you so fuckin' righteous now that you're above all that?" Angel spat.

Rahman took a step towards her, arms open.

"But you don't have to get it that way! All that talk about somebody gotta sell it is garbage! What if you don't sell it and don't allow it to be sold. What do you think happens to all that money? It's still in the community. It can still be made! Look at the Italians, the Irish, the Asians. You don't see that bullshit in their communities, do you? Yeah, they started out as criminals to establish themselves, but now most of their money is legit. Niggas been on the corner for fifty years and what we got to show for it? Platinum chains? Slaves chains!" he cried with passion. "It ain't too late, yo. Ride wit' me. Yeah, we are just alike. We understand power. Let's use it to build, not destroy."

Angel silently acknowledged his point, but she had a personal vendetta that her heart wouldn't let her abandon. "Do you still trust me, Roc? Regardless of where we stand, do you still trust Dada?" she asked him, using the nickname Dutch had given her.

Rahman remembered it, too. Dutch called her that because he said she was as vicious as Jaws and nicknamed her after the theme music. Dada...dada...dada... Roc smiled at the memory.

"Yeah, Dada. I trust you. I trust your heart."

"Then trust me when I say my thing with Roll is almost over. He's finished. All I gotta do is put the icing on the cake. When it's done, then we'll talk, okay? For now, let this bully thing go, and we'll respect your territory to the fullest. I got the coke up on Springfield. I'll clear the block and relocate. It's yours. Just let this go and don't expand on Roll. This way we all happy. You get a drug-free zone, and we get our paper. Do it for Dada."

Rahman looked at Angel and hesitated before he spoke. In his heart they would always be family but he couldn't subject his plan to his emotions. He replied, "A hundred grand. Take it or leave it."

Angel closed her eyes, then slowly opened them.

"If you do this Roc, I can't help you."

"Help me?" Rahman chuckled. "I don't need help. Roll does."

"You can't win, Roc. You... can't... win," Angel emphasized because she knew his weakness.

"But I can die tryin'."

The conversation was over. There was nothing left to say. Angel hugged him again and this time he hugged her back. They broke their embrace and went their separate ways.

"Two for five! Two for five!"

"I got that fire over here, yo!"

"Gimme one for fifteen!"

"No shorts!"

The block was booming despite the hour. It was 2 a.m.

Hustlers and scramblers, crackheads and dope fiends filled the sidewalk in front of Brick Towers. Expensive whips were double-parked and shorties in tight skirts and bootie shorts leaned through windows and on car hoods. Everyone was so caught up in the rhythm of the night that they paid no attention to the U-haul truck pulled up in the middle of the street.

Until it was too late.

Rahman, Salahudeen and seven other masked Muslims came out of the bed of the truck and opened fire with automatic extended chips.

"They shootin'!"

Everybody finally looked. Girls screamed and ducked while hustlers ran for cover, pulling weapons from bushes and stash boxes.

Bullets tore through flesh, glass and brick, sending blood, shattered fragments, and sparks flying.

The Muslims stood mercilessly in the middle of the street, blazing the block, taking no prisoners, while on the roof, three Muslim snipers picked off hustler after hustler, painting the streets with blood. Police sirens filled the air. Rahman shouted, "Let's go!"

The Muslims continued to fire, backpeddling into the U-haul, and closed the bed.

Seconds later, police cars from everywhere converged on the scene and surrounded the U-haul.

"They in the truck. They in the fuckin' truck!" a wounded nigga snitched in agony. "Call an ambulance! I'm hit!"

The police turned their weapons on the U-haul.

"Come out now! Throw out the guns and come out with your hands up!" an officer with an itchy trigger finger bellowed.

The U-haul remained silent.

"Last chance! Get out of the fuckin' truck!"

Silence.

The commanding officer gave the nod and the police pumped the U-haul with so many shots that the truck rocked back and forth on its axles. The police continued to fire until the U-haul looked like a hunk of Swiss cheese. They were certain no one inside it could have survived, but took no chances and slid up on the side of the U-haul with guns aimed, locked, and loaded.

In one fluid motion, they threw open the bed's door and screamed, "Don't move!"

All they found inside was gun smoke and street light bleeding through the bullet-ridden truck body.

"What the fuck?"

"No way!"

"Move! Move! Move!"

"They aren't here!"

Completely baffled, the police didn't see the board on the truck's floor for a full five minutes. Under the board was a hole and directly under the hole was the escape route.

An open manhole.

"Son of a bitch!" a policeman cursed and mobilized his units to block off the area for twelve blocks.

Rahman and his team emerged on Howard Street. They crept out of the manhole like shadows and split up in separate directions. They jumped into their vehicles and disappeared into the night.

When all was all said and done, eight hustlers and two females were killed, six were injured, and one guy would be paralyzed for life.

Rahman had struck first.

Roll laid back on his double king-size bed watching Leslie's fat ass bounce and grind as she rode his dick backwards. He spread her ass cheeks and inserted a thumb in her asshole. She squealed with delight.

"Oooh, daddy! Fuck me, daddy," she moaned, leaning back on her palms.

Roll noticed that since Leslie had been fucking with Angel, she had gotten extremely freaky. He loved it. She was like a nymphomaniac now, ready to fuck anywhere, anytime. She even let him fuck her in the ass. It blew his mind.

But Leslie was just playing her position, that position being to keep Roll on his back while Angel handled the operation. Angel was slowly isolating him from his power.

The phone rang, and Roll answered.

"Yeah," he grunted watching his dick slide in and out of Leslie's tight pussy.

"Yo, Roll! They shot up the bully! Police everywhere and bodies everywhere! Lil' Nut, Doo-Doo, Teflon..."

Roll sat straight up in the bed almost knocking Leslie on the floor.

"Who shot up the block?" he asked, but before the man could answer, the name popped in his head.

Rahman.

"I told that bitch!" Roll growled, cursing Angel. "Aiight. I'll be in Newark in an hour."

He hung up and called Nitti. Leslie tried to slide back on top of his magic stick but Roll pushed her aside.

"Not now."

Nitti picked up.

"Where you at?"

"A.C."

"Meet me in Newark as soon as you can and bring them peoples!"

Roll slammed down the phone. It was true that Rahman struck first, but Roll planned on striking back hardest. What Roll didn't know was that Rahman had already struck again.

"Ay, yo. Crackhead just pulled up wit' a van full of custom Timbs!" the hustler shouted. "Sellin' 'em twenty a pop!"

The Plainfield corner flooded with niggas tryin' to cop the fresh kicks from the skinny smoker.

"I got all flavors. Gucci Timbs, Louie Timbs, Powder blue, dark blue, burgundy, dark gray, light gray, black and, of course, tan. If I ain't got it, they don't make it!" The smoker boasted as he nervously pulled on his cigarette.

"Yo, you said twenty? Gimme five pair," a young hustler said, negotiating the boots for crack viles.

"Gimme ten!" another added holding out two Benjamins.

The crackhead filled order after order until he sold at least one pair to each of the twenty-plus cats on the block.

"Check this young blood," the crackhead said, stepping to the cat he knew as the block lieutenant. "I be gettin' this shit like water. Rollies, leathers, all that shit. Gimme your number, and I'll make sure you get first cut."

The lieutenant jumped at the chance. "Now that's what's up!"

"Holla at cha, boy. I'll take care of you," the crackhead mumbled to himself on the way back to the van. He got in and pulled off.

Twenty minutes later, Salahudeen called the lieutenant from a nearby pay phone.

"Who this?" he barked into his cell phone.

"I got a message for Roll," Salahudeen replied calmly.

"Who?" the lieutenant fronted.

Salahudeen laughed. "Look around you."

The lieutenant felt a set-up and glanced around, alert to anything out of place. All he saw were his runners, workers, and other hustlers milling around, comparing the new Timbs most of them were wearing. He didn't see anything unusual.

"Yeah, and?"

Then, right in front of his eyes, those same cats began to explode almost simultaneously. Their bodies burst like human piñatas at a child's birthday party. Blood and body parts flew everywhere, and the screams of men with half their bodies blown away, holding leaking intestines, made his stomach weak. He fell to his knees and vomited. He had never seen anything like it in his life. He was truly terrified.

"Tell Roll As-Salaamu Alaikum," Salahudeen said and hung up.

Roll, Nitti, Angel and Goldilocks were in front of Brick Towers talking to a young cat who had seen the shoot out.

"Then they got in the U-haul and disappeared," the young cat emphasized.

"What you mean, disappeared?" Roll was in no mood for exaggeration.

"Just what I said, yo. They had cut a hole in the floor and dipped through a fuckin' manhole."

He pointed to a manhole across the street, feeling the way Rahman and his team escaped and planning to use the same tactics if the opportunity ever presented itself.

Another young dude ran up carrying a portable DVD.

"Here, I got the DVD."

Roll had cameras on all his blocks to monitor who came and

went and any potential stick-ups before they went down.

The tape showed an elevated view of the block. Angel watched the U-haul truck pull up.

"Who the fuck is supposed to be watchin' the camera?" she asked.

The cat who brought the DVD looked nervous. "I... I... I don't know."

"You're lyin'," Angel accused him. "Was it you?"

"Naw. It was... JD."

"Where he at?"

"Dead."

Angel shook her head in disgust. She watched the nine men get out of the U-haul and open fire. She focused on the figure she knew was Roc. He had definitely come out, like she said he would. Only he had come out against her.

Before she could comment, Roll's cell rang.

"Roll! I got somebody need to holla at you," the man spoke. It was his man who supplied Plainfield on his behalf.

"Yo Blue, I'm busy ri..."

"Naw, Roll. I'm tellin' you, you need to hear this shit. Hold on."

Roll sighed in aggravation. A younger came on the line. "Roll?"

"What?" he barked.

The young black lieutenant, still in shock, replied, "Man... man... they blew up! They just... blew up!"

Roll shook his head, trying to figure out what the hell he was talking about. "Yo, son, you ain't makin' no sense. Fuck, is you high?"

The lieutenant shook his head no like Roll could see him, then answered, "Some dude called and said he had a message for Roll."

"Who called? What message?"

Salahudeen sat in a car across the street from the two Plainfield dealers. He lifted the small black box and pressed the green button.

What Roll heard on the other end was inexplicable. The short agonizing scream that echoed through the phone before it went dead was so intense, he knew whatever happened was extremely painful and fatal. The blast killed both men instantly.

Roll's head spun like a top as he lowered the phone from his ear. Angel saw the look on his face and asked, "What was that?"

Roll looked at her blankly. "Plainfield. Nigga said somebody blew up everybody out there, individually..." Roll remembered the scream and it rattled his spine.

"C4. Rahman laced them cats with C4. Probably sold 'em a watch, a phone or some shoes loaded with C4. If it was shoes, he put the C4 inside the heel of the boot or under the sole."

Angel smirked because she knew the tactic. He had taught her how to use it. Rahman was using his old tactics against her.

C4 in boots and watches? Roll thought to himself, fully realizing that Rahman was still every bit as deadly as he had ever been. He turned to Nitti.

"C4 in boots?"

Nitti couldn't believe it either. *C4. Now that's an ill assassination weapon,* he thought to himself.

Angel took charge.

"Look, put somebody on the roofs in every major spot we got. Two men with scopes, one at each end of the block."

She turned to the cat who brought the DVD. "You. Mount the camera to face the stoplights. Every car, you better know who's drivin' it and how many is in the car. If you leave this camera to shit, I'ma kill you my muthafuckin' self. Si?"

The cat nodded.

Angel prepared the troops, knowing in her heart it was futile. Roc would surely already know what she'd do and wouldn't fall into her trap.

Roll got on the phone and implemented Angel's orders like she was the boss and he was the flunky. He relayed the message.

"Oh," Angel grinned. "And tell 'em not to buy any more cheap shoes."

"And don't buy no clothes or watches or nothing from nobody until I say so!" Roll ordered.

Roll did the predictable thing and sent a team to run over Roc's spots, but the Muslims were prepared. Their spots were small and easily defensible, so once they cleared the area of women and children, all Roll's people found were rounds of shells raining down on them like deadly hail on the cars. Roll's men were fortunate to escape with their lives. The only damage done was to Roll's ego.

"And they call me a killer," Dutch laughed as he and Roc exited the Perth Amboy Multiplex.

They had rolled down on a rival dealer and his girl inside the theatre. They waited for the girl to go to the bathroom then they slid in the row behind the dealer. Dutch put a gun to his head and whispered coldly, Remember me, nigga?"

The dealer's blood ran cold. "Dutch, man. It wasn't me. I swear! It..."

Roc wrapped his big arms around his throat and squeezed

*like a python. The dude gagged and kicked violently while Dutch
sang him to sleep.*

"Relax. The more you fight, the longer it takes, yo."

*Roc was in a zone, feeling the man's life spasm in his grasp
and sputter like a dying flame until it was finally extinguished.*

They silently left like nothing had happened.

*"Some niggas is made to kill if put in the wrong situation,"
Dutch said as he sat in the passenger seat. Mobb Deep played
through the Blaupunkt speakers. "But some niggas is born
killers, Roc." Dutch looked at him. "Like you. You a born killer,
nigga. A natural born killer."*

After all these years, Rahman was forced to acknowledge the
truth in Dutch's assessment. And while he loved Islam with all
his heart and had disciplined himself to the best of his ability,
he knew deep down that the virus within him still existed and
that he was still a killer.

He felt it when he beat Jerome and heard his bones crack
and splinter under the force of his boot. He felt it when he
aimed for his head, ready to burst it like a ripe melon. It surged
through him as he stood in the middle of High Street, bullets
flying and bodies dropping. The killer was in him and it was in
him deep. Dutch was right. One-eyed Roc was a natural born
killer. It was Rahman who searched for truth and righteous-
ness. But it was Rahman or One-eyed Roc or whoever he was
who was not to be fucked with.

Rahman heard about Roll's retaliation on his way back
home. Salahudeen told him that no one had been hurt. He
thanked Allah and continued home, taking his usual precautions.

When he entered the house, he was greeted by the TV. He

caught the reporters in mid-sentence. "...bizarre tragedy. Sixteen men here in Plainfield were found dead in an area known for rampant drug activity. The police are baffled as to the cause of their deaths but it appears that they were the victims of C4 explosives that had been inserted into the soles of their Timberland Boots. Two of the sixteen were found a few blocks away in the same condition. Police say it appears to be drug-related but the methods employed made one policeman say it looked like something he'd seen in Vietnam. More later as details develop."

Ayesha and the kids were sitting on the floor in the living room when Rahman walked in. Ayesha turned to him with fire in her eyes. She could hardly keep her voice steady when she sarcastically quipped, "Look kids, Daddy's home! Long day at the office, huh?"

Rahman could hear Ayesha's accusations in her tone. He replied in a low, firm tone, "Turn off the TV. It's time for Salat."

The family performed evening Salat together as they always did when Rahman was home. Ayesha stood on his right and the children stood behind them, following them through the prayer positions. In Islam, children under 10 weren't required to make Salat but the children loved to pray with their parents. When they were finished, Ayesha turned to the children and said, "Ali, you and your sisters can watch TV until dinner."

The kids ran out of the room with glee, already arguing over what they would watch.

Ayesha turned to Rahman. "I hope you asked for forgiveness."

Rahman rubbed his eyes, trying to avoid the confrontation.

"I always ask for forgiveness."

"I hope you really asked... no, begged... and you need to

make sixteen Ra'kas the next time you pray," Ayesha spat, referring to the sixteen victims in Plainfield.

"Don't start with me, Ayesha," Rahman replied quietly, folding up his prayer rug.

"No, Rahman. I want to know. Did you? Did..."

Rahman's voice boomed like thunder. "Woman! I said don't start!" he yelled.

Ayesha knew her man's anger, but he knew her intensity was just as fierce. Their eyes locked in a silent battle until Ayesha shook her head.

"And you said it was over. You said it was over, and I believed you. Just like before."

"I ain't gonna be doin' this forever. Just a few million and I'ma get out of the game."

"You got out of the game the last time, alright? You went to prison!" her voice quivered and tears of frustration welled in her eyes.

"What do you want me to do, huh? What? Just sit by and watch my people die in the streets?" he stressed.

"I guess killing them yourself is better?" Ayesha shot right back.

"Pimps and pushers! Pimps and pushers, Ayesha. They live off our blood like leeches..."

"You used to be one," Ayesha challenged. "Right? Don't use Islam for an excuse to be a gangsta, Rahman."

He paced the floor, agitated by his wife's accusations.

"Is that what you think I'm doing? Okay, since you're the expert on Islam, tell me, what do I need to do?"

"Be a father to your children and a husband to your wife," Ayesha said, folding her arms across her chest, giving him the simplest of answers.

"And I haven't?"

"When you're here! Which is becoming more and more infrequent. I'm tired of being the woman you come home to instead of the woman you share your life with!" Ayesha sobbed. "I know you're doing a lot for the community. In those neighborhoods, children are safe, women are respected, and bills are paid. It's beautiful. But I need you home. We need you home."

Rahman knew she was right. He had not been coming home on purpose, trying to protect his family from his actions on the streets. He knew he hadn't been fair to his family, but he had to put the cause first.

"Listen, Ayesha. I'm fighting a war out there and I'll be damned if I'ma fight one in my own house!"

"Then go fight," she heaved. "Go fight your war. That's what you want to do anyway!"

She started for the door but Rahman grabbed her and pulled her to his chest. "Listen... I know it's hard, but I told you. Freedom comes with a price, and this is it. I need you to be with me right now. Okay?"

Ayesha didn't respond. He gently lifted her chin with his palm.

"Okay?"

"I am with you, Rahman. But I need you to be with me," she pleaded, pulling at his heartstrings.

"I am baby girl... I am."

"That was a lame-ass move you made," Angel said, laughing through the phone at Roll as she pushed the Viper 90-plus across Highway 1&9. Goldilocks laid back in the passenger seat with closed eyes behind Chanel shades, chilling to the sounds of La Belle Mafia.

"Them niggas seen you comin' a mile away," Angel added.

Roll was also on the road on his way back from Plainfield.

"I know one place I won't miss. Branford Place," Roll threatened, referring to the Masjid where the Muslims congregated. "I'll really give them muthafuckas something to pray for!"

"Don't be a fool, Roll," Angel casually warned. "There's too many Muslims in Jersey in the game, too. Right now, they don't give a fuck about Roc and his cause. But if you shoot up a Masjid, you'll give Roc an army that'll come from everywhere. Keep it in the streets and we'll break 'em."

Roll nodded to himself. If the Muslims got involved, it could get ugly.

"Besides, I know Roc, and if everything goes as planned, I'll kill the muthafucka myself," she lied, trying to put Roll's mind at ease. "Family or no family, this is my paper too."

Roll smiled.

"That's what I'm talkin' about. What's the plan?" he agreed, foolishly thinking he had a monopoly on her loyalties.

"We'll holla at you after your birthday party tonight. I say after because tonight, we party. We worked too hard for this paper not to enjoy it, no?" she grinned like a black widow spider before a manly meal.

"No doubt, no doubt. I definitely need a party," Roll answered.

"Happy birthday, baby boy! Relax. You got an Angel on your shoulder," she smiled.

Roll laughed.

"I wish I had an Angel on me," he flirted.

"Be careful what you wish for," she responded.

"One."

"Siempre."

The Noise Factory, Roll's multi-level club on the outskirts of East Orange, was packed to capacity. Everybody knew Roll's birthday party would rock, but the only heads being admitted were members of Roll's clique around New Jersey, as ordered by Angel who put herself on security. She used her team of young wolves to secure the perimeter just in case Roc showed up. She also wanted to make sure that no one got out as well.

Angel watched whip after whip pull into the parking lot, flossing to see who had the sickest ride. Gators mixed with Air Ones, platinum with white gold, Bentleys with baby BMWs, and money filled the air. It was going to be a night no one wanted to miss.

Inside, the party cranked. The music was live, and Roll's team were out in full force. Attached to their arms were the women who Angel had recruited to carry out her plan. Smiles and winks exchanged between Angel and her co-conspirators as she passed through the crowd. She found Goldilocks by the door.

"Everything good?" she asked, giving Goldi a kiss.

"Couldn't be better," Goldilocks smirked, "Roll and Nitti are in the VIP room."

"What about the champagne?" Angel questioned.

"Ready when you are, baby," Goldilocks answered, brushing a lock of Angel's hair out of her face.

Angel surveyed the scene.

"Look at these cats, boo. They make it easy, don't they?" Angel was feeling good because her plan was on the verge of completion. "Go get Capo and tell him I'm ready."

She smacked Goldilocks on the ass as she sashayed off to get Capo. Angel made her way to the stage and signaled the DJ to lower the volume.

She took the mic in her hand. "Can I have your attention for a second, please."

The crowd buzzed then silenced, turning their attention to her. She looked into all the unaware faces and felt a twinge of regret. *Like sheep to slaughter,* she thought then cleared her throat.

"Y'all havin' a good time?" she yelled to the crowd.

"Hell yeah!"

"No doubt!"

"It'd be better if I was havin' it with you!"

Angel looked for the face in the crowd and laughed at the comment.

"Yeah, aiight. Better not let your baby mama hear you say that!" she hollered back. The crowd laughed.

"On the real, though. Y'all know why we're here. To make sure Roll's 35th is a night to remember, right?"

"Fo' sho!" the crowd agreed.

"Yo, Roll! Roll! Get yo' old ass out here and holla at your peoples!"

The crowd shouted for Roll, and a few moments later, he was onstage with Leslie, dressed in an Armani suit, black silk shirt, derby gators, and Dutch's dragon chain. Leslie was at his left in a tight-fitting purple Prada dress. Nitti stood to his right. Angel's eyes fell on the chain.

"Aiight, aiight. Y'all know the routine! Y'all ain't too big to sing my man happy birthday, are you?"

Angel started singing and the crowd joined in.

Roll was feeling himself as he surveyed the crowd, like a politician before his supporters. The world was his. Every nigga in front of him would kill for him, and there wasn't a bitch in the house who he couldn't fuck. Except for Angel. He couldn't even fuck with her, as he would soon find out.

The song ended with cheers. Goldilocks, Capo and the wolves passed out bottle after bottle of Cristal.

"Yo, we gonna pass these bottles out for you to drink. I want you to share 'em with your friends. There's enough for everybody," Angel said into the mic. "Yeah, everybody make sure you got a bottle because we gonna toast my man!"

Once all the bottles were handed out, Goldilocks brought out a bottle of Remy Martin for Angel.

"Roll, ever since I came home, you ain't shown me nothin' but love, yo, and I appreciate it. To Roll. May this birthday be the best one yet!" Angel chimed as she held up the bottle of Remy.

"Happy birthday, Roll!"

The bottles turned up and everybody in the club got tipsy. No one noticed that the females weren't drinking Cristal. They were all drinking Remy.

"Come on, Roll. Let's take our party to the VIP lounge," Angel suggested, and they made their way to the Roll's office.

Angel, Leslie, Roll, Nitti, Goldilocks and Capo entered Roll's plush office overlooking the club. Roll closed the door.

"Angel, I'm feelin' this party you put together for a nigga. Word. I won't forget it."

"I know," Angel chimed.

"And yo," Roll began, sitting on the couch and lighting a cigar, "I got a surprise for you. Your man Roc? I just made a move that I know is gonna break his shit up."

"Later for that. Right now, let's discuss the future," Angel said as she held up her hand and popped a bottle of Cristal.

Angel seductively slid over to Nitti and wrapped her arms around his neck. "Roll, your man Nitti here is my kind of nigga..." She caressed his cheek, tracing the scar on his chin.

"Damn, Nit," Roll responded with more than a tinge of jealousy. "I thought it was MY birthday."

"You'll get your turn, boo," Angel assured him, eyes dancing over Nitti. He eyed her back, licking his lips. "What's the deal, ma? You tired of bein' a vegetarian?"

Angel snickered and held the bottle under his mouth, tracing his bottom lip with her index finger.

"Slow down, baby. Drink to Angel," she said as she tilted the bottle against Nitti's mouth. He drank until she lowered the bottle. She wiped his mouth and kissed him gently.

The kiss of death.

She turned her attention to Roll and poured some champagne on the floor.

"To my niggas who ain't here."

She toasted to herself, thinking of Dutch, Zoom, Shock, Craze and Roc. "This game is ours."

Roll held up his cigar.

"Ours," he repeated and Angel laughed in his face.

"Ohh, Roll. You're such a fuckin' joke," she spat.

"Joke?" he frowned.

"A fat, stupid, trick-ass..."

"Bitch, is you drunk? Who the fuck you talk..." Roll began but the look on Nitti's face caught his attention.

His face was twisted like he had just tasted something bitter. When he grabbed his stomach, Roll knew something was wrong. "Nitti? You aiight?"

Nitti couldn't speak. His throat muscles tightened like he was throwing up but nothing came out.

"Do he look aiight?" Angel laughed triumphantly.

Nitti fell to his knees as green mucus bubbled out of his mouth and nose. Roll jumped to his feet. Goldilocks and Capo whipped out pistols and pointed them at him.

"What the fuck did you do to him?" Roll asked, rushing to Nitti's side.

Nitti's insides were on fire like he had swallowed hot lead. He collapsed to the carpet, dead.

"This the new millennium, Roll. Gangstas don't bust guns no more. We just let you kill yourselves!" Angel declared, pulling out a .38 revolver. "You ever play chess, Roll? You ever seen the queen checkmate her own king?"

Roll shook with rage. "I'll kill you, you pussy lickin' bitch! I'll murder you!"

Angel ignored his rants and looked at Leslie.

"Leslie, where you going?" Angel asked as she saw Leslie heading for the door out of the corner of her eye.

Leslie had never watched someone die before. She was anxious to leave. "I'm goin…"

"Nowhere, bitch. Nowhere," Angel calmly ordered and pumped two slugs into Leslie's voluptuous body. Leslie slumped on the couch, just another expendable pawn.

Roll knew he was next, but he fought not to let his fear show. "You think you can just walk in here and kill me in my own club? You dumb bitch! My whole team is out there! You'll never make it to the door!" Roll boomed arrogantly, but Angel could smell his fear.

"Your team, huh? Let me show you your team, yo," Angel replied.

She snatched Roll by the dragon and led him to the window.

She tore down the blinds and gave him a bird's-eye view of the dance floor. Roll didn't recognize what was going on at first. To him, cats just looked drunk and slumped at the booths. Then he recognized the bodies strewn on the floor. All of them were sprawled in puddles of green vomit, just like Nitti. He saw a cat stagger and fall while others grabbed their throats and stomachs and vomited up their lives.

"What the..." Roll whispered in a breathless gasp. He couldn't believe his eyes. Angel had used his birthday to gather all his people under one roof and then eliminated them all, at one time.

"What you mean, what? That's your team, nigga! You ever hear the phrase *dead drunk*?" Angel grinned.

Body after body, hustler after hustler, dropped to the floor. Even the DJ was slumped over his turntables, a Busta Rhymes record skipping and repeating itself.

Most of the females had cleared out, although some had been foolish enough to drink the Cristal Angel warned them against.

"See how easy it is, nigga? Throw a party, pop the cork, add untraceable arsenic, and voilá! Tell them that ain't gangsta," Angel boasted, pointing at the death scene. "While you were laid up lettin' Angel handle your business, I ate away at your home, from the inside."

Roll dropped his head in defeat. "What do you want?" was his only question.

Angel leaned in close to his ear and spoke through clenched teeth, "Nigga, what the fuck you got that I ain't already taken?"

Roll had nothing to lose. Angel had leaned in too close. Roll lunged for the gun, snatching it out of her hand and shoving her down. He knew he was about to die. His last wish was to take the conniving bitch with him.

He never got a chance.

Goldilocks and Capo riddled his body with so much force, the shots lifted him through the plate glass window and he dropped like lead to the floor below.

Angel stood up and brushed herself off. "At least he tried, huh?"

Goldilocks and Capo chuckled.

"Let's finish this shit and be out," Angel said, looking at the both of them.

They left the room and descended to the floor below. The smell of acid death was nauseating. Niggas were dying in so much agony that Capo randomly executed the groaning bodies and put them out of their misery.

"He... help me..." a dying hustler begged, green vomit on his chin. Capo lifted the gun to his face and helped him with a bullet to the head.

Angel saw that Roll's body had landed on top of two poisoned dead bodies. He was still alive. Angel kneeled beside him and removed the chain from his neck. She held up Dutch's chain with lust in her eyes. The jewels winked at her. She kissed the dragon.

"Welcome home."

"Fuck you... bitch... Kill me you piece of shit," Roll moaned.

Angel ignored his plea for death, her eyes set on the dragon chain. "Finish him."

Goldilocks spread out and began pouring alcohol everywhere, on live and dead bodies alike. Angel approached Capo.

"Tu verlo! Tu verlo? This is what happens when you slip. In this game, nothing else matters. Any weakness can be exploited! You understand?"

Capo looked around at the squirming bodies. It was a sight he would never forget. "Si," he replied solemnly.

Angel studied his eyes for any weakness in him. Satisfied, she patted his cheek and kissed him on the forehead.

"La familia."

Angel placed the chain around her neck, feeling the weight of it against her breasts. Goldilocks approached her and said, "It's done."

Angel lit a cigarette with a wooden match, grabbed half a bottle of Remy, stood over Roll, and emptied it on him. "Happy birthday, nigga. Let me see you blow out this candle."

As she strolled away, she tossed the match over her shoulder. Roll watched the small deadly flame arc through the air and land on his chest. In seconds, he was a human inferno.

"Noooo!" he shrieked as his flesh ignited.

From his body, the flames spread through the club and cries of pain and burning bodies filled the air. Angel, Capo and Goldilocks turned and exited Hell.

By the time they reached the Jag the club was fully engulfed in flames.

In one night, Angel had succeeded in doing what had taken Dutch a month to accomplish. She had locked down the streets without firing a single shot. She had proven that pussy was the most dangerous weapon of all.

Goldilocks caressed Angel's thigh. "You were right. Pussy does control the game."

She kissed Angel on the cheek, then on the neck, then put her knees in the seat and faced Angel's lap. Angel cocked her right knee up on the gearshift, giving Goldilocks easy access to her golden sweetness.

While Angel was celebrating her success orally, back in Newark Roll's final order was being carried out.

Salahudeen closed up his martial arts shop and pulled the metal awning down over the window. He squatted to lock it in position. His fingers worked unconsciously as he thought of

Rahman. Salahudeen didn't disagree with Rahman's tactics, only the motives he felt was behind them. He felt Rahman was losing focus on the overall goal and getting caught up in the objectives designed to obtain them. He planned on having a long talk with him.

"Yo, nigga!"

Salahudeen's razor-sharp instincts told him to react. He reached for his gun and spun out of his squat in one smooth motion, ready to blaze, but he was met by four assassins, all dressed in black and carrying AR-15's.

BBBRRRAAAAHHHHH!

A chorus of flying bullets sang Sal to sleep. His body jerked and twisted like a puppet on a string.

When the gunbursts finally ended, he fell to the ground.

"There is no God but Allah, and Muhammad is his messenger..." Salahudeen spoke before closing his eyes for good.

WAR

Chapter Eight

Dwight and Nina laid in bed, both staring at the oscillating ceiling fan, lost in their own thoughts.

Their relationship was rapidly deteriorating. They didn't laugh and joke like they used to and every date seemed to be more tense and awkward. Their sex life was all but non-existent. It had all started to go down hill ever since Nina's birthday. For whatever reason, things had taken a turn for the worse.

Dwight thought it all stemmed from his marriage proposal. He had taken the biggest step of his life the night he asked Nina to marry him. But judging by the following weeks, it was also the biggest mistake of his life.

Nina remained torn between reality and hope. The reality was that she had a good man who cared for her, who vowed his commitment to her on bent knees. And even though she had accepted Dwight's proposal, her hope for Dutch ate at her incessantly. Her long dead feelings were attacking her with a vengeance.

What if?

In his absence, Dutch loomed larger in her life than he did when he was with her. Thoughts of him consumed her to the point that she could no longer make love to Dwight. But then, she had never really been making love to Dwight, insisting that he turn off the lights to help her fantasies unfold. She couldn't reach orgasm with Dwight but the mere thought of Dutch fucking her aroused her and moistened her desire day and night.

It had gotten to the point that she cringed at the thought of Dwight. Even his touch made her uncomfortable. She felt like she was being unfaithful to her dreams, her hopes, herself and, of course, to Dutch.

They laid in bed like inmates of a glass house, scared to throw stones and shatter the illusion of their relationship.

"You know... we can't go on like this," Dwight said softly.

"You're right."

"Baby, I've searched my heart and my mind, trying to... It's like it just happened... I wonder if I did something to trigger this, whatever it is between us..." Dwight struggled to find the words. "Do you love me?" he finally asked, leaning on an elbow, peering through the dark at her.

"Yes," Nina answered, wanting to want to love him.

"Do you still... want to... to marry me?"

"I do..." Nina replied, wishing that she could.

"But?" he probed. He detected hesitation in her reply.

Nina sat up, pushing a wisp of hair from her face, and wrapped her arms around her knees.

"Dwight... so much has been going on lately that it's just..." she sighed. "You wouldn't understand."

Dwight leaned forward and caressed her cheek and smiled sweetly. "How can I understand if you won't talk to me? Haven't I always been a good listener?"

She looked into the comfort of his brown eyes and wished she had never known Dutch so she'd be free to love this wonderful man. But Dutch had a lock on her heart and refused to release the key.

"I'm not sure I understand myself."

"Whatever it is, it hasn't changed how you feel about me because you do love me and I do make you happy. Right?"

Happy?

Happiness was a feeling she hadn't truly felt for a long time. Nina knew she being unfair to Dwight by not telling him the truth but she couldn't let him go because she didn't want to lose him. She felt selfish, greedy, guilty. She felt many feelings but happiness wasn't one of them.

"Nina... do I?" he asked again, feeling a tightness in his chest because she didn't answer.

Nina lowered her head and buried her face in her knees. Dwight put his feet on the floor, his back to her, and palmed his face.

"So when did I stop making you happy, Nina? When I put that ring on your finger?"

Nina heard bitterness in his tone. She lifted her head and attempted to speak.

"Dwight, I don't know. I..."

Dwight stood up and faced her. "No, Nina. I really wanna know. Was it when I asked you to be my wife? When I thought enough about us and what we have to want to commit to it, to you, to us, for the rest of my life? Is that what made you so unhappy?"

Dwight was visibly hurt. He fought to hold back his tears. It killed Nina to hurt him.

"Dwight, you're important to me too," she emphasized, instantly regretting her choice of words.

"Too?" he echoed. "Too?" It was almost too much for him to

ask the next questions. "So, you're saying there's someone else? Is that why every time I touch you, want to make love to you, you act like I'm a stranger? Like you're repulsed?" Dwight turned away, balling his fists tightly, trying to restrain his emotions. He regained his composure and slowly came around the bed and sat next to her.

"Listen, baby. We're not the only people who have problems. The key is working through them. I'm willing to fight for us because what we have is worth it fighting for. But if you won't talk to me and let me in... if you don't trust me enough to confide in me... then what do we really have?" he asked sincerely.

I'm in love with a ghost, and I'm going to lose the real thing. He's right here in front of me. I can keep him if I want or I can lose him, let him go.

"I'm going. It's obvious that we're not getting anywhere. Maybe you need some time to think, to decide. I can't make you choose, Nina. But, I love you. I do and... I hope it's enough because it's all I got."

Dwight turned away from her with his head bent down.

His words stung and brought tears to her eyes.

"Dwight, I love you, too, but..." she looked down at her left hand. She slowly slid the ring he gave her off her finger. "I can't marry you. Not... not now."

Nina placed the ring in his palm and folded his fingers around it. He looked down at his hand, feeling like Nina had just handed him back his heart.

A lesser man would have shrugged her off but he remained a gentleman. He leaned over and kissed her on the forehead.

"What's meant to be, will be. Take care of yourself, baby. I hope he's as good to you as I would've been."

Nina watched him gather up his clothes and get dressed. He stopped at the door with a tear tracing his cheek.

"I'll... I'll come back for the rest of my things later," he said to the door, not turning around.

Dwight didn't wait for a reply. Nina listened to his fading footsteps descend the stairs, then out the door.

Why are you doing this to me? Why?

She remembered one of their conversations.

"Why would you be what I can't have?" Dutch asked.

"Because I'm not a possession," she replied.

"What are you then? Possessive?"

She was indeed possessive. Dutch had made her greedy for him, and as long as he was alive, he would remain hers.

Nina remained wide awake in bed after Dwight left, lost in thought until the ringing phone brought her back to reality.

"Hello?"

"Nee! Get up girl," Tamika said on the other end.

Nina looked at the clock. It was twelve past seven on a Sunday morning. Tamika must have been up all night and wanted to gossip. But Nina was in no mood.

"Tamika, I'm up, but I really don't feel like talking right now."

Tamika shrugged and checked herself in the mirror. She was wearing only a slip. "I don't feel like talking neither. I just called to see if you want to go to church with me."

"You going to church?" Nina asked, mildly shocked.

Tamika rolled her eyes at the phone. "Don't even go there. It ain't like you beat down the door every Sunday either, okay? When's the last time you been?" Tamika asked.

Nina snickered. "Point made."

"So let's go."

Tamika was right. Nina couldn't think of the last time she had been to Sunday service, and after a moment of thought, realized there was no reason not to go.

She sat up in the bed and replied, "Let me get dressed."

Since Tamika and Nina weren't regular church-goers, they went to the one nearest Tamika's apartment. Church had always been good for the soul and was still the same. The choir was still uplifting and soulful. The older women still wore fancy hats, and the collection plate still circulated at regular intervals.

The sermon was 'The Prodigal Son Returns' and Nina and Tamika both would have sworn the message was for just them, even if for totally different reasons.

Overall, it was a good service. Nina could understand why churches were filled on Sundays. The sermons were comforting.

After church, she and Tamika went out for brunch.

"I gotta hand it to you, Mika. That was really good for me. I needed it more than I realized," Nina remarked, sipping her coffee.

"You? Girl, you just don't know what I've been going through," Tamika said, her eyes filled with frustration and worry.

"You okay? What's up?" asked Nina, concerned. Tamika wiped her mouth and gazed out the window at the passing cars.

"Nina, you ever feel like you're going in circles? Like you need a change?"

Tamika didn't know how much Nina could relate.

"Did you hear about that club burnin' down about a week ago?"

"Club? Where? Was anybody hurt?" Nina frowned.

Tamika's face took on a solemn expression. "Everyone was killed."

Nina felt a chill run up her spine. "What do you mean everyone was killed. I don't understand."

"They say that they all got trapped inside. Somehow a fire started and with all that alcohol... Girl, can you imagine burning to death?" Tamika stressed.

"No, I can't," Nina said.

Nina didn't want to imagine it either. Surrounded by flames, doors melted shut, people clawing and stampeding to get out. She recalled how the hot comb used to blister her ear when she was a child and couldn't imagine anything worse than that.

"Nina, that coulda' been me. I was supposed to go with this guy from Linden. It was a big drug dealer party for some kid named Roll. It was his birthday party and only his people could get in. The guy, Ronald, from Linden worked for Roll. He was supposed to pick me up at nine. Girl, I was all set to go. I had my hair and my nails done, even went and bought this Roberto Cavalli blouse for like $750. Honey, I was ready! Wasn't no way I was gonna miss it but..." Tamika rubbed her forehead. "I got sleepy. I'm talkin' I couldn't keep my eyes open. Sleepy."

She closed them at the table.

"I woke up at one in the morning and Ronald had left me six messages. I tried to call him but I couldn't reach him. I thought he was mad at me or somethin'... until I heard he was dead."

Nina saw how badly the incident had shaken Tamika. She reached over and grabbed her friend's hand.

"I just... I can't get over it. I coulda been in the club, you know? That shit made me realize that there's gotta be a better way. Niggas shootin' each other like there's no tomorrow, all of 'em going to jail, locking girls up too just 'cause they were in the house with a nigga, clubs burnin' down..." Tamika took a deep breath. "What good is money if you ain't around to spend it?"

"Now ain't that the truth. Amen to that," said Nina, letting her friend vent.

I think we both might need a change. A big change, Nina thought to herself.

"Don't worry, Tamika. It's going to be okay. I know exactly what we need to do."

While Nina and Tamika were having Sunday brunch, the Muslims were holding the Janazah ceremony for Salahudeen.

The Muslims lined up, prayed over his body, then took him to the cemetery and buried him facing Makkah, the Muslim Holy City.

The women were dressed in black, and the Muslims blocked all entrances and exits to the cemetery. Rahman wasn't taking any chances with his enemies. He knew them all too well because he had once been one of them and hadn't hesitated blazing several funerals in his past. So he prepared himself for all possibilities.

He stood stone still, watching as Salahudeen's body was lowered into the ground. They were all well aware of the risks. They all knew death was a strong possibility and sometimes a consequence of what they were doing. Still, losing Salahudeen was painful. Rahman would miss his longtime friend.

Rahman felt someone looking at him. He glanced up and met Ayesha's gaze. She had been watching him and knew he was hurt, but she also knew he was angry. She could see him boiling inside. But somehow he found the strength to maintain his composure. He flashed her a slight grin to let her know he was alright.

Haneef approached him. "As-Salaamu Alaikum, Ock. How you?" Haneef inquired, giving him a hug.

"All praise is due Allah. To Allah we belong and to him we return."

"True indeed," Haneef agreed. "But are you okay?"

Rahman didn't respond.

"Rahman, I need to know. We got a lot of brothers upset and ready to flip for the wrong reason. We can't change from fighting for Allah's cause to fighting for revenge. That, my brother, is not Islam. Justice yes. Revenge no. The difference is intention."

Rahman understood what Haneef was saying. He had already been to war within himself. He wanted to avenge Sal's murder but knew the fallacy of reacting on emotion. Anger clouds and love blinds, but a thinking man remains unswayed. He was prepared to turn up the heat on the streets, not for revenge but for justice.

Before he responded, his cell phone rang. He excused himself from Haneef and answered his phone.

"Speak."

"I'm sorry about Sal," Angel said with true remorse.

"We ain't got nothin' to say to one another," Rahman said and hung up on her.

A few seconds later his phone rang again.

"Roc, listen. I know you're upset, but on my WORD, I had nothing to do with it. I didn't know anything about it. That was all Roll," Angel explained.

Truthfully, Angel wanted to solve the problem not squash it like Roll had tried to do.

Rahman knew Angel was telling the truth but there was no way back, no way to return.

"Roc... Roll is gone. He ain't a problem for neither one of us. I took care of it. I just wanna make this right. I really do," Angel offered.

"There's nothing..."

"The area we discussed, the one you wanted. It's yours. Period. I'm in control now and it's yours. You take it and you handle your part of the city. I'll handle mine."

She was trying to compromise but that was a luxury he didn't have. His cause wouldn't allow him to. Outside, he remained stone but inside, he was in turmoil. He had to say no, but to do so brought him one step closer to what he dreaded. An all-out war with Angel.

"No deal. I want all the drugs out of Newark. Anything less, I won't accept. You wanna pick up where Roll left off, then you inherit his beef," Rahman said calmly.

"I remember a time when your beef was mine, yo. Now the same vow means the exact opposite."

Rahman closed his eyes tight against his emotions before speaking evenly and firmly. "The next time we meet, we meet as enemies."

Silence filled the air for a moment.

"I... I know there's no way we can avoid that now. Either you gonna kill me or I'ma kill you. But regardless, we both lose. But know this, Roc. Whatever happens, I love you."

His heart silently returned the sentiment.

"Salaam."

"Siempre."

Angel sat on the couch in Capo's safe house, staring at the

money counters. The machines counted endlessly until the rickety sound became meaningless to her. With the money coming in since Roll's death, they didn't count it as often as they weighed it. They had calculated that a million dollars in small bills filled a duffel bag made to hold two basketballs.

Capo sat across the room with headphones strapped to his head, feeding the machine then taping the stacks and depositing them in bags.

Angel looked into his eighteen-year-old face. He was a brown-skinned Puerto Rican but his features were clearly Latino right down to his curly brown hair and bushy eyebrows. She watched him, wondering how long he would live before the life took him under.

Goldilocks came out of the kitchen with a glass of water for Angel. Her shapely figure swayed as she walked. She smiled when she noticed Angel watching her.

"Here you go, boo," Goldilocks said, handing her the glass then curling up on the couch next to her.

Angel didn't respond. She just sipped her water and wondered when Goldilocks' love for her would make Angel kill her too. She wondered when love would cloud her vision, blind her judgement, and cause her to make emotional mistakes. In the high stakes game of street survival, Angel could not afford any mistakes.

Angel remembered a time when Dutch, Craze, Zoom and Roc occupied a room like this. There used to be laughter and arguments, love and trust, and nobody's mind was exclusively on the money. But with Dutch, Craze and Zoom gone and Roc her sworn enemy, the taste of success curdled in her mouth like spoiled milk.

"Fuck!" she bellowed so loudly that Capo heard her over his

music. She stood up angrily.

"Shut that fuckin' machine off! It's drivin' me crazy!" she exclaimed, holding her hands over her ears.

Goldilocks stood and wiggled up to her. "Baby, you..." but Angel's eyes silenced her.

Capo saw the abrupt change in her demeanor and quickly shut the machine off.

"What... what is we doin'? What are we here for?" Angel wanted to know, looking from face to face.

Capo was puzzled. "Countin' paper like we always do?" he replied.

"No," Angel retorted, Dutch's dragon chain swinging with her movements. "What are we doing here? In this position, huh? Where we at, who we are?"

Neither could understand what she meant so they didn't say anything. Capo thought Angel was losing it, and Goldilocks tried to soothe her.

"Baby, sit down and relax. You just have a lot on your mind. Let me give you a massage," she offered, but Angel yanked away.

"Relax? Relax?! Bitch is you crazy? Don't you know right now there's a hungry muthafucka out there goin' all out to come to get what we got, and you want me to relax?!"

Angel appeared hysterical yet her mind was totally clear.

"When they come, we got 'nuff guns to go around!" Capo boasted.

Angel snatched the headphones off of his head.

"You dumb fuck! You think we the only ones wit' guns? Huh? Kazami had guns, and Dutch took him out. Dutch had guns, and the mob pushed him out. Young World had guns, Roll slumped 'im. And we slumped Roll. Do you think that's it?

You think one day you won't get slumped?" she asked him, staring in his eyes until he looked away.

"Do you? Digame!" Angel screamed. "Do you think I could be slumped, Capo? Would you slump me, Capo?"

Capo knew Angel was crazy, but he never saw her like this before. "Naw, yo. We family, la familia, remember?" he replied, shifting in his chair.

Angel laughed in his face. "You lyin', Cap. You lyin' and you know it."

Capo hated to be called a liar, but he feared the consequences of being judged one even more.

"My word, Angel. Death before dishonor, you know that," he vowed.

"That ain't got shit to do wit' what I asked," Angel retorted. "Push come to shove, you better slump me because I won't hesitate to slump you," she hissed, then looked at Goldilocks, "Or you."

Goldilocks' heart jumped. "I would never do anything to hurt you, lover, you know that."

"Do I?" Angel asked, then again to Capo, "Do I?"

"Let's hope it never comes to that," Capo replied.

"Fuck hope! It better not come to that because I promise you all, I won't lose," Angel replied, sitting back down, laying her head back and closing her eyes.

"Count the money."

Chapter Nine

In the next days after Sal's funeral, Rahman made it a point to spend more time at home with his family. He didn't neglect his responsibilities on the streets, but he kept his word to Ayesha. His home was like another world. He cut the grass, went to his son's little league games, and cooked dinners with Ayesha. Despite the turmoil in the cities of New Jersey, home was his sanctuary, his shelter in the storm.

Rahman sat on the sofa in the living room, watching Ali and Aminah play while Anisa slept peacefully in his lap. He looked at his children and understood what it was all about. Everything he was trying to accomplish revolved around them. Peace.

To be able to raise his children in a safe neighborhood and to send them to good schools was what it was all about. Creating a legacy that could be passed down through the bloodline of establishing an economically, socially, and morally sound community was what it was all about. Rahman didn't want only for his children. He wanted for all ghetto children everywhere. Not everyone was fortunate enough to make it out of the ghetto. People became doctors, lawyers, stars and politicians, but instead of staying in the community and utilizing its resources, they took their talents and finances to the sanitized suburbs and left their old neighborhoods to wallow in the mire.

If it wasn't for the imminent threat to his family, Rahman would have moved them back to Newark. But he was street enemy number one and the risk was too great.

He prayed he would see the day when Newark would be cleaned up and safe, a place where old people didn't have to worry about being robbed or assaulted and where women didn't have to exploit themselves to get by. His mission was to change things for the better, and he was willing to kill and die to make it happen.

"Abu, are you goin' back to jail?" Ali asked as he looked up into his father's face with the questioning eyes of a puppy.

Ali's question took Rahman by surprise. But before he could respond, Aminah sucked her teeth and said, "You stupid boy. Abu ain't leavin', are you Abu?"

"Don't call your brother stupid, Minah," he gently scolded. Then turned to his son, "What made you say that, Ali?"

Ali shrugged his shoulders, afraid that he had said the wrong thing.

"Ali, are you lying to me? You do know what made you ask."

He hesitated for a second before replying. "Mommy. I heard her praying to Allah that you don't go back to jail."

Rahman didn't know what to say or how to respond. Of course going back to prison had crossed his mind. Every time he grabbed his guns, he took his chances with the law. He had killed in spite of the cause he claimed, and in court it was be called one thing... murder. The judgement would be ife without parole, or worse, the death penalty.

"Ali, do you know how much I love you and mommy and your sisters?"

"A lot?" Ali smiled.

Rahman smiled back. "A whole lot. With all my heart. I'll do anything to protect you. I'd die for you. And yes, I'd even go back to prison."

"But I don't want you to die, Abu! And I don't want you to go to prison," Ali begged. "Allah will protect us, right?"

How do you explain to a child that sometimes in life people have to die to be free, that sacrifices must be made, and sometimes that means giving up everything?

Rahman picked Ali up off the floor and put him on the couch beside him.

"I don't want to die either, Ali, and I don't want to go to prison, but... what if somebody tried to hurt us? What would you do?"

"Fight," Ali barked, balling up his little fists.

"Even if you got hurt, too?" Rahman asked.

Ali nodded vigorously.

"I'ma fight too, Abu," Aminah added, swinging at an imaginary opponent, making Rahman chuckle.

"I know you would, baby girl. But sometimes when we fight, we don't always win, do we? But that doesn't mean we stop fightin'?"

"No," Ali and Aminah said in unison.

"That's right. We keep fightin'. You can never give up," Rahman paused to consider the consequences of losing. "I have to keep fighting. You understand?"

They both nodded their little heads.

"But you won't lose, will you Abu?" Ali asked, looking up to his superhero, the master of his universe.

Rahman smiled, but inside, he trembled.

"Insha Allah. I won't."

While Rahman savored his time at home, the summer blazed in the inner city for more than the obvious reasons. A sweltering heat wave had blanketed Jersey along with a heat wave of gunplay.

Bodies piled up on all sides, both Muslims and gangstas. From Newark to Atlantic City, niggas died or came up missing as the two opposing forces waged war for control of the streets. Bombs were planted and people were kidnapped in retribution. The Muslims fought for peace in the hood, and the gangstas fought for a piece of the hood. The police had their hands full but understood very little of the underlying causes. They could clearly see, however, the effects of the war being waged.

The Muslims were determined to stop the flow of drug money, so Angel decided to stop the flow of their money as well. *They want to fuck with my paper, let's see how they like it when I fuck with theirs.*

Angel and her gang broke up vendors and pushed them off their street corners, making it just as hard to sell oils as it was to sell drugs.

Both sides took losses. It came down to who would break first. Angel was relentless and Rahman was resistant, both keeping it hot but avoiding the obvious target.

Each other.

"Ock, if you kill the head, the body will die," Haneef tried to tell Rahman one Friday after Jum'ah prayer service. They were standing outside the Masjid on Branford Place. "If anybody knows how to hit her, it's you," Haneef concluded.

Rahman had been thinking the same thing, but he knew it wouldn't be easy. Angel had the same thoroughbred instincts he did. Too many Muslims had been hurt and killed so the time had come to strike at the top. With Angel out of the way,

Rahman knew he could squash the petty wanna-be gangstas like roaches.

Yet Rahman couldn't help but feel uncomfortable for thinking about murdering someone who had been so close to his heart. He looked at Haneef and asked him the question that had been heavy on his mind since the Timberland hit.

"Haneef, I know our cause is just. But do you think we're serving it justly?"

"I remind you of the people in the boat, some on the top, some on the bottom. If the people on the top don't stop the fools then everyone will drown."

Rahman knew the story well.

"They are sinkin' our society, Rah. How else can we stop them?"

"Set it up," Rahman ordered without another thought. "But I gotta be the one to do it," he added, knowing to send someone else would be cowardly.

Haneef had already figured as much.

Angel had one weakness, her love of shoes. She had always been a sneaker fanatic. Her favorite spot to shop was the Newport Center Mall in Jersey City. Rahman knew this and planned to use it against her. When a person indulges their desires, their defenses are down.

It took several days of surveillance before he received the call.

"She's here."

He had been staying in Jersey City, a few blocks from the mall, waiting for his team to call.

Angel, Goldilocks and Capo pulled up in Capo's chrome 745. The mall was moderately crowded but the two gorgeous killers still managed to turn heads in their short shorts and multicolored tanks. Angel both hated and loved the attention. She hated it because she'd rather be who she really was, but she needed the attention. The clothes were the bait, or at least that's how she wore them.

Since her conversation with Rahman, Angel's demeanor had changed, and Goldilocks was worried. Everything became strictly business and money. She took no shorts from her team, and Goldilocks was no exception. Any little thing set her off. Angel was like a walking time bomb. Goldilocks didn't understand why.

For Angel, all she had ever loved was Dutch and the family. Rahman had come to represent all that to her since everyone else was gone. True, they had irreconcilable differences which she understood, but for Roc to tell her they were enemies extinguished whatever feelings of love she held in her being. For Angel, there was no more loyalty, therefore no more trust. So she trusted no one nor could she be trusted. All she had left was money, power and respect she extorted from the streets, and she held it all down with an iron fist.

Goldilocks had watched in horror one night as Angel made Capo beat a nigga to a bloody death with a lead pipe because he had fucked up fifty grand, peanuts in their operation. It was then Goldi realized that Angel was walking a very dangerous edge.

"Baby, I've been thinking," Goldilocks said as they walked through the mall. "Why don't we go away for a while. Take a trip somewhere. Anywhere. Just you and me."

"Maybe in a couple of months, ma. Shit is too hectic right now for me to get away," Angel replied.

"Which is exactly why you need to go. Capo can handle things, right Capo?"

"No doubt. There's nothin' I can't handle," he confirmed, trying to convince a leery Angel. Angel grinned slightly, but her eyes remained stone.

"Callete, okay?" she spoke calmly.

Capo and Goldi knew not to push the point so the conversation was over.

Angel looked at Capo then at Goldilocks. She just couldn't figure it out. *Goldi never thinks about the paper. Capo's a thirstball but Goldi acts like the money is nothing.* Angel didn't know if that was a good thing or a bad thing. If she took the 'love' issue out the equation, then what was Goldi doing with her?

Angel no longer believed in love so she doubted the authenticity of Goldi's. If Roc could turn against her, then anybody could. Angel decided to let the relationship run its course. She was on point, now more than ever, and even Goldi would fall under her magnifying glass.

They entered Angel's favorite sneaker spot in the Newport Mall and began to browse. The walls were covered on all four sides with the newest editions and retro throwback styles. Angel came to spend even though she already had over a hundred pairs of sneakers and hadn't worn even half of them.

"Good afternoon, Ms. Alvarez," said a white guy in a referee-striped shirt. He welcomed her like the regular she was. "Glad you dropped by. That special order of Air Force One's arrived two days ago," he smiled, then disappeared in the back to get them.

"Now, these are hot," Goldilocks remarked, removing the silver and black T-Macs from the display. "You like 'em, boo? You gonna cop 'em for me?" she chimed.

"Why? So you can walk away from me in 'em?" Angel retorted sourly.

Sourpuss, sourpuss, Goldi thought. "Yo, what the fuck is wrong with you? You got a real fucked up attitude."

The man returned with four boxes of sneakers and set them on the counter. "Here you are, Ms. Alvarez."

"Yo, Duke! What color you got these in?" Capo asked the salesman across the floor as he held up a pair of shell-top Adidas.

The man squinted and replied, "I'll have to check."

"Just give me every color you got in a size ten," Capo ordered. He loved shopping 'cause he was able to order around the salespeople.

Just as the clerk started off for the back, a loud, irrationally high-pitched alarm filled the mall, startling everyone.

"What is that?" Goldilocks cringed, covering her ears.

The clerk rushed over to the register and picked up the phone.

The P.A. announcer came over the system.

"Mall shoppers, may I have your attention please. At this time, we ask that you calmly move towards the exit nearest you. There is no need for alarm but we do request your immediate cooperation. Thank you."

The alarm continued to scream. Despite the calm announcement, shoppers moved at a rapid pace, bordering on panic. On the way out, Goldilocks commented to Capo, "What the hell is going on? Terrorists attacking the malls now?"

Her comment sparked a dèjá vu in Angel, stopping her dead in her tracks. During the 'Month of Murder', Roc and Zoom had used the same tactic. Create confusion, murder, and then escape in the chaos. It was a timely thought that made her instantly aware of her surroundings. She felt her life was in danger, saw it coming for a split second, and then all hell broke loose as the mall erupted in gunfire and screams. The first shot from Rahman's bullet grazed her in the upper arm as she pushed people out of her way. The second shot shattered the window behind her as she dove for cover.

"Fuck!" Angel cursed at the sight of her own blood, adrenaline pumping too fast to feel the pain.

"Angel!" Goldilocks screamed, not knowing how serious her wound was.

"I'm good! Move! Where's Capo?! Capo!"

Angel came up firing recklessly, almost hitting two young girls.

The mall was in total chaos. Six shooters and Rahman were all trying to take Angel down.

Capo pulled his gun and popped the safety.

"Angel!" he called out, peering from between a rack of t-shirts.

His voice and words were rewarded with a barrage of gunfire. He returned the shots, but the next round found its way into the flesh of his neck. Two more shots finished him off.

"Capo!" Angel screamed from behind the counter. She and Goldilocks were using it for cover. She watched as Capo was gunned down and fired on the killer.

"Move with the crowd! He won't shoot into a crowd!" Angel commanded Goldi, then reloaded her nine. "Let's go!"

Goldilocks emerged from their hiding place first, gripping her pistol like a trained gunman. Two of her three shots found fatal homes in the flesh of two of the shooters. As she and Angel ducked and dodged through the crowd, Angel was amazed at her accuracy. *Damn, this bitch shoot better than me.*

Rahman and his team circled the mall trying to cut Angel off and fish her out of the crowd. The mall police were looking for the shooters in the midst of the madness.

Angel saw the police at the door and made a decision to dip through the exit that lead to the subway that ran under the mall.

"She took the stairs!" Haneef shouted to Rahman. They both headed in that direction.

"Freeze, or I'll shoot!" a cop screamed at one of the shooters, before catching two shots in his face from a second shooter to his left.

"Ock! Let's go!" Haneef screamed.

Angel and Goldilocks jumped down the steps three at a time and fired back up to keep Roc at bay.

The people waiting on the train platform screamed and ducked as Angel and Goldilocks ran down to the far end.

"Go back, Haneef! I got it from here! Police is everywhere! Let me do this," Rahman ordered.

"You sure?"

Rahman nodded and Haneef moved in the opposite direction away from Rahman.

Rahman skipped down the steps staying close to the wall as he reached the platform. The train hadn't arrived yet and the people were hiding behind whatever they could.

"So this is how it ends, Roc, huh?" Angel screamed from behind a steel support column. She fired two shots that struck the wall inches from Rahman's head. "I know you can hear me, muthafucka!"

Rahman remained quiet, inching closer to the pinned down Angel. She peeked around the column, and he let off three shots in rapid succession. She nodded to Goldilocks next to her, who hunched down low and crept along the opposite side, attempting to circle around and trap Roc.

"You wanna kill me Roc? You want me dead? After all we been through?" Angel saw that Goldilocks was ready.

Angel came out from hiding, her gun lowered. "Here I am."

Rahman slipped out from behind a beam and was about to squeeze off a shot when he felt a powerful thud in his upper back that slammed him face first into the pavement.

It was Goldilocks. She had crept up behind him from the other end of the platform. Once Roc came out, he was so focused on Angel, he was a sitting duck for Goldilocks. But he had come prepared. The bullet crumbled on impact as it hit his Kevlar vest instead of penetrating his flesh.

Goldilocks was about to fire on Roc again, but Angel yelled out. "Goldi, behind you!"

Two police officers were at the top of the stairs. Angel fired over Goldi's head and her bullets caught the cops dead in their tracks, dropping them to the floor. The distraction, however, was enough to give Rahman a chance to roll his body onto the tracks just inches from the third rail.

The platform rumbled as a train steamed in on the other side. Angel and Goldilocks jumped on the train.

"You missed me, Roc! But, I'm not gonna miss you. Holla back!" she yelled, holding her wound as the doors shut and the train pulled off.

Rahman sat with his throbbing back to the concrete wall, listening to Angel's taunt. He had missed. Now all he could do was wait until she hollered back.

He struggled to his feet and disappeared down the dark tunnel, making his escape.

PEACE

Chapter Ten

"I'm going to miss you, Ms. Martin," Susan, her secretary, confessed warmly.

They stood in Nina's office among cardboard cartons waiting to be removed.

"Me too, Susan. I know we got off to a bad start and all..."

"No need. It was all a misunderstanding. I know I can be a bitch sometimes. But we worked it out and that's all that matters," she said. "So what's the plan? Got a better offer somewhere else?"

What is the plan? I don't even know.

Nina didn't have a better offer. In fact, she wasn't looking for one. She had impulsively handed in her two week's notice almost at the spur of the moment. She needed to get away.

After the break up with Dwight, she tried to refocus on work but just couldn't pull it together. She knew Dwight was perfect for her and she had been a fool.

So she had to get away. She felt it was her only choice. Her financial investments were sound enough to live off of. What wasn't sound was her peace of mind. She knew the only way to move on with her life and be free of the ghosts of her past was to relocate. Maybe down south, maybe out west. But first, she booked a Caribbean cruise vacation. She would sail around the islands, figure out a plan for her future and decide what she wanted out of life. Money wasn't the issue. She had enough in savings to cover her relocation, and Nina didn't have to work. She worked because it was what she had chosen to do with her life.

"Well, whatever you decide, I wish you the best," Susan said, sensing Nina's hesitancy to discuss her future plans.

"Thank you Susan. I really appreciate that."

Susan walked to the door and put her hand on the knob. She turned around and faced Nina.

"Even though things didn't work out with Dwight, I think you are a good person and you deserve the best. Don't let disappointments make you not believe in rainbows. There's a pot of gold for everybody. You just have to find it."

I just have to find it? Yeah, maybe she's right or maybe I just lost my pot of gold when I let Dwight go.

Susan walked out leaving Nina to ponder.

Three days later, Angel retaliated.

She drove silently in a blue Taurus rental and a blond wig, her arm in a sling. Every time she moved it, she felt pain, and every time she felt pain, she thought of Roc.

Angel had to hate him. She had to despise him. She knew what she had to do, and the only way she could carry out what she had to was to let hate boil inside of her. The look in his eyes on the subway platform played over and over again in her mind.

"Here I am," she had said to him, stepping into his path.

Angel thought of how he hadn't hesitated to raise his gun, eyes focused like a hawk's, ready to shed her blood like she meant nothing to him.

Who the fuck is he? Fuck him! Fuckin' sell out! she chanted in her mind trying to convince herself that she hated him.

And, oh, how she wanted to. But something in her heart wouldn't let her. Several times, she fought the urge to turn back. But pride pushed her forward as she headed to the conclusion of her mission.

Roc had to die, and she would kill him. But it wouldn't be out of hate.

Angel hit the Trenton exit off the Turnpike and drove through the city looking for the Muslim girls' school on East State Street. She remembered Roc telling her about it in his prison letters and how good he felt at the accomplishment.

The school wasn't difficult to find. The small brick building was on a corner, a playground and a parking lot in the back. At was nine on a Saturday morning, only a few girls were in school for special Qur'an and Arabic lessons.

Angel had planned on attacking Ayesha first, but Roc covered his tracks well and protected her whereabouts. Even when she ran the plates of his car, her connect said the address was 25 Branford Place, the Masjid in Newark. Angel settled on the next best thing.

His cause.

She knew how to get a Roc from the start but held her trump card, hoping she would never have to use it. When he made the fatal mistake of trying to kill her, she put it in play. The move was like everything else was to her. Business. Nothing personal.

Angel got out of the rental, threw on dark tinted shades and looked around. The area was quiet and peaceful. She adjusted her sling which held a concealed revolver and approached the school.

"Okay, Rasheeda. I want you to draw me alif," the female teacher instructed. She wore an orange khimar and white niqab. On the floor around her were nine young girls between the ages of eight and ten, struggling to learn their religion.

Rasheeda, tall for her age, approached the board and took the chalk from the teacher. She drew a straight line that resembled the letter L.

"Very good, Rasheeda. Class, this is an alif. Say it with me. Al-lif."

"Al-lif" the class repeated.

"Alif is like the letter A in English. Can anyone tell me a word that starts with the letter A?" the teacher asked.

"Allah," one girl said.

"Asad which means lion," another suggested.

"Angel."

The teacher looked up to find a strange woman in an obvious wig and a large golden dragon dangling from her neck leaning with her arm in a sling on the inside of the door frame. She knew she wasn't one of the girl's mothers.

"Can I help you?" the teacher asked.

"I was wondering if I could speak with you for a moment," Angel requested politely.

The teacher looked at Angel then at all nine little faces.

"Al... Alright. Class, keep studying your lesson book."

The teacher walked over to Angel. "How may I help you?" she politely offered, trying to mask nervousness behind hospitality.

"Please, don't be nervous. I just need to meet someone here, and I need you to wait with me until he arrives," Angel said softly.

"I... I don't under..."

Angel slid the pistol out of the sling. The teacher gasped with fright. "Please don't..."

"Shh..." Angel quietly silenced her. "Don't alarm the girls. I won't hurt you as long as you cooperate. If you don't, I will kill everyone here."

The statement was simple yet so menacing that the teacher knew the woman meant business. Her eyes glazed over with tears as she contemplated the safety of the children.

"I'll... I'll do whatever you ask. Just don't..."

"Hurt the children?" Angel finished her plea. "We already discussed that." Angel pulled out her cell phone and handed the teacher the phone.

"Dial this number."

Rahman closed his cell phone. He did it without emotion, without words and without choice. He had no choices because Angel had left him none. He listened to the Muslim sister's trembling voice.

"Brother, Angel is here," the teacher said as tears streamed down her cheek. She finished reading the note Angel had passed her. "She has a gun and there are nine little girls here."

Then Angel got on the line and finished. "I know you won't call the police, but if you've changed that much, you know the consequences. Come alone and unarmed, one hour, your life for theirs. A minute late, start subtracting from nine. You bring a gun, I'll kill them with it."

Click.

Rahman resigned himself to his fate. The game was over and Angel had won.

You can't win, Roc, he remembered her saying, but he had brushed it off as an empty threat.

You missed, but I won't, nigga, she had promised that day on the train platform.

Angel had laid at his feet his entire cause, represented by nine little Muslim girls, the ultimate sacrifice.

Your life for theirs.

Anyone could live for the cause, kill for the cause, even die for the cause in the heat of battle. But to be asked to trade your life for another's when you could sit safely at home was what separated the faithful from the false.

Do you think that you will be left alone, saying you believe, and not be tested?

Rahman recited the Qur'anic verse over and over again in his mind. There was nothing he would not do for a cause that involved Islam. Nothing.

Your life for theirs.

Rahman didn't hesitate. He had to do what he had to do. Only one obstacle remained. His family.

Rahman grimaced over what he had to say to Ayesha. Could he just kiss her and walk out, leaving her with the impression that he'd be back, and then go to Angel, never to return?

It would be a lie, and their relationship had never been based on lies. Of all the blood he had shed, lives he had ruined and money he had made, he never lied to Ayesha about anything. She had stayed with him through thick and thin, through his wickedness, his incarceration and his re-birth, each time sacrificing a part of herself to accommodate his intentions. All she ever asked in return was his love and support. All she wanted was for him to be a good father to their three children. She would sacrifice for her family. She already had.

Didn't Ayesha and his children deserve his presence? Hadn't he put them through enough? How could he leave his children fatherless, taking life from them to give to nine more? What if he didn't go?

He shook off the cowardly thought because he realized he had created the situation. If he didn't go, blood would surely be on his hands.

He had no choice.

Rahman rose from his stupor and went into the bathroom to make wudu for prayer, his last prayer. He unfolded his prayer rug and stood before his Lord to offer the two ra'kahs of prayer Muslims do before imminent death.

He bowed and fell on his face. As he prayed, tears lined his face and wet his beard. He cried not out of fear of death but because he had failed.

As he prayed, Ayesha came to ask him to go to the store to get some milk. She found him in prayer, sobbing hard, and it made her want to go to him and embrace him. Instead, she waited by the door until he was finished.

"Baby, are you okay?" she asked.

He couldn't even look her in the face. She approached him and touched his shoulder.

"We're out of milk. I wanted you to go to the store for me," she said, not knowing what else to say.

Rahman wrapped his arms around her waist and cried against her stomach. The force of his tears ran down Ayesha's cheeks and they cried as one even though she didn't know what she was crying about. She held her husband's head nervously. She had never seen him cry like this before and couldn't imagine what had caused him to be so emotional.

Rahman rose to his full height and continued to hold Ayesha tightly. Finally, he said, "I... have to go."

The way he said 'go' she knew it wasn't the type of go she had heard before. It made her search his eyes frantically for answers.

"Rahman, what do you mean 'go'? Go where? Where do you have to go?"

"Ayesha, something has happened that... that I can't stop and I can't let it go on either," he said, trying to explain rationally what her emotions would never allow her to understand.

"No! No, Rahman! Wherever it is, whatever it is, no! You can't go!" she said trembling, fearing the worse.

"Ayesha..."

"Then I'm going, too! If you go, I'm going, and the children are going. We're all going, Rahman."

Ayesha was hysterical. Her instincts told her that something terrible was threatening to rip their lives apart.

He grabbed her arms with force and shook her, hoping to make her understand.

"Nine little girls, Ayesha. Nine little girls are going to die unless I do! If I don't go, they die! Do you understand? I have to go!"

Ayesha would hear none of it. She wrapped her arms around his neck like a vice.

"You promised me, Rahman! You promised me you wouldn't leave me! What about that? You can't leave me now, leave us," Ayesha pleaded selfishly.

"Ayesha, please. There's nothing I can do. Please. Don't make it harder for me. Don't let the kids hear us," he pleaded softly, but Ayesha was in hysteria's grip.

"No! They will hear if that'll keep you here! Ali! Aminah! Anisa!" she yelled, tearing herself from Rahman's arms and running into the living room.

"Ayesha!"

Rahman followed her into the living room.

"Go to your father! Go to Abu and tell him not to go! Tell him not to leave us!" Ayesha cried from the depths of her soul.

The children understood nothing but their mother's tears. They ran and wrapped their little bodies around Rahman's legs and each other.

"Abu? Where are you going? Don't go. Please!"

"Abu, don't leave us!"

"Daddy!"

The chorus of young pleas tore Rahman in two pieces, father and man.

"Tell them, Rahman. Tell them! You tell them where you're going!" Ayesha screamed. She fell to her knees, pleading and praying. "Nine little girls... but what about your own three? You can die for strangers but you can't live for your own family?"

Rahman knew if he didn't pull himself away he'd never leave. He hugged and kissed his begging, wet-faced babies and embraced his wife for the last time.

"How could you do this to me, Rahman? How?" she repeatedly asked as he rocked her in his arms.

"I'll meet you in Paradise. Insha Allah," he said before pulling away, leaving his children wrapped in their mother's arms, not knowing why their daddy was leaving.

Rahman looked at them once more and said a silent prayer for their protection. Then he was gone.

Nina pulled up to her house and climbed out of the car. It was still morning but the sun was already scorching.

She looked at the For Sale sign on her lawn. This was the first home she had ever purchased and she couldn't believe she was selling it. She never thought she'd move. She never thought this wouldn't be home. Luckily, the market was strong with the low interest rates and the house sold within 90 days after being placed on the market.

"Really good, Nina. Really good. And we got our asking price. What more could you ask for?" asked her real estate lawyer with papers in hand for her to sign so he could close the deal.

She inhaled deeply and exhaled slowly, looking at her house one last time, hoping she was doing the right thing. It felt like the right thing. The burden on her already felt lighter. She ascended the porch and had already taken out her keys when she noticed that the door was open a crack. Her heart skipped a beat thinking that there was a burglar or an intruder inside.

Maybe it was Dwight. But he had left his key the night they broke up.

Maybe she had left the door ajar. She had become absent-minded lately. Just the other day she left a cup of mocha on her car roof only to have the hot liquid spill all over her windshield when she backed out of Dunkin' Donuts.

Nina gingerly pushed the door wider and yelled, "Hello?"

She got no response.

Nina peered into her house, afraid to go in, not knowing what could be waiting for her. When she reached for the knob to close the door and call the police, she saw a rose petal on the foyer floor.

It was blood red and unmistakable, just inches from her Nike sneaker. It was too fresh to have been there long, and she couldn't remember the last time she had flowers in her house. She opened the door a little wider. Her heartbeat accelerated when she saw another rose petal and another and another.

Nina was frightened. She felt in her heart that Dwight didn't leave the trail of rose petals. Only one man would leave such a subtle and alluring message. Only one man, and that's what petrified her and excited her all at the same time. The trail of rose petals became one long rainbow, the rainbow Susan said to believe in, the one with the pot of gold at the end. Nina's first step confirmed her belief and each shaky step after urged her to run in the other direction.

He's toying with you.

Run.

She reached the steps.

All he's ever brought you is pain.

Run.

She reached the landing where the steps turned and climbed to the second floor.

He left you when you loved him most.

Run.

He lied to you. He's here.

Nina reached the second floor and the rose petals continued to her bedroom door.

Run.

She saw the sun shining on her pillow through the slightly open door. Her knees trembled, her stomach fluttered, and her lips quivered in anticipation.

She wanted to call out his name but couldn't will her voice to work. The sunlight took on a surreal aura inside her room. She approached the door and stared at the knob.

Run.

But she didn't run, she couldn't run. The mystery of what awaited her magnetized her. She pushed the door open slowly and what she found stopped her breath.

"Hello, Rahman," Angel said as he stepped into the classroom.

Angel sat on the floor with her legs folded under her and was reading a book to the nine little girls circled around her. Her gun rested on the floor between her legs.

The teacher remained in Angel's line of vision but was not part of Angel's little circle. The girls looked around and saw Rahman.

"As-salaamu Alaikum brother Rahman," said one of the little girls. The others shouted out the same.

Rahman looked into their smiling faces and could see that they didn't have any idea of what was happening. He half expected to find them tied up and gagged. But thanks to Allah they weren't. But the situation couldn't have been much worse. They were sitting next to a loaded cannon. Rahman glanced at the teacher. As he expected, Angel had scared her half to death. The teacher was visibly shaken.

"What are you doin', Angel?" Rahman asked.

"Just tellin' 'em a story," Angel smiled at the girls sitting around her so happily.

"Miss Angel, tell us about the dragons and the prince again," one little girl chimed.

Angel gripped the chain. "Not now, little ones. I need to talk to mi amigo. Si?"

"Si," they all repeated as if Angel had just taught Spanish 101. The little girls giggled as Angel brushed their heads as she stood up, her gun once again cleverly hidden in her sling. She took a seat on one of the hard wooden chairs and faced Roc.

"Can... can I take the children now, please?" the teacher asked.

"Of course you can go now, but don't get stupid. Don't get anyone else hurt," Angel replied, nodding to Rahman.

"Come on girls. Let's go," the teacher said and quickly hurried them out of the room.

Angel took out her gun and cocked the hammer.

"Didn't I tell you you couldn't win, Roc? I told you that. Remember?"

Rahman kept his eyes on her without speaking. Angel rose from the chair and crossed the room towards him.

"You a true gangsta, Roc. Or should I say, a true Muslim? You're like a Tupac song, playin' no games, right?" Angel smiled. "But that was your weakness, the one I knew I could use against you at will."

"I'm here. I fear nothing except Allah, not even death. So, if you gonna shoot... shoot. I ain't got all day," Rahman calmly said. He was completely at peace with the death he was about to meet.

Angel raised the gun and held it sideways to execute a head shot. Rahman braced himself.

"Tell... me... why," she growled.

"Why what?" Rahman replied, the smell of death burning his nostrils.

"Why? We made a vow, Roc. All of us. We vowed never to turn on each other!" Angel shouted, trembling with rage.

Rahman then saw Angel do something he had never seen her do before. She cried. Fat tears ran down her face. Rahman closed his eyes.

"We were family Roc... family! And you threw it all away!"

He took a deep breath. He was ready for it to end. "If you gonna shoot," he opened his eyes and locked his gaze with hers, "shoot." He didn't give a damn about her, their past or anying she was saying. It was too late. Nothing could save him or her from what she was about to do.

She steadied her arm and said, "I still love you, Roc."

"I love you, too."

It was his reply but it didn't come from Rahman. The familiar voice rang in her ears. She just couldn't believe she was hearing it.

Nina pushed the door open, and her heart fell and leapt at the same time. Fell because he wasn't there. She had expected to open the door and see the only man who made her body smile all over.

She expected to see Dutch.

She had imagined running into his arms, sticking her tongue down his throat, feeling his warmth all over, both inside and out.

But he wasn't there.

What made her heart do double-time, however, was what lay on the bed.

Nina had followed the rose petal trail to her bed. Spelled across her white comforter was a question.

Will you marry me?

Even the question mark was formed in petals but the dot below was a one-way ticket to France. Nina covered her mouth. Her hands were shaking hands. She prayed that if it was a dream, she would never wake up.

"Yes," she whispered to herself. Then in a louder voice as if he could hear her she shouted, "Yes! Yes! I will marry you, Bernard. I love you!"

Dutch had managed to romance her like no man had ever done before, from the shadows without ever speaking a word. Nina knew she was in love with fire, a very dangerous, all-consuming fire, but the burn was the sweetest thing she had ever known.

"I leave and come back... to this?"

Angel and Rahman both looked into a face they knew so well but hadn't seen in a long time.

"Cr-C-Craze?" Angel spoke in a hushed whisper as she lowered her gun hand.

It was Craze, second in command in Dutch's empire. It had been over three years since they had seen him, but he was still the same Craze. Same soft brown skin, same chipped tooth, same smirk, same dress code. The custom-made crème colored linen suit draped his frame, showing he had gained some weight but had chiseled it into an athletic physique.

Angel's intention to kill Roc was immediately forgotten. "Where's Dutch?"

Craze chuckled. "Same ol' Angel... What? Craze don't get no love? Damn! What about me? Why you ain't been worried about ol' Craze?"

Craze smiled and Angel knew it was all real. She ran into his arms. "Crazy!"

Angel's high-pitched squeal snapped Rahman out of his zone. When she hugged Craze and wrapped her arms around his back, Rahman quickly snatched the gun out of her hand.

Craze, with his back to Rahman, never turned around and never let go of Angel's waist.

"What now, Roc? You gonna shoot me, too?"

Craze turned to face his former lieutenant with his arms around Angel's neck.

"Behold the black messiah," Craze remarked sarcastically. "You wanna clean up the hood? Then forget everything that's happened between you and Angel and take a trip with me."

Rahman held the gun on his side, not pointed, but poised.

"A lot's changed since we last saw each other, Craze."

Craze took his arm from around Angel's neck and approached Rahman. Rahman was a head taller so Craze had to look up to see him eye to eye.

"Look, Roc. You want Newark? Okay. It's yours. All yours. Every spot under Angel's control is yours. Now... what you gonna do wit' it? What you gonna do when the crooked cops, crooked DA's and judges, the mob and the cartels all come at you at once? Huh? Because you'll be eatin' off their plates if you stop the drugs in Jersey."

"I'll worry about that when it happens," Rahman said, stunned that Craze seemed to know every little thing that had been going on. He handed the gun over to him.

"It's gonna happen so you better worry now."

Then he turned to Angel.

"And you..." he kissed her on the forehead and smiled at the chain around her neck. "You so busy tryin' to take back what we left for dead... We been there, done that, ma, then moved on, left the scraps for the dogs."

He gently lifted the dragon chain from her neck and held it up to watch it dangle in front of his eyes.

"You shoulda buried this wit' World," he said before he let it drop to the floor with a heavy thud. Angel went to pick it up but Craze stopped her.

"Leave it. Just like we leavin' this petty street paper to the pawns who think they playas." Craze turned once more to Rahman.

"You want the streets? Take 'em. See how long you can keep 'em. 'Cause to the Feds, you the worst kind of gangsta. But you come wit' us and we'll show you how to really change the game. No more hood gangstas, no more street gangstas, but international gangstas. Then you can make your own decision from there," Craze proposed.

Rahman looked at the gun in his hand and realized he had made a major miscalculation. He was so caught up in the battle he had forgotten about the war. Craze was right about the judges and cops and district attorneys. They all had a piece of the drug pie, either directly or indirectly. Cops were either paid under the table or promoted to detective or captain after a big bust. DAs got convictions and become senators or presidents. One black man in prison could launch and elevate the careers of four white men.

The streets weren't his enemy. They were his army. His only regret was all the blood that had been shed for this one valuable lesson.

"The trip," Rahman began, "where we goin'?"

Craze smiled, threw his arm back around Angel and said, "We're goin' to see an old friend."

The three of them walked out, leaving the tangled dragon chain in a pile on the floor, glittering in the morning sun.

Chapter Eleven

The VA hospital in Newark smelled of sanitized pain. Amputees and invalids lined the linoleum halls.

Nurse Shirley had been working there for fifteen years and it pained her to see how her government treated the men who risked their lives. The government tossed them in half-rate medical facilities with inadequate health care coverage and left them to rot. Yet every year they held mock memorials for so-called Veteran's Day. It reminded her that everyone was expendable.

The only reason she remained at the job was to try and bring her own sense of comfort to the people under her care. She had seen many die, but she had also helped many survive, physically as well as mentally. Her current priority was an old Vietnam vet. He needed dialysis three times a week for his deteriorating liver, an organ destroyed by many years of cheap liquor and poor diet.

He was a homeless man who usually ranted and raved about the war he had yet to win, a war he said he would die fighting. Nurse Shirley knew death was upon him and went to see him daily, hoping to ease his sufferings.

She entered his room with a pitcher of cold water to find him lying in his bed with his eyes closed. She didn't try to wake him.

Shirley studied his wrinkled face and furrowed brow. Even when he was asleep, he was deep in thought. His lips were usually pursed or turned down in a frown, but when he smiled, she tingled inside. Despite his unkempt appearance, his smile told her that he had been a fine man in his day. Until, like so many others, he was destroyed by the war.

Shirley went to put the pitcher down on his bedside table. She jumped a little when she felt his cold, clammy touch on her wrist.

"Did you make the call?" he rasped.

"I thought you were asleep," she said, catching her breath.

"You know what they say? Every closed eye ain't asleep," he told her before breaking into a coughing fit.

She helped prop him up in the bed and poured him a cup of water.

"Thank you," he said gratefully.

"My pleasure," she smiled.

"Now... did you make that call, Ms. Shirley?" he inquired again after taking a deep drink form the cup.

"No," she admitted with regret. "This place has been a madhouse. Two of my nurses called in sick and I..."

He held up a big yet feeble hand. "No need to explain, Ms. Shirley. You've been so good to this old man, I hate to press you, but... I know I ain't got much time and the time I had, I wasted. But you see... I got some makin' right to do with my Lord, and the people I keeps in my heart."

She gazed into his brown eyes and smiled warmly.

"I promise. After my rounds, I'll make the call."

"Thank you, Ms. Shirley," he replied and flashed a smile that would tickle any woman's fancy.

"You are a mess, Mr. Man," she said rubbing his thin, fragile thigh before leaving the room.

As she promised, she sat down at her desk with the phone book after her rounds were completed. She flipped to the white pages in search of M, until she found Murphy, then fingered the rows of names until she reached D. Shirley dialed the number but got the answering machine.

"This is Delores Murphy. I'm not here right now, but please leave your message... BEEP!"

"Ms. Murphy, this is Shirley Green at the VA hospital. Please call me as soon as you can at 555-9...3...2...6. I'm calling about one of my patients who believes you're his wife. His name is Bernard James. It really is... urgent."

Shirley hung up, happy to have done a good deed, but not knowing the Pandora's box she had just opened.

QUANTICO, VIRGINIA, 10:05 AM E.S.T.

Chapter Twelve

The director of the FBI held court at a large round wood table. Around it, several field agents sat with thick files and binders placed in front of them. Behind the director on a large white screen were mug shots of Dutch, Craze, Angel and Rahman.

"For many years we've tried to pin him down, but all was in vain. Even when faced with multiple life sentences, Angel Alvarez and Rahman Muhammad refused to give him up. We had him in custody. Then the tragedy he orchestrated at the Essex County Courthouse. After that, he disappeared."

The director debriefed his staff with bitterness in his voice.

"Under our directive, the Newark police department concealed his successful escape from the courthouse from both the press and the public. For obvious reasons, we needed them to believe he was dead. We fabricated the technicality that allowed Angel and Rahman to be released from prison. We wanted them to lead us to him. And that is what we are here to discuss today."

The director looked around the table to make sure he had everyone's attention.

"Years before we orchestrated their prison releases, we placed an agent in deep cover, an agent none of you know."

Several of those in attendance at the meeting snapped their heads up and raised their eyebrows.

"Only I and a handful of those who needed to know are aware of the agent's identity. This agent has been on the case for over three years, and we're finally seeing some light at the end of the tunnel."

He pressed a button on the intercom.

"Please bring in Agent Reese."

The pressurized door slid open with a smooth whoosh and agent Kimberly Reese walked in. She was dressed for business in a navy blue suit, nude stockings and sensible navy blue shoes. Her demeanor was all business, too. The only things out of place were the gold-tipped dreadlocks sticking out from the bun she wore at the nape of her neck.

"Let me introduce Agent Kimberly Reese, also known as Goldilocks."

The director smirked and there was a smattering of laughter.

Goldilocks smiled politely and turned to the business at hand.

"I know the director has briefed you so I'd like to bring you up-to-date. I spent two years in a federal penitentiary getting close to my contact, Angel Alvarez." Goldilocks pointed to Angel's mug shot. "Angel is the only woman in James' organization. At that time, we believed that there was a romantic connection between her and Bernard James for us to exploit but I have subsequently learned that there is none."

Goldilocks pointed to the other mug shots.

"These are James' last two remaining players. A third, Qwan Taylor, was murdered by Angel herself upon her release from prison," Goldilocks said, remembering the blood she wiped from Angel's cheek.

"We were beginning to think James had abandoned Alvarez, and we were prepared to re-indict her under the Rico Act. Since she's been out of jail, her murder rate alone would incarcerate her for life. But fortunately for her and for us, James reached out to her through Christopher Shaw, better known on the streets as Craze, a few days ago," Goldilocks explained, smiling triumphantly.

"We are one hundred percent certain that Craze will lead us to James. We, as in myself, Angel, Craze and Rahman, are scheduled to leave on a plane the day after tomorrow. I haven't been told the destination, but I am included on the journey."

A young Asian man asked, "I'm sure this case has been grueling, and I commend you on your work, but isn't this a little much? Despite the courthouse fiasco, he was just a kingpin, correct? Why all the extra muscle for a criminal the public believes is dead anyway?"

Goldilocks looked at her boss. "Director?"

The director stood up and addressed the question.

"Mr. James is still very much a threat. There are things we are privy to but aren't at liberty to discuss. Whatever his agenda is, we need to know it, now, and at all cost." The director punctuated his statement by hitting his fist on the table.

"You have been brought in for an extremely covert assignment. I'm counting on all of you to do your best work. Thank you."

The meeting broke up and all except for the director and Goldilocks left the room.

"Two days, huh?" the director questioned.

"Yes, sir," Goldilocks replied with a smile.

"Understand, Reese. Whoever and whatever you have to do, it must be done. Do not let James get away from us now. He is our number one priority," the director affirmed.

Goldilocks nodded. Dutch was her number one priority as well.

Excerpts from
two recent releases from
Teri Woods Publishing

TRIANGLE OF SINS
and
TELL ME YOUR NAME

NOW AVAILABLE IN BOOKSTORES

TRIANGLE
of
SINS

Nurit Folkes

"I told you that I wanted to be alone!" she shouted as she ran upstairs into the darkness.

She entered her bedroom and was about to flip on a light when, from behind, a strong hand suddenly grabbed her arm. In an instant, the arm belonging to the hand was around her throat. A muffled voice whispered in her ear, "Don't scream, bitch."

Natalia's heart raced. A different voice from across the dark room shouted, "Where's the safe?"

"I-I..." she stuttered.

"Where is it?" the voice commanded. "We know you got one."

"I-I don't have a safe," she stammered.

"Bitch, don't lie to me!" the same voice shouted. The man holding her yanked her hair. Natalia was petrified.

"I don't have a safe!" she screamed back, nervous tears streaming down her face.

"Shut up!" And then a swift punch pounded her cheek. The sound of the blow rang unbelievably loud in her head. The sting kept her from passing out.

"Take her out to the car," Shawn ordered.

"What?" Nut asked in disbelief.

"Just take her out to the fuckin' car," Shawn shouted again.

"What the fuck you talking about? That's not the plan."

"Just do it!" Shawn ordered.

"Aiight. Pick her up y'all," Nut commanded.

Spank and D.L. tried to pick her up together, but their heads collided, and Natalia fell to the floor.

"Forget it! I'ma get her. Y'all just go ahead!" Nut yelled. He scooped her up from the floor and headed for the door. When he was almost there, she reached up and grabbed his ski mask, pulling it off. Then she bit into his cheek, hard.

"You fuckin' bitch!" he yelled and dumped her onto the parquet foyer floor.

"You gon' get it now b..."

Natalia hopped to her feet and rammed into him like a bull. Nut slammed into the stair rail and slumped down, writhing in pain. She turned back to the kitchen and bolted to the patio doors. Old memories flooded her mind. She was nine again, running to her neighbor's house. But her closest neighbor was more than two miles away. She was trapped on her own property, but she ran anyway. She ran towards the gravel road. Just as she was within a few feet of the road, Spank tackled her to the ground. Shawn ran over and grabbed her by the arm, pulling her to her feet. He towered over her. She looked up into his masked face but could hardly see his eyes through the slits. She trembled in his tight grasp, and as he brought his face close to hers, she felt his warm breath seep through the mask onto her cheek.

Shawn pulled her close, pressing his chest against hers. Her breasts were heaving from terror and the exertion of her attempt to escape. Realizing that she was trapped, Natalia broke down and cried.

"Shhh. Just do as I say, and I promise we won't hurt you," he assured her.

She spit on him and shouted at the top of her lungs, "Go ahead and kill me, you bastard! That's what you're gonna do right? Just get it over with!"

Shawn calmly wiped the spit from his shirt. "I don't wanna hurt you, lady. But if you do some stupid shit like that again, I'ma have to."

Nut ran over to Shawn with a bloody piece of tissue balled up in his hand. He grabbed Natalia's long tresses, balled up his fist and swung at her. Shawn blocked the blow.

"No!" he shouted.

"The crazy bitch bit me," Nut complained.

Shawn chuckled. She had spunk. It made him want her more.

"Don't worry, she'll get hers." He patted Nut's shoulder.

"Now, are you gonna be a good girl?" he asked as her turned to Natalia.

"Get your hands off me!" she spat, trying to wriggle free.

"You better calm your ass down," he warned. "Go ahead to the car y'all. I got this." He twisted Natalia's arm behind her back and put her in a loose headlock. He didn't put any force into it, though. In fact, it was more playful than threatening.

"Don't push me. Be a good girl, and it'll all be over before you know it," he whispered in her ear.

In a shaky voice, she asked, "What will all be over?"

He turned her to face him and simply stared at her. She, in

turn, glanced down at his crotch, raised her knee and began to strike. With a chuckle, Shawn blocked the blow with his right hand and off-balance, she fell down onto the grass. Shawn jumped on her, straddling her with his knees and effectively pinning her down. He held her wrists firmly against the dewy grass.

"You like to fight, huh?"

She ignored the question and continued to struggle.

"You really think you can get up? Go ahead get up then," he challenged. Realizing her efforts were in vain, she stopped struggling.

"Please, just take the money in my purse and leave. I won't report this...Please just go."

"I want more than that." His lustful eyes were hidden in the darkness.

"I don't have a safe, I swear."

"I know you got money stashed."

"I don't have a bank card. You can't get anything. All I have is a checkbook."

"Stop lying to me. I'm trying to be nice."

"I'm not lying. Check my purse. You'll see." Shawn stared at her for a couple of minutes. *Maybe she's telling the truth,* he thought. He looked over at the car. Spank, D.L. and Nut were watching and waiting for his next move. He got off her and pulled her up. Then he ran his gloved fingers across her lips. Leaning down, his face just inches from hers, he warned, "You better be telling the truth."

"Where's her purse?" Shawn shouted. Nut looked at Spank. Spank looked at D.L., and D.L. looked at Nut. None of them knew. Spank volunteered to go back in the house to get it. He rushed back outside a few moments later empty handed.

"I didn't see no purse," he shrugged.

Natalia panicked. *Where the hell is my purse?* Then it dawned on her that it was still in the Louis Vuitton bag in the Navigator. "It's in the car!" she shouted like a student in class with the right answer. Shawn looked over to where her SUV was parked.

"Where're the keys?" he asked.

"Duh! In the house."

He smiled under the ski mask at her sarcasm.

"You're something else, you know that? I guess I don't scare you, huh?"

He did. But she wouldn't let him know it.

"All I want is for you to leave," she looked him straight in the eyes. "Is this personal?"

Shawn couldn't believe his ears. She must have a lot of enemies to have asked such a question. He looked away.

Nut turned on the radio in the Navigator and strolled over, bopping to the sounds blasting from the jeep.

"Yo, that shit is mad nice," he smiled.

"What is wrong wit you?" Shawn yelled.

"What now niggah?" Nut asked.

"Go turn it off."

Nut sucked his teeth, "I found this bag," he threw the bag on the ground. It landed in front of Shawn. "I ain't see no purse."

Shawn looked at Natalia waiting for an explanation.

"It's in there. I swear," she said as she pointed to the bag.

Shawn unzipped the bag and rummaged through her clothes, depilatories and undergarments. He pulled out thongs, bras and cosmetics and threw them all to the ground. When he pulled out the white leather clutch, she shrieked, "That's it!"

He dropped the cumbersome overnight bag and opened the clutch. In it, he found a leather covered checkbook, a change purse, three one hundred dollar bills and two twenties. He looked at her suspiciously. "I thought you only use checks?"

"Well, I do go to the bank occasionally to get some cash. You do need cash every once in a while, you know," she rolled her eyes at him.

"You always leave the house with this much money?" he asked, throwing down the purse.

"Not really," she answered nonchalantly. She hoped that having some money would make him leave. "Take it and go. Please."

Shawn shook his head. "This is chump change, ma. This can't do nothing for me."

"It's all I have. Please take it and go. Just go!"

"Not without you."

Tell Me Your Name

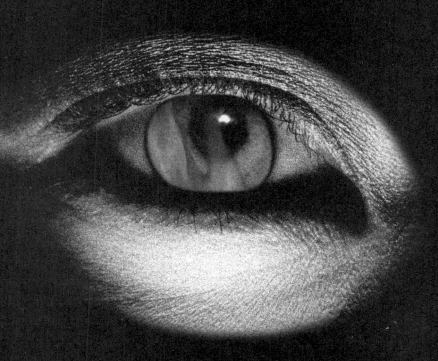

Eric Enck

The path leading to the front of the medical building was bathed in blinding white light. It bled out in long shadows between the foliage and reflected off the building's windows. The detective's heels clicked loudly on the hard marble floor as he approached the front desk. He flashed his badge at the clerk behind the window and signed in. The clerk smiled as she snatched the clipboard from him and signed her own name below his.

"Do you know where you're going, sir?" she asked.

"Yes, unfortunately I do."

"That's fine. Just remember to stay to the left at the bottom of the stairs. We wouldn't want you walking into the blood room now, would we?"

"Thank you, ma'am," replied Detective Holloway as he passed her, keeping to the right of the hall until it ended at a metal door. He opened it and went down the stairs.

Once on the lower level, Trent found Autopsy Room 2 and pressed the intercom button.

"Identification, please," a hollow voice requested.

"Spring Garden Police, Homicide Division, Detective Trent Holloway."

After a brief pause, the automatic lock disengaged. Holloway stepped into the room.

It was very large and very bright. A team of examiners worked intently at a central chrome table. A microphone wrapped in plastic hung from the ceiling. On the table lay the naked body of Cassandra Evans. One of the medical examiners approached the detective with his hand extended.

"Detective Holloway, a pleasure to meet you," greeted the compact, bald-headed ME. His name tag read DR. DERRICK MOORE. His smile was subtle, and his manner, though professional, was a little uneasy.

"What have you determined, doctor?" Holloway asked as he approached the corpse. Two members of the team looked up from their work and glanced at the detective.

Moore replied, "The subject is female, African American, age twenty-seven, eye color brown, hair black. No known diseases or complications prudent within diagnosis. We ran a blood test on her, all counts normal. There is no trace of poison or proximity."

"Notice the bluish contusions around her neck. These indicate..."

"Strangulation," Holloway interrupted.

"Yes, very good. She was strangled, but strangulation is not the cause of her death. This was done to her post-mortem."

"Jesus." Holloway grimaced.

"Oh, it gets even stranger," Moore continued, "The victim was raped repeatedly after she was killed. She suffered lacerations and massive internal hemorrhaging from multiple stab wounds inside her vagina. We were lucky to find traces of seminal fluid. It is possible that her husband or lover was involved in her murder. I would like to get samples from both of them for comparison."

"We're not going to bother with tests at this time, Doctor. Both the men in her life have substantial alibis for the night she was killed."

"Yes, of course. Well then, Detective. Both of them are going to have to be notified that she was six weeks pregnant."

Feeling terrible as he did so, Holloway silently congratulated himself on his intuition. It was not right to see this woman laying on a slab of chrome, naked, shredded, with staples closing the wounds in her abdomen.

"Her attacker used a sharp instrument on her. He actually severed her intestines. I suspect the weapon was an axe," Dr. Moore said.

Detective Holloway could see her eyes from where he was standing ten feet away. They were dark and glossy and seemed to be peering at him from their emptiness, desperately seeking an answer. *Why? Why did I have to die, Trent? Why did you let me die?*

Dr. Moore continued with his findings. "The victim's throat was literally torn out."

"How do you mean?"

Detective Holloway watched from where he stood as the doctor approached the chrome table. Dr. Moore motioned to Holloway to come closer as he adjusted the victim's head to for better viewing.

"Her throat was chewed, not cut or lacerated by a blade, as we first suspected. This is difficult for me to say detective, but under the microscope, we found the imprint edges of teeth."

"Teeth?"

"Yes, sir."

"You're saying this fucker killed her with his mouth?"

"That's exactly what I'm saying."

"How big are they?"

"They are consistent with the size of lower incisors and canines of an Alaskan wolf." Moving to the victim's fingers, Dr. Moore said, "Ms. Evans managed to scratch her attacker before she was murdered. We found skin samples underneath her fingernails."

Holloway stared at the young woman's neck. Under the ligature marks from the strangulation, an open gash of flapping skin hung from ear to ear. Detective Holloway could see that the windpipe had been severed.

How would a wolf attack? By first tearing open the throat so its prey could no longer make any noises then continuing to maul the best parts.

"This was found in her mouth." Dr. Moore held an unfolded but heavily creased 5x7 piece of white paper between surgical tweezers.

Holloway hesitated. He looked down at the piece of paper, then at the writing. He slipped on a pair of latex gloves and gently took the slip of paper from the ME.

"You'll find it intriguing, I'm sure."

And coming soon from
Teri Woods Publishing

Deadly Reigns

AVAILABLE IN BOOKSTORES
IN MARCH 2005

Ricardo Dominguez loved the Bureau, lived for the Bureau, and shortly, he would die for the Bureau.

Dante Reigns tried to clear the air by waving his hands in front of his face. He frowned and coughed slightly to show his displeasure. He despised smoking. He despised drinking as well. To him, both indicated a lack of discipline, a slothful indulgence, a weakness in willpower.

Weakness. A concept Dante found difficult to comprehend. Life's glory came from power, and the more absolute that power, the more glorious life's rewards. Nature rewarded the strong and killed off the weak. So why did people gave in to their weaknesses and make themselves even weaker? Dante just couldn't grasp the concept. Power was the key to life's treasures. And glory rested in power.

"Twenty million means five thousand a kilo," Dante clarified. "But no. Make it four thousand a key and we'll do business."

"Four thousand a key! Are you crazy?" shouted Mickey Moniavaiz, Dominguez's partner. "Five thousand a key is the price, same as you were paying Ramon."

Both agents watched for Dante's reaction at the mention of Mexico's largest drug dealer. Anxious to know Dante's source, they both silently begged for his expression to betray him.

But Dante's face remained the same, his golden eyes windowless to his soul because he had none. His baritone voice remained neutral as he repeated almost mechanically, "Four thousand a key and we'll do business."

"Godammit, Dante! If you couldn't make the deal, or didn't have the juice to negotiate with us, then your brother should have been here instead!" Moniavaiz complained. His role was Mickey Rodriguez, an up-and-coming star in the drug underworld with lots of merchandise to move. Tonight he was also playing the role of the pushy, take-it-or-leave-it, in-your-face drug dealer, a role he relished. "Or maybe that sister of yours.

Princess. I heard she's the one with all the balls in your family anyway. Have her call me so I can do business with a real player and not the family flunky!"

Dominguez winced. Mickey had laid it on too thick. Agent Moniavaiz had been pulled from the Vegas field office, and although had been briefed on the Reigns family structure, but had obviously not been briefed on each member's psychological profile. Or, if he had, he was taking Dante's lightly. Dominguez tried to restore the situation.

"OK. Forty-five hundred on this one, forty-seven hundred on the next one, five grand on the rest. You win a few times, we win a few times," Dominguez suggested.

Dante looked to his right where his cousin Mina stood and waved for her to come closer.

Mina Reigns was the youngest daughter of Dante's uncle and the most precocious member of the Reigns family. Dante brought her along because she was also the most gullible.

When she stepped within arms reach of her cousin, he slapped her and pushed her so she fell over a stack of large cardboard boxes. The roar of tumbling boxes and Mina's surprised shriek echoed throughout the vast corrugated steel warehouse. Not loosing a step, Dante calmly approached his beloved cousin and began to kick her in the stomach and back.

"Holy Jesus," slipped from Agent Dominguez' lips.

"Okay, enough! Five thousand!" Agent Monciavaiz shouted. "Now would you stop already!"

Dante continued to brutally kick Mina. The toe of his brown wingtip struck her face and blood flew from her nose and lips. She cried out in gut-wrenching pain for him to stop.

"Hey! Hey!" Monciavaiz shouted as he raced forward to stop the brutal assault. As he reached out and gripped Dante's shoulder, his hands were shaking. With all of his strength, he spun him around and brought him face to face. Dante Reigns was smiling.

"Lay off her, man," Monciavaiz said. "If you got personal problems, deal with them on your own time!"

Dante bent down over Mina and rolled her on her back. She was unconscious. As he pushed her body aside, he quickly reached into her waistband and pulled out the .40 caliber, semi-automatic pistol she had hidden there. He slid the barrel up his sleeve and nestled the handle in his palm to hide it.

"So you care about her, huh?" Dante asked Agent Monciavaiz as he stood up. "You care about what happens to her, right? And you want to save her?"

Dante's suspicions had been confirmed. Whether undercover or in uniform, the first reaction of a law enforcement officer was to save lives. These two "business associates" were desperate to save Mina. The thought made Dante smile.

"You know, Dominguez, cigar smoking is a very nasty habit. I used to tell my former business associate, Reuben Palacios, the very same thing all the time. You see, Reuben had a taste for these especially disgustingly putrid Cuban cigars. They were these big, thick suckers with a green and gold band around them... much like the one you're smoking right now. Odd. Reuben was busted by the FBI, what, a few weeks ago? And now you turn up smoking one of his specially blended, illegally imported, disgustingly putrid, handmade Cuban cigars."

Dominguez reached for his weapon, but with the speed of a cheetah, Dante adjusted his weapon, fired two shots into Agent Dominguez's chest and leveled it at Monciavaiz's head.

"Do not move unless you wish to join your friend," Dante told him. "Who are you? Better yet, which are you? DEA, FBI, Customs, Treasury, or just some really stupid locals?"

Mickey Monciavaiz raised his hands slowly into the air and

began to plead.

"Look, I don't know what you're talking about, man. I just came to do a deal."

"Where is the leak in my family?"

"I don't know what you're talking about."

Dante lowered his weapon from the agent's face to his foot. "Where's the leak?"

"I don't know!"

Dante fired his weapon. The sound echoed in the large space and reverberated in his ears. Agent Monciavaiz grabbed his shattered and bloodied right foot.

"Where is the leak?" Dante repeated softly.

Beads of sweat and tears of pain dripped profusely from the agent's face. "I don't know!"

Dante shifted his aim from Agent Monciavaiz's right foot to his left and squeezed the trigger again. The bullet streaked downwards and struck Agent Monciavaiz's left foot. The agent fell to the ground and cried out in agony.

"I don't know...what...you're..."

Dante stepped closer to the fallen agent and pointed the weapon at his right shoulder. Without asking a question, he fired again.

"Help!" Agent Monciavaiz writhed in pain on the ground, holding his wounded shoulder. "Help...help me..."

"What was that?" Dante asked. "You want to help me?"

Agent Monciavaiz shook his head. "I...don't know..."

Dante leaned forward and placed the barrel of the gun on the agent's kneecap and pulled the trigger. Bits of bone fragment and soft tissue exploded into the air. Blood gushed from the fresh wound.

Dante laughed and turned to his cousin, Kevin, and said, "Seems like we really struck a nerve with this guy."

Agent Monciavaiz held up his hands submissively. "I don't

know who the...leak...is. I was...pulled in from...the Vegas field office...at the last...minute."

Dante turned and looked at the dying agent in disgust.

"I didn't ask you any more questions, did I? I was rather enjoying our little test of wills, but now... you've really brought our fun and games to an end." Dante raised his weapon and pointed it at the agent's chest. "I hate party poopers."

Dante's weapon coughed twice. Agent Monciavaiz's body jerked, and he was dead.

Dante then turned to Kevin. "Take the bodies to the cement factory and drop them in the acid vat. Make sure there's nothing left. Remember, no bodies, no crime."

Kevin Reigns nodded and immediately set out to complete his assigned task.

Dante turned to a now conscious Mina and grabbed her by the hair. "The next time you want to help the family, you better damn well make sure that the people you're hooking us up with aren't federal agents. Do you understand me?"

Mina nodded.

"Good. Now get this place cleaned up!" Dante turned, and headed for the exit. "And stop all of that damn whimpering, you stupid bitch."

Teri Woods Publishing

an Entertainment Investment Group

ORDER FORM

Teri Woods Publishing
Greeley Square Station, P.O. Box 20069
New York, NY 10001-0005
www.teriwoods.com

DUTCH II: ANGEL'S REVENGE	**$14.95**
Shipping/handling (via U.S. Priority Mail)	**$ 3.85**
TOTAL	**$18.80**

Order additional titles from TWP: YES

True to the Game by Teri Woods	$14.95	☐
B-More Careful by Shannon Holmes	$14.95	☐
The Adventures of Ghetto Sam and The Glory of My Demise by Kwame Teague	$14.95	☐
Dutch by Teri Woods	$14.95	☐
Triangle of Sins by Nurit Folkes	$14.95	☐
Tell Me Your Name by Eric Enck	$14.95	☐

Purchaser Information

Name_____

Reg.#_____

Address_____

City_____State _____ Zip_____

Total number of books ordered _____

For orders shipped directly to prisons, TWP deducts 25% of the sale price of the book. Costs are as follows:

TITLE OF BOOK	$11.21
Shipping/handling	$ 3.85
TOTAL	$15.06